D0803974

"Are you seducing me?" I blurted the question against her lips.

Her voice was low. "You built the fire. I thought you were doing the seducing."

Wind roared in my ears, although the breeze coming off the water was mild. The spitting fire sounded very loud. I lay back, pulling her on top.

Our lovemaking happened fast. My hands were dirty, my clothes full of sand. I was afraid to touch her with anything but my mouth. I hiked up her sweatshirt and gobbled her breasts, then pulled her shorts down. She stayed above me the whole time. As I lifted my head to suck her in, I saw the fire burning behind her, the flames leaping high into the night . . .

LOOKING FOR NAIAD?

Buy our books at
www.naiadpress.com

or call our toll-free number
1-800-533-1973

or by fax (24 hours a day)
1-850-539-9731

THE TOUCH OF YOUR HAND

EDITED BY

BARBARA GRIER

AND

CHRISTINE CASSIDY

THE NAIAD PRESS, INC.
1998

Copyright © 1998 by Naiad Press

All rights reserved. No part of this book may be
reproduced or transmitted in any form or by any means,
electronic or mechanical, including photocopying, without
permission in writing from the publisher.

Printed in the United States of America on acid-free paper
First Edition

Cover designer: Bonnie Liss (Phoenix Graphics)
Typesetter: Sandi Stancil

Library of Congress Cataloging-in-Publication Data

The touch of your hand : erotic love stories / by Naiad Press
authors : edited by Barbara Grier and Christine Cassidy.

   p.   cm.
   ISBN 1-56280-220-8 (alk. paper)
   1. Lesbians – Fiction. 2. Lesbians' writings, American. 3. Erotic
stories, American. Love stories, American.   I. Grier, Barbara,
1933 –   . II. Cassidy, Christine.
PS648.L47T68 1998
813'.01083538'086643—dc21   98-13236
                                            CIP

ABOUT THE EDITORS

Barbara Grier

Author, editor, bibliographer; writings include *The Lesbian in Literature, Lesbiana, The Lesbian's Home Journal, Lavender Herring, Lesbian Lives* as well as contributions to various anthologies, *The Lesbian Path* (Cruikshank) and *The Coming Out Stories* (Stanley and Wolfe). She is co-editor, with Katherine V. Forrest, of *The Erotic Naiad* (1992), *The Romantic Naiad* (1993), *The Mysterious Naiad* (1994). She co-edited *The First Time Ever* (1995), *Dancing in the Dark* (1996) and *Lady Be Good* (1997) with Christine Cassidy.

Her early career included working for sixteen years with the pioneer lesbian magazine *The Ladder.* For the last twenty-five years she has been, together with Donna J. McBride, the guiding force behind THE NAIAD PRESS.

Articles about Barbara's and Donna's life are too numerous to list, but a good early overview can be found in *Heartwoman* by Sandy Boucher (N.Y.: Harper, 1982).

She lives in Tallahassee, Florida.

Christine Cassidy

Christine Cassidy is the Director of Marketing and Circulation at Poets & Writers, Inc., a contributing editor to the *Lambda Book Report* and an editor for the Naiad Press since 1988. A poet, she is the recipient of a New Jersey State Council on the Arts grant in poetry. She also writes reviews, essays, articles and stories, and has been published in *The Persistent Desire: A Femme/Butch Reader,*

The Lambda Book Report, Our World, Poets & Writers Magazine, and *On Our Backs,* among others. She can be seen, courtesy of photographer Morgan Gwenwald, in *Butch/Femme,* a lively collection of photos edited by MG Soares. She lives in New York City.

TABLE OF CONTENTS

Long Odds
Ann O'Leary

The alarm woke Lee Browne at eight o'clock on Tuesday morning. Drowsily, she reached across and turned off the buzzing clock, vaguely aware of the feathery remnants of a dream floating away from her consciousness. She yawned and snuggled back down under the quilt. She couldn't recall what the dream had been about, but it was set against a background of her childhood home. She wanted to enjoy these memories that had been floating into her mind frequently in the last few months. The images she recaptured for a few moments — of rosellas, flashing red and green in flight across the river, and the eerie sea-like sound of hot summer wind whisking through the Casuarina trees in the schoolyard — were oddly comforting. As a child and adolescent, she couldn't wait to grow up and leave her sleepy country town in southern New South Wales. She yearned, back then, for faraway places where exciting things happened. Now, the memories of that time were warm and nurturing. But she couldn't lie there all day. Today was Melbourne Cup Day and she was going to the races.

She threw back the quilt and got out of bed. She opened the blind and saw that the sky was overcast, but that didn't worry her. She smiled as she headed for the shower. She had moved down to Melbourne from Sydney only a few months ago, and like most people from other places, she found it incredible that Melbourne actually had a public holiday on the first Tuesday in November every year, for a horse race. Of course, the Cup was no ordinary horse race. Thoroughbreds were brought in to compete from all over the world — the U.K., the States, Hong Kong and Europe. The stakes were high and it was the highlight of Melbourne's prestigious Spring Racing Carnival, which went on for a week. Lee looked out of the bathroom window as she stood under the shower. There'd be plenty of people disappointed at the sight of the gray skies. They were the ones who weren't really interested in gambling but considered Cup Day just as a fashionable day out. They spent thousands on their designer clothes and hats and dragged crates of Bollinger from the trunks of their cars to drink with their gourmet picnics prepared by society caterers. But Lee hoped it might rain a little as had been forecast, because she liked the chances of a mare called Inspiration, which was good on a damp track.

As a child, Lee learned from her father the thrill of racing — the tingling excitement of placing a bet, of taking that chance, and she still often enjoyed the entertainment of racing and betting. But she was aware she'd been betting more heavily and more often since she left Sydney and Jessica.

Oh, God. Jessica. Lee massaged mousse through her brown, medium-length, layered hair, scrunching it as she blow-dried, and patiently rode out the storm in her mind, of Jessie's darkened eyes, her mouth murmuring her desire, her body drawing Lee further into her own illicit desire that she'd tried in vain to suppress. These painful, melting memories invaded her mind constantly. Nothing matched the excitement, the thrill, the high she got from Jessica, but betting was the best substitute Lee knew of.

Glancing outside, she saw a break in the clouds. If it was going to fine up, she thought, she'd put her money on Courageous Lady. She remembered when she was little, her father betting with his mate Pete who owned the pub and ran a book on the side. Sometimes on Friday nights, Dad and a group of other blokes played poker in Pete's back bar and Dad didn't come home until very late. He used to say he was only having a "little flutter." Lee often sat on the front porch on hot nights and waited for him, until Mum, stony-faced, told her to go to bed. The worst part of his occasional Friday night flutters, Lee remembered, was having to tiptoe around the house all day Saturday because Mum always spent the day in her room having a lie-down and Dad stayed in his shed. Lee would sit on the back step drawing in the dust with a stick, or have a swing on the clothesline, while the cicadas moaned monotonously and the sulphur-crested cockatoos screeched overhead, alighting in a flapping white cloud in the gum trees at the end of their yard. Those baking hot, yellow summer Saturdays, when the iron roof groaned and every floorboard creaked, seemed interminably long.

On other Saturdays or some nights after school in the summer, Dad often said, "Come on, love, let's go down to the park for a swing." This was always accompanied by a sly wink and a grin, and Lee, pleased to be Dad's confidante, accompanied him down to Pete's where she learned how to bet. Lee recalled how Dad and the other blokes gathered around the radio to listen to the races, and the way their eyes shone with excitement. "Ahh, Jeez," Dad often said after a good race, "win or lose, there's nothing like it. You can feel the blood pumping through your veins and you know you're bloody alive."

He died young at forty-five when Lee was twelve, and for years she missed him terribly. According to his mate Dave, he came tearing out of Pete's pub waving around a fistful of cash, yelling, "Fuck me dead, Dave! I've won the bloody quaddie!" Then he collapsed and died on the footpath — just like that.

Lee remembered the horrible responsibility she felt as Dave stuffed the two grand into her hand. "Don't tell yer Mum, love, for Christ's bloody sake."

Not knowing what else to do, Lee buried it in the

backyard near the dog's kennel. After a year or so, Lee began taking small amounts from the tin she'd buried and dropping in to Pete's. She was only thirteen but Pete let her have a little bet in memory of her Dad. He was a bloody great bloke, they all said, and it was his money she was betting with, after all. Lee studied the form guides and took her chances for as long as the money lasted. When she lost, the defeat felt like a crushing blow in her chest. But when she won, she was so exhilarated, she felt like she could fly.

Lee went into the kitchen and had her usual breakfast of a chocolate bar and a glass of milk. Sitting at the bench, gazing out of the window, she pictured her mother sitting at the kitchen table years ago at home. Lee was leaving that day for Sydney to go to university. Mum had a cup of tea in front of her and the steam and the heat of the day made Mum's face moist and dreamy-looking. The afternoon sun was streaming in through the slats of the venetians painting golden stripes across the room, and Red, the dog, was barking in the yard.

"Your father," Mum said, "was always looking outward — his eyes were always focused on the horizon, like yours. He had a restless spirit like yours, and he couldn't find contentment in real life. That's why he gambled. It gave him the illusion of accomplishment, but he was really only avoiding the things in life that were too hard for him to face."

Lee was eighteen and she felt impatient with her mother. Mum could never understand the excitement Dad got from betting — the excitement that she'd been secretly enjoying too. She was going to get away and find adventure — she wanted some bloody fun. Dad had settled for betting in Pete's back bar, but she wanted a lot more than that. She gazed outside at the sheets on the line being tossed around by the hot wind, cracking like whips, as if trying to tear away from the pegs that held them back, and she had just nodded to her mother, as if she understood.

For years, first at university, then at work, Lee found the adventure and excitement she'd been craving. Her life was full of friends, occasional lovers and good times, and although she kept in touch with her mother, she never thought of home or had a care in the world. But then last year, not long after her twenty-eighth birthday, she met Jessica and everything changed. All the things she ever wanted or thought mattered were suddenly personified by Jessica. Loving her, but unable to be with her, created an aching void inside her that seemed impossible to fill. She knew her restless days would be over and she'd be perfectly contented if only she could have Jessie. Perhaps that emptiness and loneliness explained her recurring sentimental thoughts of home in the country, Lee thought, where life had once seemed so boring but had at least been innocent and uncomplicated.

She was spending today alone at the races. She'd turned down an offer to go to a Cup Day party being held by one of her new friends. She'd had to leave Sydney quickly because of Jessica and found it hard to settle down in Melbourne. The company she worked for as an accountant had fortunately managed to arrange a transfer for her to their Melbourne office, she was renting a nice apartment, and she'd

met some nice women. But her outgoing nature had
dimmed and she found it hard to take much interest
in new friends, and any idea of a new lover was out
of the question.

Lee went into her bedroom and dressed in her
light gray suit, with a white camisole underneath.
The jacket and pants were a blend of lightweight
wool and silk, and the fabric had a fine herringbone
weave and the slightest sheen. The long-line jacket
draped softly from the padded square shoulders to
the two buttons at her waist. She pinned a rose to
her lapel. It was deep pink, exactly the color of the
lipstick Jessica always wore, and Lee was suddenly
overwhelmed by the melting memory of Jessica's
luscious mouth. She trembled and took a deep breath.
The rose-pink lipstick looked perfect with Jessie's
deep blue eyes and long blonde hair. She usually
wore her hair in a French braid and there were
always little wispy bits that curled around her
forehead.

Lee had met Jessica at a party last summer. She
noticed Jessie across the room talking and laughing
with another woman, and couldn't take her eyes off
her. When they were introduced, Lee felt an
overpowering and instant attraction that set her
heart racing. Jessica held Lee's gaze as she smiled
enticingly. But Lee soon discovered Jessica had a
lover — a woman called Prue, with whom she lived.
Lee liked Prue, and the three of them became
friends. As time went on, Lee's attraction for Jessica
grew stronger and she began to dream guilty dreams
— unsatisfying, burning dreams of having Jessie in
her arms. Her friendship with Prue became stunted

by her guilt and warped by jealousy that grew with the same intensity as her desire. Lee should have stayed away from them, but Jessica's inviting eyes and private smiles beckoned irresistibly. It all culminated on that fateful, wonderful night three months ago, when Lee watched herself walk to the edge of the cliff with Jessie's hand in hers, and Jessie whispered, "I can't," and breathed, "I want you," and murmured, "No," against Lee's mouth as she tore off Lee's clothes with a desperate urgency. Lee had stepped over into the abyss and she was still falling.

Lee grabbed her keys and wallet. A day on her own at the races would do her the world of good, she thought. It should be an exciting day and perhaps she'd get some relief from the melancholy memories and yearnings that haunted her. The Melbourne Cup was race eight later in the day, but she had selections for each race and wanted to be there in time for the first. She locked her apartment and headed for her black Honda Prelude parked out front.

As Lee crossed the immaculate lawns of Flemington racecourse, she felt the tension of race day begin to tingle in her body. The enormous rose garden was in full bloom, the sun was shining brightly, and everywhere people were congregating, laughing and excited, dressed extravagantly in the latest fashions or outrageously ludicrous outfits. Lee smiled at two gay men walking hand in hand, dressed in beautifully tailored white suits with tails, complete with sequin-studded bow ties and rainbow-striped top hats. They gave Lee a grin as they passed. On rugs on the lawns, hampers were being opened, chocolate croissants were being passed around for brunch, champagne corks were popping like firecrackers, and in the background, bands were playing. Lee decided to head for the Mounting Yard to inspect the horses in the first race.

The horses looked magnificent — glossy in the sunshine, their muscles rippling as they were walked slowly around by the strappers. Lee fancied the chances of a horse called Paradise. She saw the jockey who'd be riding Paradise; she was wearing a deep purple silk and was decidedly cute. Liking the look of both horse and rider, Lee decided to check out the bookies next and see the odds, but fifty bucks each way felt pretty right.

There was a while to wait before the first race was run, and Lee decided to stop for a coffee on the way to the bookies' enclosure. She sat down at a table in the sun and ordered a café latté. She gazed around at the milling crowd as she sipped her coffee. Suddenly, from the corner of her eye, she glimpsed a woman in black with blonde hair in a braid, and her heart skipped a beat. She was a distance away and Lee had only glimpsed her for a moment, but she looked an awful lot like Jessica. Her mind instantly shimmered with deliciously erotic but painful memories. *God, would this ever end?*

Lee had gone to their house for a barbecue one evening. When she arrived, Jessica told her Prue was away in Western Australia working for a couple of days and wouldn't be back until tomorrow night.

Jessica cooked the steaks but they never got to eat dinner. Lee couldn't recall exactly how it started, but suddenly, Jessica kissed her with a breathtaking passion that unleashed the desire Lee had only just been managing to restrain. Lee reeled backwards and found herself pressed against the latticed wall of the gazebo dripping with white jasmine, and her senses were flooded with the combined heady fragrance of the flowers and the erotic scent of Jessica. Jessie was reckless, gasping, as she slid her hands inside Lee's T-shirt and groaned a long, throaty, lustful groan into Lee's mouth as Lee reached under her skirt. They made love there under the jasmine, quickly and urgently before they went inside to the bedroom.

As the first gray light of dawn filtered through the bedroom window, Jessica reached for her again, and Lee surrendered with an insatiable thirst that couldn't be quenched. Every fiery stroke of Jessica's fingers, every touch of her lips and melting caress of her tongue only made Lee want her more. Lee gazed into Jessica's darkened, blazing eyes, wet with tears, and wondered tremulously how much of the mysterious darkness was desire and how much was guilt. While the first birds began their morning song, Lee made love to Jessie again with a passion that was shocking — in their house; in their bed. Later, with her body on fire and her face wet with tears, Lee asked Jessica, who lay trembling in her arms, "What do you want, Jessie? Tell me."

Jessica wept softly in the half-light. "I don't know," she whispered.

Lee left before it was fully light. She had to avoid

Jessica's eyes. She didn't want to see the sun shining on Jessica's beautiful face revealing her remorse, or the honest light on Jessie's body, misted and flushed with passion from loving the wrong woman.

Lee stayed away from Jessica and Prue during the following few weeks while she arranged to leave for Melbourne, and she hadn't spoken to either of them since. There wasn't anything else she could have done. She was desperately in love with Jessica and Jessica wasn't in love with her.

The memories vaporized gradually while Lee sat in the sting of the springtime sun. She focused on the passing colorful parade of people, the ripples of desire in her body slowly stilling. The number of people passing by was increasing and Lee thought the expected crowd of 100,000 looked likely. She drank some coffee and thought she'd better do something about placing her first bet. Suddenly, she saw another glimpse of the woman in black. Her face was turned away but her hair was just like Jessie's and her body, dressed in tight black pants and a tight, black long-sleeved top, looked achingly like Jessica's gorgeous body. Then she vanished into the crowd. Lee's heart began to pound and she felt herself break out in a sweat. It couldn't be Jessica — it wasn't possible. But she got up and began to follow the woman. The crowd became thicker, but Lee surged forward, catching occasional, quick glimpses of the woman in the distance and wondering fearfully what she would do if it was Jessica. She might be here for a few days holiday with Prue, and what in God's name would Lee say to either of them? She completely lost sight of the woman and stopped in her tracks. Get a grip, she told herself. Of course she wasn't Jessie. Place a bet, for God's sake, and try to enjoy the day.

She chose a bookie and put her fifty dollars each way on Paradise. She found a place in the stand with a good view of the track and watched Paradise romp it in, turning her fifty bucks into a hundred. She felt the exhilarating thrill of the win — she got her high and forgot for a while about Jessie.

The morning progressed with more exciting wins and a few aggravating losses. Early in the afternoon, an amplified voice rang out around the course, announcing that the time was approaching for race eight — the running of the Melbourne Cup. A murmur of anticipation rumbled through the crowd and people rushed toward the bookmakers to place their bets. Lee put two hundred dollars on Courageous Lady for a win, and as she moved away from the bookie's stand, she glanced around and saw the woman again. She was closer this time, and Lee nearly fainted. *The woman was Jessica.* Lee froze — her heart was pounding violently. Her impulse was to chase after Jessica but fear held her back. Jessie would be with Prue; she would smile warmly at Lee and kiss her cheek. She would say, "It's lovely to see you, Lee," or something terrible like that, and Lee knew she'd just die.

Lee heard the announcement blaring across the course, that the Cup race was about to start. In a daze, she headed toward the track, pushing through the throng. The atmosphere was electric with anticipation — the huge crowd was still, waiting for the gates to open — and people murmured in low anxious voices. Lee heard the crash of the gates and the thundering of the horses as they took off. The crowd began to roar, and suddenly, seized with panic, she began to run, looking for Jessie. Maybe Jessica was with Prue, but maybe she was alone. She had to find her. The Cup race was a long one and the tension rose as the minutes passed. Lee, breathless and tearful, ran with the horses, pushing, rushing, growing desperate as her chance seemed to slip away. She couldn't see Jessica anywhere.

Lee paused, panting, not knowing what to do. She glanced toward the track and saw that the race was nearly over. She stood transfixed watching Courageous Lady pounding down the straight, neck and neck with Shadow Prince. This used to be the blissful illusion, where for a few moments nothing else in the world mattered and everything focused on the simplicity of the outcome of the race. But this time, the usual magic wasn't there for Lee. The crowd behind her was cheering and people close by were weeping with elation or cursing in disappointment, the sky was a perfect clear blue, the horses' movements were a marvel of synchronized muscle and sinew, their hooves pounded and tore up the turf that showered around them, Courageous Lady was a nose in front, then a head, then she was past the post in a clear win, and Lee felt the tears of a terrible loss trickle down her face. Then she shuddered as the cool silkiness of a familiar hand slipped into hers. Lee gasped, and turned to look into Jessica's eyes, filled with tears.

"I've been looking for you." Jessie's voice was low and husky.

Lee began to tremble and couldn't find her voice. She took Jessie into her arms and held her tightly.

Jessie slid her arms around Lee's shoulders. "I didn't know where else to find you, but I knew you'd be at the races on Cup Day." She kissed Lee's neck, and Lee quivered as a wave of desire washed over her. "I love you, Lee, and I came down here to be with you if you still want me."

Lee's brain seemed to be wrapped in cotton-wool. She felt lightheaded with happiness. "God, baby," she breathed in Jessica's ear. "Do you have any idea of how long the odds are of your finding me in this crowd?"

Jessica looked into her eyes and gently wiped the tears from Lee's face. "No, darling, I don't," she said softly with a smile. "Why don't you take me home so you can work it out. I'm just dying to know."

We Fit So Well
Linda Hill

Those eyes. Larger than usual. Darker, somehow. Unwavering as they seem to be searching. Beckoning to me.

My knees are shaking as I lean closer. Anticipation. My lips quiver ever so slightly, and I hope she doesn't notice. Our lips meet — just barely. Softness. Luxury. Her tongue hinting, as always. Such a sweet greeting. *We fit so well.*

It crosses my mind to pull back now. To be content with the offering. But that mouth welcomes me, lures me in. Captures me, and I cannot resist.

I hear something between a sigh and a quiet moan escape her, and my eyes open, our lips still melded. There are those eyes again. But they are different now. Cloudy. Questioning. Unbelieving? Smoldering.

My stomach flutters. The stirring rises, swelling. I want so much to be inside that mouth. The kiss deepens. Our tongues entwine. She pulls me in, and I follow eagerly, intoxicated. We cannot press close enough. *We fit so well.*

My hands rise and I want to touch her. Feel her skin. Melt into her softness. I struggle to maintain control. But the kiss, her mouth — I cannot think. I am paralyzed, crippled.

Fingertips brush skin and now my knees will not support me. My hands drop. Rise again. Drop.

Again the moan. Is it hers or mine? I cannot tell. Does she hear my struggle? Does she hear the battle in my mind?

Fingertips find a safe place in the crispness of her hair and press against the softness of her neck. My sensibilities are leaving me, and I know I must stop now.

The pressure of our lips lessens. The kiss is gentle again, lingering. We are reluctant to let go. *We fit so well.*

My eyes open as I lift my head. She is unmoving. Her eyes still closed. Her mouth still open. It is a brief moment in which she gives herself away. I cherish the glimpse, knowing the look belongs to me. My heart begins to swell with hope. Is she relishing? Savoring? Or is she regretting?

Silently, she is talking to me. Whispering, and I

cannot possibly walk away. My mouth covers hers. Answering. Saying words I cannot speak. I pray that she can hear me.

We somehow press closer, our mouths creating a vacuum. Sucking. Urgent. Needy. Hungry. Insatiable. We are greedy. *God, we fit so well.*

I want her. I cannot.

Cannot.

My throat tightens, and I know I must let go.

Cannot.

I must. The anguish is too familiar.

The kiss softens. Releases. I read her clearly now. There is sadness in those eyes, regret tugging at the corner of her mouth.

I search her face, her eyes, believing she can read my thoughts and know my words.

She knows. I read her easily, and am sobered. *It is over.* I know that now. Even though I don't want to believe it. She has a lover. I've known that. Watched from afar. Waited for years. She had told me, warned me months ago. Even as she kissed me. Even as she touched me. Her words told me that she'd never leave her. But everything else told me differently. Her lips said she wanted me. Her touch said she needed me. Her eyes said she loved me.

Those eyes.

I must break the gaze that holds me, has always held me. Even though it is the very last thing I want to do. I know that I must.

Cannot.

I do.

Arms drop and I turn, lifting leaden legs and putting one foot in front of the other *Keep walking.*

I glance back quickly. The sadness again. Still *My God, those eyes.*

I keep walking. Until finally, she's out of sight. Beyond my reach.

Keep walking. Just keep walking.

With each step I relive our past, relive that moment. My body shudders, betraying me again. I am overwhelmed by my reaction, the impact of her touch. Her lips. Those eyes. I can't remember ever wanting — or loving — more.

My heart rises and a smile finds my lips as I remember how well we fit together. Then it sinks again as I'm reminded — we cannot.

Hand in Hand
Catherine Ennis

Clair opened her eyes slowly, squinting a little because of the light over the bed. Eva was still sleeping, her face tight, a faint frown creasing her forehead.

"Eva," Clair whispered. "Eva."

A sigh, then Eva's eyes, blurry with sleep, focused on Clair's smile.

"How are you, darling?" Clair asked softly.

Another sigh. "I didn't mean to fall asleep. I just got so comfortable."

"I'm glad you were able to rest. I only woke you

because —" Clair's voice broke, recovered. "Because the children will be here soon, you know. Have we decided to tell them?"

"No." Eva frowned. "I'm not going to say anything. It would be too much of a burden, I think."

"You're right as always." Clair's smile widened, remembering how many times she'd said that to Eva. "You're right, of course," she whispered again, reaching for Eva's hand.

They stayed like that, not speaking, Eva's large hand clasped in Clair's smaller one.

The night nurse swept into the room, her starched uniform crackling. She inserted the needle from a full syringe into the line by the bead. "There's more where this came from. Just hit the button if you need me. I'll be here all night." She leaned to pat the clasped hands, nodded, smiled and left the room, her rubber soles hushed on hospital tiles, the huge door closing quietly behind her.

"Unless someone stumbles in here by accident, the children will be our only company for the rest of the night. We —" Her words interrupted, Clair's face brightened with welcome. "Come, babies. Hug Mama." She held out her arms to the two who hurried through the door.

"We almost missed visiting hours, Mama. Wouldn't you know my sitter was late?" The young woman, her hair the same red as Clair's except for the white at Clair's temples, hugged and kissed her mother, then leaned into Eva's ample arms. "Y'all doin' okay?" she asked, throwing her purse and gloves on the bed.

"Can't you see? Of course they're okay." Bravado,

a shallow pretense. The man's eyes misted. He, too, had Clair's silky red hair. He also shared the deep brown eyes and generous, laughing lips.

"Lonnie, I can see perfectly well they're okay." The girl ducked her head. "You won't be in here much longer." The appeal in her voice, followed by streaming tears, gave lie to her words.

Eva finally spoke, her voice choked. "Everything's fine. You two don't have to worry. And, Millie, please stop crying; you're going to get the rest of us started."

Her words set the tone. The rest of the visit was full of family things, especially of the four grandchildren who were not present.

Finally alone, Clair reached for Eva's hand again.

"I don't like to keep reminding you, but you asked, remember?"

Eva nodded. "There's something else I remember," she said. "Your dragging the kids in that little wagon, the rain and lightning coming down like forever . . ."

Clair remembered that first time, too. The house assigned to her by social services had not one dry area in any of the four tiny rooms. She tried to shield the babies, but their squirming and wailing proved too much. Finally, loading them in their tiny wagon, she headed down the road.

She was aiming for the white house she'd seen when the family-aid truck had deposited her at the door of the rent-free place which was supposed to be her new home. She brought with her only the children's tiny wagon and a plastic bag containing all their belongings. The rain, which showed no sign of quitting in her lifetime, had flooded the rooms, so she slipped and sloshed down the red-clay road, children under the plastic, with no money, not even a towel to cover her head.

Even through the driving rain, Clair remembered, the white house had looked snug and dry and welcoming. The gate wasn't locked so she walked boldly to the door and banged with all her strength, hoping she was making more noise than the rain.

The woman who answered the door was tall, sturdily built, and smiling. "Yes?" she asked.

"I have no place to stay, no transportation, and my babies are wet and hungry. Can you help me?" Tears, unbidden, streamed down her cheeks.

"Come in," Eva said.

Eva worked the night shift at the local hospital so that she could care for her ailing mother during the day. It had worked out just fine when Clair offered to cook and take care of Mother and the house, in return for room and board. They became a family. Mother died; Eva changed to day work, and the children grew.

"Eva, I've fallen in love with you." After a while Clair knew what she wanted. She also knew what Eva wanted. Eva's strong arms around her, her head pillowed on Eva's ample bosom. Clair found that life was generous after all. The memory of an abusive, drunken husband, now safely dead, faded.

The years passed. They made a loving home for the two children. There were birthdays and graduations and vacations and soon, there were grandchildren to love. Clair's silken hair began to go gray; Eva's arthritis made movement painful. Cancer came as a surprise.

They had looked at each other then, dumfounded. Both clearly recalled the pact they had made when Mother died.

"Whichever one of us, the other will end it before the pain becomes unbearable." They had both agreed. Clair remembered how they had held each other in a tight embrace, hearts racing, tears falling.

Now the time was here. Clair felt that her heart would burst. She pictured the quiet evenings, the soft laughter and the joy in sharing happiness. *I must be strong,* she thought, watching the pain on Eva's face. Over all the years Eva had been Clair's strength. Now, Clair knew, she must be the strong one. Delay would only make it harder.

Keeping the heartbreak from her expression, her smile calm, Clair squeezed Eva's hand. "No one will come now. It's time, my darling."

Eva shifted, imploring. She whispered, "Please, no. I'm not ready."

Clair felt tears begin to stream. Her lips quivered, making speech difficult. "We promised, remember? You have to be brave."

"Tomorrow, Clair, please tomorrow."

"No, it's time. If we don't do it now, I'm afraid we won't be able to do it at all." Clair tightened her fingers to stop the shaking. "There won't be any pain," she said quietly, reassuringly. "No more pain, ever. And we'll be together one day, I promise."

"I'll love you forever," Eva whispered. Then she

stood, inserted the needle of a large syringe into the infusion line and slowly pressed the plunger.

Clair reached for Eva to say, "I love you, too." But Eva never knew. She saw only the faint twitch of Clair's fingers. With a sob, Eva grasped the still hand and held it to her lips.

Coming Home
Frankie J. Jones

Blood soaked into Diana's lab coat. How could this be happening to her on her first day in private practice? She gently laid the limp body of the terrier on an examining table and tried to avoid looking at its distraught owner, Chris Dolan — the woman she had kissed in a childish fit of passion fifteen years earlier.

"Will she be all right?" Chris asked, her voice a shaky whisper.

This isn't about you, Diana reminded herself, forcing herself to meet the dark, tear-stained eyes that had haunted her dreams for years. Unable to bear their intensity, she returned her attention to checking the dog's vital signs. "I won't know until I examine her," she answered.

"She's never run out of the gate before," Chris said, her voice trembling. "I went out back to feed her, like I do every evening when I get home. She darted out the gate and into the road. The car came around the corner before I could catch her." She started to rub her face but stopped short at the sight of blood on her hands. She swayed slightly and Diana reached out to steady her. When her hand came into contact with Chris's warm, smooth skin, the intensity of emotions rocked her.

"Julie," Diana said, snatching her hand away and turning to her assistant who was entering the room. "Take Ms. Dolan into my office." She didn't want Chris to have to sit in the waiting room, in case anyone else came in.

After Diana had graduated, Chris had worked her way into the position of principal at Clayton High, which meant she was known to most, if not all, of the inhabitants of the small town.

Diana began scrubbing her hands. After pulling on gloves, she turned to find Chris still staring at the terrier.

"It would be better if you waited in my office," Diana said. "This will probably take a while and you'll be more comfortable. There's a restroom where you can wash up, too."

"Can't I stay here with her?" Chris pleaded.

"That's not a good idea." Diana raised her head

and forced herself to look at Chris. "I'll let you know the minute I know something."

Julie stepped forward and took Chris by the arm. "Come with me," she murmured.

Chris placed a hand on Diana's arm and squeezed. Again, a surge of electricity shot through her, and for a moment their eyes locked. Chris's gaze drifted down to rest on the small, gold labrys that lay in the hollow of Diana's throat. A thin shadow of a smile formed before she turned and followed Julie out.

Diana felt a sudden rush of dizziness and realized she was holding her breath. As the door closed behind Chris and Julie, she exhaled loudly and turned her attention to her patient. A quick examination told her that the terrier's injuries were extensive.

The glint of a metal tag caught her attention. She eased it to where she could read it. "Well, Alice B," Diana said, "you have to lend me a hand here, girl. We don't want to let that wonderful woman of yours down, now do we?"

The surgery on Alice B lasted two hours. Julie took Alice B's front paw in her hand. "What are her chances?"

Diana sighed and made a final check of the dog's blood pressure before answering. "If she makes it through the night, she'll probably recover. As you saw, there were extensive internal injuries. If she survives she'll have a permanent limp due to the damage in her left hind leg."

Diana tore off the bloody gloves and smoothed the dark, curly hair down between Alice B's ears. "Julie, will you please tell Chris that I'll be right out to talk to her?"

Julie left and Diana stripped off the soiled lab coat and began to scrub. As the water sluiced over her arms she recalled the enticing feel of Chris's hand and was transported back fifteen years to when that hand had first caused such a riot of emotion within her.

Diana had been a senior in high school and Chris Dolan was her English teacher. Fresh out of college, Chris had returned to her hometown to teach. There was only five years' difference in their ages, but at that point in their lives, five years might as well have been five decades.

Since that time, Diana had often wondered why she had never noticed Chris before. They had grown up in the same general neighborhood and their parents were acquainted.

Diana's crush on Chris developed around mid-year and by graduation she was a stuttering, stumbling mass of raging hormones.

On Diana's final day of school, Chris had asked her to stay after class. As the last student left, Chris walked back to where Diana stood rooted to the floor by her desk.

"I wanted to congratulate you on your acceptance to Texas A & M," Chris said.

In the small town of Clayton where everyone knew everyone, it wasn't a secret that Diana wanted to be a vet like her father and his father before him. "Thank you," Diana managed to squeak.

"Some city will be lucky to have a vet as caring as you. I know you will be wonderful." Chris gave her the small lopsided smile that Diana had dreamed of so many times.

"I'm coming back here to practice," Diana pledged.

A frown creased Chris's forehead. "A small town can be very confining for someone like you," she said and then hesitated. "But I understand how you feel. After all, I came back." The frown faded, and she gave Diana's arm a squeeze.

Some inner voice screamed to Diana that it was now or never. Without stopping to think of the possible consequences, she leaned in and kissed Chris. The kiss ended as quickly as it started. Diana still didn't know which of them had pulled away first. She waited for the disgust or anger that she was certain Chris must feel, but all she saw was that slightly puzzled look on Chris's face again.

A terrorizing span of silence hung between them until Chris nodded and said, "I'll eagerly await your homecoming."

Before Diana could respond, Chris had turned and left the room.

Fifteen years later, Diana was still carrying a torch for this woman. She shut the water off and growled in disgust. "This is ridiculous. Chris didn't literally mean she would wait." Diana ripped a paper towel from the dispenser and continued to berate herself. "There was nothing to wait for. She was just being nice to a love-struck kid." She glanced in the mirror and automatically smoothed down her short, auburn hair.

"And it's not like I waited," Diana admitted. She had been in and out of a couple of relationships.

Affairs, she reminded herself. The truth was, she hadn't met anyone who could measure up to her expectations of what she imagined Chris Dolan to be. In those rare moments when total honesty prevailed, she was forced to admit her greatest fear — that even Chris probably couldn't meet those expectations.

With a last brush of her hand through her hair she squared her shoulders and went to go face Chris.

She opened the door to her office and found Chris staring into space. At the sound of Diana's entrance she jumped up.

"How is she?" she asked. "Julie wouldn't tell me anything."

Diana held up her hand. "I told Julie I wanted to talk to you."

"Oh, God," Chris cried and gripped the back of the chair she had been sitting in.

"No. No. She's okay for now," Diana said and rushed forward to reassure her. When her hands come in contact with Chris, the physical jolt again hit her, and she snatched her hands away.

Chris's frown was stopped with Diana's assurance, "Alice B's surgery went well." Back in her familiar realm of medicine, Diana felt calmer. "There were serious internal injuries and a compound fracture —"

"Stop," Chris interrupted, holding up her hands and stepping closer to Diana. "In simple terms, is she going to be all right?"

Diana focused her attention on her own hands. She couldn't look into Chris's eyes without telling her how much she wanted another chance to kiss her. Chris turned away and Diana's eyes roamed the length of her back, downward over rounded hips that were pleasingly clad in dark linen slacks. The ache building within her told her she wanted much more than a kiss.

"Will she be all right?" Chris asked again, without turning to look at Diana.

Embarrassed that she had momentarily forgotten about the trauma that had brought Chris back into her life, Diana cleared her throat and made herself focus on Alice B.

"I won't lie to you," she began. Chris turned to face her, but Diana put a clamp on her emotions and continued. "She's badly injured." She took a deep breath. "If she makes it through the night, I'd say her chances of recovery are about ninety percent. But she will have a permanent limp."

"Do you think she'll make it through the night?" Chris asked in a small voice.

Yes! Diana wanted to scream. Anything to take the look of anguish from Chris's face. "I don't know," she answered honestly.

"I'd like to stay with her."

"She's heavily sedated and will sleep for several hours," Diana explained. "You should go home and rest. I'll stay and call you if there's any change in her condition."

"No. I'd rather stay." Chris gave an awkward laugh. "I know this sounds silly to be so attached to an animal . . ." She let the sentence trail off and shrugged.

"I understand," Diana replied, knowing that if it were her own dog, she too would want to be there with it. "There's a sofa in the recovery room. My dad spent several nights in there, so I guess it's comfortable enough to sleep on. He always kept pillows and blankets in the back. I'll go find them for you."

Diana spent the night trying to nap on the sofa in her office and went in several times to check on Alice B. Each time she found Chris sitting by the cage holding Alice B's front paw and talking to her.

When Diana checked in just before daybreak, Alice B was awake. Diana did a quick exam. "Her vital signs are stronger." She gave the small dog's head a caress. "I'd say Alice B is on her way to a strong recovery."

"Thank you," Chris said, stroking Diana's wrist as she followed her into Diana's office.

Diana remained perfectly still and let the pleasant sensations of Chris's touch course through her. Several seconds ticked by and neither woman moved.

"You've been snatching your hands away from me all night," Chris said at last. "I was beginning to think you found touching me offensive."

"You should know better than that," Diana answered in a voice thick with emotion.

"Why would I know that?" Chris prompted.

Diana felt the blood rush to her face as she again recalled the awkward kiss she had given Chris a lifetime ago. "Because I . . ." Diana floundered. Without sounding like a complete fool, how could she tell this woman she had loved her all these years?

"Because you had a schoolgirl crush on me?" Chris asked softly. Diana found she was having trouble concentrating as Chris's thumb began making slow circles on her hand. "That was a long time ago."

"Time doesn't change everything," Diana managed to say.

"That's not true," Chris argued. "Time changes everything."

"I still feel the same way about you." *There.* Diana told herself. She had said it.

Chris turned her head to the side slightly and smiled. "I don't think so." Her smile faded. "When you didn't return after graduation, I knew you had changed your mind about moving back."

"Dad wasn't ready to retire and the town isn't big enough to support two vets," Diana replied lamely, unable to tell her she had been too afraid of Chris's rejection to come back. And afraid of what she would do if she had to see Chris on a regular basis.

Chris's thumb stroked the back of Diana's wrist. "A few weeks ago I ran into your mom at the supermarket. The small-town social center," she added and again smiled.

"I remember," Diana said. The supermarket had always acted as an unofficial gathering place. She felt the tension begin to melt away.

"Your mom mentioned that your dad was retiring and you were coming home to take over his practice. All I could think about was your coming home." She turned Diana's hands over and softly stroked her thumbs over Diana's palms. "It was time for Alice B's shots, but I waited so I could bring her by after you came back." Chris took a deep breath and glanced through the doorway at the sleeping terrier. "You were so brave that last day of school," Chris said, pushing a lock of hair from Diana's forehead.

"I was petrified," Diana admitted. "I'm surprised I didn't knock our teeth out with that god-awful kiss."

"It was the sweetest kiss I've ever had," Chris said as her palm caressed Diana's cheek.

"I was a gangly, love-struck kid," Diana said, trying to control the flood of sensation that was washing through her.

"I wasn't much older," Chris reminded her. She shook her head and again captured Diana's hands. "The whole thing seemed so wrong to me then. With me being a teacher and you a student. At that time the five years' difference in our ages felt like eons."

"And now?" Diana prompted, her hands moving to Chris's wrists.

"Now," Chris repeated and stared into Diana's eyes. "Now, we're both grown women who live in a small and very observant town." Her hands slipped to Diana's elbows.

"I'm out to my parents. They've both been supportive of me," Diana assured her and moved her hands to Chris's shoulders.

"My family has known about me for years, too. And I don't think the school board would be very shocked. You aren't the first," she added hesitantly. "There's bound to be talk if we start —" Chris hesitated and smiled. "I was going to say dating, but that sounds like a term that should only apply to the kids at school."

"I think I will enjoy dating you, Ms. Dolan," Diana teased.

Chris's hands dropped to Diana's waist as their gazes met and held.

"I believe we've waited long enough for this,"

Chris whispered, and pulled Diana to her. The kiss that had begun fifteen years ago resumed with a slow meeting of lips. Hands tightened their respective hold and pulled their bodies together. A groan escaped Chris's throat as Diana's hands moved up into her hair. The kiss deepened and grew more frantic. Chris's knee pushed between Diana's legs.

Diana's hand cradled the back of Chris's neck and pulled her closer. Diana's body ached as Chris brushed the side of her breast. When the hand closed over it, Diana had to pull away to breathe. "Too much," she whispered as Chris's other hand inched its way up the inside of Diana's thigh.

"Nowhere near enough," Chris replied. "I've waited too long. This is only the beginning." Her hands slipped under Diana's shirt and in one smooth motion the shirt and bra landed in a pile behind Diana. Chris's mouth burned a trail down Diana's neck and across her throat, while her hands teased Diana's swollen nipples.

"I need to feel you," Diana said, fumbling with Chris's blouse. Diana wondered briefly how so many buttons could be on one item of clothing.

Chris stopped long enough to help Diana. They attempted to remove the blouse without unbuttoning the cuffs and one sleeve clung with stubborn determination.

"Damn," Chris growled and yanked the sleeve harshly. The stubborn button yielded and pinged across the floor. The bra gave way to their urgent demands, and Diana's lips captured the object of so many of her dreams. The nipple grew harder at the touch of her tongue. Diana sucked with greedy need until her mouth filled with the sweet tender flesh. Her hands moved to where the button on Chris's slacks should have been, and she was surprised to find that sometime during their struggle Chris had already kicked off the remaining barriers of clothing.

Diana gathered the damp curls into her hand and felt her knees weaken in anticipation. How many times had she dreamed of doing this? Could this moment possibly be real? Or would she wake to find it was another dream?

"It's real," Chris whispered.

Diana started, unaware that she had spoken out loud.

"Don't stop now," Chris begged and again captured Diana's mouth with her own. Chris's tongue began a slow rhythmic stroking.

Diana found her fingers matching the smooth insistent strokes. She grew dizzy with desire as her fingers pushed deeper into Chris's silky wetness. Diana's fingers grew more demanding and Chris rested her head on Diana's shoulder.

"Now," Chris begged, pushing Diana's fingers deeper inside her.

Diana's mouth recaptured a swollen nipple and sucked hungrily.

A small cry started deep in Chris's throat and tore through in a loud moan as she grabbed Diana's hand and rode it to wave after wave of pleasure. With one final thrust against it, she shuddered and leaned heavily against Diana. "I don't think I can stand alone." She sighed.

Diana led them to the sofa and helped her stretch

out. "Rest now," she murmured and kissed Chris's forehead.

"Not so fast." Chris grabbed her, pulling her down. "I said I couldn't stand." She maneuvered her body onto Diana's. "Why do you still have your pants on?" she demanded as she unfastened the button and slowly slid the zipper down.

"I had my hands full," Diana informed her with a wicked smile. She raised her head and captured Chris's dangling breast between her lips.

"Enough of that." Chris rose up on her knees to pull Diana's jeans away. She remained kneeling for several seconds, gazing at Diana's naked body. "You have no idea how many times I've dreamed of doing this," she said.

Diana stared up at her. "Why didn't you say something then?"

Chris shrugged. "You were a student. You were about to go away to college. I thought you'd be better off."

"Why didn't you try to find me? I came home for holidays. You had to know I'd be here."

Chris nodded and idly ran her hands over Diana's stomach. "Yeah, I always knew exactly when you arrived and when you left town."

"You never came by the house or tried to find me."

Chris's hands moved slowly down Diana's torso. "You never tried to see me either. I guess I thought it was just a schoolgirl crush and you had forgotten about me."

Diana was having trouble concentrating on anything but the feel of Chris's hands teasing the inside of her thighs.

"I was too scared of what you might think of me. But I didn't forget and I never got over you," she said, her voice husky with desire.

Chris eyed her and smiled. "Maybe I should make sure you never forget," she teased and bent forward to let her tongue replace her wandering hands.

When Chris's tongue slipped between Diana's swollen lips, Diana's vision faded to a blur of bright colors and sensations. She screamed out when Chris placed her hands beneath her hips and pulled Diana still closer to her devouring tongue. Chris's hand moved in to claim her, and Diana knew she was at last truly home.

A Touch, a Kiss

Lyn Denison

The whole town was excited, according to the headlines in the local newspaper I had spread out in front of me.

Mornings were a rush of making lunches and getting the kids off to school, and the half-hour or so I had before I left for work I spent with a quiet cup of tea and the daily news. Perhaps I thought the calming effect of the tea would negate the usually unsettling roundup of world events in the paper.

Today no amount of tea was going to still the

racing of my heartbeats. They were skittering around like marionettes gone mad.

I glanced at the headlines again, hoping I'd hallucinated or something. "City's Golden Girl Returns Home." I swallowed painfully. No. It was no dream. Chrissie Wilson was coming home.

The trouble with this town was its isolation. It was a hundred miles or so from the nearest town to the west and about the same distance eastward to the coast. It was one of those places where everyone knows everyone else and we all sort of mind one another's business. There wasn't much else to do and it had become a local habit.

Everyone in town knew Christina Jane Wilson. She was born here, grew up here, made good and left here. And now she was coming back here.

I made myself read the rest of the article.

Chrissie was the fourth of the six Wilson children, now all adults. Her elder brother had taken over the local family business; her twin sisters had married and lived in Brisbane. Her younger sister, Stacey, had been in my year at school, and she was also married and lived at the coast. The youngest, Tony, always a show pony, was a sports commentator on one of the commercial television networks.

But Chrissie was the really famous one. Like all of us she'd started to play hockey at school and by the time she was in her teens everyone knew Chrissie was going to be more than an average player.

I wasn't a bad player myself and if I'd set my mind to it I might have been able to take it further

than the State Schoolgirl Championship trophy I had
on my mantelpiece. Who knows? But I didn't have
Chrissie's dedication.

Our school's sports mistress, Miss Grayson, spent
a lot of time coaching Chrissie, and Chrissie was
definitely her favorite. Nancy Grayson had only just
retired and lived with her, well, cousin, also a
teacher, who was due to retire soon as well.

I suspected the cousin story was just a cover for
Miss Grayson and Miss Hall but no one else seemed
to talk about it, especially not sixteen years ago.

That's what my current agitation was all about
really, something that had happened sixteen years
ago. And over those years I'd taken out the memories
of that incident, examined them, replayed them like a
well-worn video, stopped and fast-forwarded them.
But I'd never been able to finish the story, add any
sort of ending to it. Maybe that was the problem.

Chrissie was a year or so older than me and at
the time of the incident she was the school captain
as well as being captain of the senior hockey team.
She was tall and attractive and had a self-confidence
I used to envy as I surreptitiously watched her cross
the school grounds as though the whole world was
hers for the taking.

Yet Chrissie Wilson was a thoroughly nice person
as well. She gave her time freely to help coach us,
the junior team, and under her tutelage I began to
shine. Even Miss Grayson was impressed. I was
absolutely certain I was Chrissie's favorite.

I was nearly sixteen the year both the senior and
junior teams won places in the state finals, so

Chrissie and I had to go with our teams down to Brisbane to play. I remember hoping that we'd be billeted together but of course we weren't.

The senior team members were there in the stands to cheer us on when we played our final game. Five minutes before full time the score was locked at two all. I glanced up into the stand to see Chrissie waving me forward. I accelerated, saw space and whacked the ball. And that's all I remembered for a while. Next thing I knew I was flat on the ground and I was fighting for breath.

Apparently I'd scored a goal but collided with my opposition and taken the brunt of the impact. I was only winded, but I felt as though I was on my way out.

Then the blue sky above me darkened and when I blinked the shadowy area became a face. Clear blue eyes. A dusting of freckles across a small nose. A wide mouth that always seemed to be smiling. But not then. A frown of concern furrowed Chrissie Wilson's tanned forehead.

"Janey? Are you okay?" The smooth, honeyed tones of her voice only seemed to make my heart do a flip-flop that had nothing whatsoever to do with being knocked off my feet.

And then she touched me.

She reached out, brushed back my damp fringe, cupped my hot cheek. "Janey?"

What little breath that had found its way laboriously back into my lungs left for the second time in as many minutes.

"Get a stretcher," someone else said, and I groaned in alarm.

I made myself gingerly move my arms and then my legs. "I'm all right," I said quickly and struggled to sit up.

Chrissie put her strong arms around me to help me and I found myself slumping into her. Not that I needed to, really. I don't know why I did the dying swan bit but all I know is that when I leaned against Chrissie's body I felt something I'd never experienced before or since. It was sort of like coming home.

Then I was on a stretcher and being carted off the field. And Chrissie held my hand all the way to the dressing rooms.

While I recovered, the team went on to win the match, thanks to my winning goal, so I was definitely the wounded heroine of the match.

Then it was Chrissie's turn to take the field. I made sure I'd recuperated enough to watch her game. Her team won, of course, amid whispers that representatives from the Australian Institute of Sport were very interested in Chrissie's future.

I didn't see Chrissie again until we were back at school. By then the news was all over town that Chrissie Wilson was going to the Institute of Sport on a sporting scholarship. She'd even play for Australia, everyone predicted.

For some reason the fact that Chrissie was leaving town depressed me. I couldn't understand why I didn't want her to go. I mean, it was the opportunity of a lifetime for her.

I knew I had to congratulate her but couldn't bring myself to do it. I avoided her but at the same time wanted desperately to be with her. If I practiced hard maybe I could go to the AIS, too. I fantasized about our meeting there.

In the end it was the day before she was due to leave and I knew I had to see her. I found her in the sports room packing up her gear. I hung about waiting for everyone else to leave but of course there were two stragglers, her best friends, Margie and Carmen, and I cursed them, willing them to vanish to wherever.

Then Chrissie looked up and saw me and a faint smile hovered around her mouth. She turned to her friends. "Just give me a few minutes alone, to sort of say good-bye to the old place," she said.

The other two protested.

"No. I'll be okay," Chrissie reassured them. "I'll catch up with you."

Margie and Carmen reluctantly turned to go.

"Chrissie wants to be alone," Margie said to me pointedly when she saw me hovering just inside the room.

I blushed, wanting to run out the door, but I made myself stand my ground until they'd left. Then I walked over to Chrissie on decidedly shaky legs.

"Congratulations on getting the scholarship," I said, my voice embarrassingly squeaky.

Chrissie smiled and my heart lurched in my chest.

"Thanks," she said easily. "No aftereffects from your fall at the championships?"

I shook my head. "No. Actually I was just tired and wanted to lie down," I said with a forced laugh and I cringed, but Chrissie looked amused.

"You played a great game, Janey."

I scuffed the toe of my sneaker on the cement floor. "So did you in your game."

The silence seemed to expand in the small room.

"I — I just wanted to say good luck and I hope you get to play for Australia in the Olympic Games," I said in a rush.

"Wow! Now there's something to strive for." Chrissie chuckled.

For the first time I noticed how her blue eyes crinkled at the corners, how her full mouth curved upward so wonderfully.

"Actually, Janey, playing for Australia in the Olympics is one of my ambitions," Chrissie continued.

"One of your ambitions?" I laughed a little breathlessly. "You mean you have others?"

Chrissie nodded. "Oh, yes. A couple of others."

"You mean like getting married and having kids."

A shadow of some emotion I couldn't define passed over her face and she shrugged as she turned to zip up her bag.

Then she looked back at me and I couldn't seem to drag my eyes from the intensity of hers. My mouth went completely dry and I felt as though my heart had jumped right out of my chest and was thumping away right where my boobs had begun to develop.

I took a shallow breath. "Well, I guess I'm, well, keeping you from your friends. We'll all —" I swallowed again. "I'll miss you," I managed.

Chrissie continued to hold my gaze. "I'll miss you too, Janey," she said softly.

And then she leaned across and kissed me. Her

lips were so soft, like velvet, and my mouth opened in surprise. Chrissie drew back, her eyes dark pools, and then she kissed me again. I met her halfway this time and our lips held for indeterminable, exquisitely erotic moments.

My young breasts tingled and something delicious happened in the pit of my stomach, spiraling to center between my legs. It was the most incredible experience of my life.

I hadn't seen Chrissie Wilson again. Well, not in the flesh. But I'd watched every one of her games they'd televised. And I had a scrapbook of articles and photos I'd collected out of newspapers and magazines.

For months after that kiss I'd walked around in a daze. My mother eventually got totally exasperated with me, which was nothing new so it didn't bother me.

What did snap me out of it was an article in a magazine down at the news agency. "You Can't Play on the Team Unless You're a Lesbian," screamed the teaser on the cover.

The word *lesbian* repeated itself over and over inside my head for days until my curiosity overcame my embarrassment at actually fronting up to the counter and buying the magazine. I hurried home and locked myself in my room to read the article.

It seemed the vice captain of a netball team had been dropped from the side and now she was crying discrimination. She was convinced she was being excluded from the team because she wasn't a lesbian like the rest of the team members.

Lesbian. I looked the word up in my dictionary

just to be sure I had it right. And I remembered Chrissie's kiss. Did that make Chrissie and me lesbians? I almost hyperventilated with fright. And I worried myself sick.

So when Gary Robertson asked me out two weeks later I surprised us both by accepting. I waited anxiously for Gary to kiss me goodnight so I could see if it would feel the same as Chrissie's kiss.

It didn't. No crashing trains. No earth-shattering breathlessness. It was nothing like being kissed by Chrissie. I really must be a lesbian.

I desperately kissed Gary back, willing everything to be all right. For some time afterward I recall kissing every guy at every opportunity, until I decided that, lesbian or not, no kiss would ever match up to Chrissie Wilson's kiss.

Maybe I should have tried to kiss another girl but in a small town like this I knew I didn't have the intestinal fortitude to fly so blatantly in the face of convention. Two years after Chrissie left I married Gary Robertson. A year later my son, Coby, was born and the prerequisite two years later, my daughter, Jenna, arrived.

I knew the day I married Gary I was making a mistake, but by then I felt as though my life had been set in stone. Grow up, get married, have two kids. And I pushed Chrissie Wilson out of my mind. Most of the time.

I glanced at the clock and drank the rest of my tea in gulps. I was late. I worked part-time at the town's only bookshop but at the moment I was doing full-time. The owners were away on holiday.

I opened the doors of the bookshop just on time

and had my usual morning rush. Old Mr. Craigie shuffled in to read the morning newspaper in air-conditioned comfort sitting in what was now referred to as *his* chair by the window.

Half an hour later a couple of women I knew from PTA meetings came in and each bought a fat filthy, giggling over the lurid covers. Then, with Mr. Craigie dozing in his chair, I opened my own paper again and finished reading about Chrissie.

Seems she was coming home to recuperate after knee surgery. The knee had been giving her trouble all season and when asked by the reporter if she thought her knee would be up to a try for another Commonwealth gold to go with her Olympic medal, Chrissie had said, "No comment."

I carefully cut out the article and put it in my bag. It would be added to the scrapbook I'd kept of Chrissie's career.

Taking a stack of new releases from the box I'd opened yesterday, I began setting the books out on the shelves.

Chrissie Wilson. Her young, smiling face slipped so easily, so vividly, into my mind. Would she remember me?

There was a discreet cough behind me and I dropped the three or four books I was holding. Miraculously I juggled them and caught them before they hit the floor.

"Nice save."

I looked up at the owner of the smooth voice and this time the books did hit the floor.

"Sorry. And I can't even bend down to pick them up for you."

The blue eyes were the same, crinkling at the corners as she smiled that well-remembered smile. My eyes focused on her lips and I grew incredibly hot. Angrily I chastised myself. I was thirty-two years old, for heaven's sake. Not a blushing sixteen-year-old.

But sixteen was how I felt. And memories of that kiss in the sports room all those years ago took away what little composure I had left. I made myself bend down, pick up the fallen books. Perhaps she'd think the effort of doing so would account for my flushed face.

I had to pull myself together. Pushing myself to my feet I hurriedly shoved the books on the shelf and smiled shakily.

"Chrissie! Hi! Nice to see you again. How are you?" That's all I could get out because my tongue seemed to cleave to the roof of my suddenly dry mouth.

"I'm fine." Chrissie's smile widened. "And it's great to see you again, too, Janey."

We stood looking at each other, smiling away, and I wondered if she thought I'd changed much. She hadn't. My eyes did a swift sortie over her body. It was far more muscular now and she was obviously very fit. My gaze settled on her breasts and I had to swallow again. I dragged my gaze back to her face and I could tell by her expression that she'd been aware of my regard. I flushed again.

"I'm amazed you recognized me after all these

years," I said, disconcerted, rushing into embarrassed speech. "It must be sixteen years or so, mustn't it?" As if I didn't know.

Chrissie nodded. "Sixteen sounds right. And I'd have known you anywhere."

I laughed a little breathlessly. "You would?"

"Yes. I would."

"I would have known you, too. But then, I've seen you on television and in magazines, of course, when you won your medals. Congratulations on those."

Chrissie inclined her head. "Thank you."

"The whole town here went mad when you won your Olympic gold."

She laughed softly and I felt the prickle of awareness skim my skin like goosebumps. "As I remember, the whole team went mad, too. It was pretty exciting all round."

I nodded. "I guess it was."

"You didn't keep up your game?"

"No. Not after —" I stopped. Not after you left, I wanted to say. Somehow my enjoyment went out of the game. "Not after I left school," I finished quickly.

Chrissie leaned on the bookshelves and I remembered her knee. I pulled the stool from behind the desk. "Please, sit down on this."

"Thanks." She sat on it gratefully. "It's not too bad, really. Soon be good as new."

"Will you be rejoining the team next season? They said in the paper you might not be."

Chrissie shrugged. "It probably wouldn't be wise. I'm getting too old for it anyway." She grimaced ruefully. "I'll probably take up one of the coaching jobs on offer."

That would mean she'd be leaving again. I felt a wave of dejection wash over me. What had I expected anyway? That she would want to come back here to this tired little place when she'd been all over the world?

"They want me to take on Sports Coordinator for the secondary schools here."

"They do?" I couldn't keep the excitement out of my voice. "Will you take it?" I modified my tone a little and Chrissie shrugged again.

We were looking at each other once more and I felt so hot I wondered if the air-conditioning was failing. It was Chrissie who eventually broke the potent, swelling silence.

"Stacey sent me a photograph of you and Gary when you got married," Chrissie was saying. "She also told me about Gary's accident with his truck. I was sorry to hear about that."

"Gary and I had separated a year before he was killed," I told her, and an even heavier stillness enveloped us again.

"So." Chrissie fiddled with the bandage on her knee. "Is there anyone special in your life at the moment?"

I smiled crookedly. "Two, actually."

I watched a shadow flicker over Chrissie's face.

"My two kids. Coby's thirteen and Jenna's nearly eleven. That's the sum of it."

"Oh."

I licked my dry lips. "What about you?" I couldn't

believe the words had come out when I thought I was only thinking them.

"No. No one."

My heart did a decided flutter. "You've never felt the urge to marry?" I asked carefully. I mean, I could hardly ask her the other question that loomed dangerously in my mind.

"Marry?" Chrissie laughed and shook her head. "No. Never." She paused, her gaze holding mine. "Not to a guy anyway."

My heart leapt again and I felt myself blush hotly.

Chrissie raised her eyebrows. "Have I shocked you, Janey?"

"Oh, no. No, of course not," I said hurriedly. In truth I'd shocked myself with my reaction to her honesty.

"I've had a couple of relationships, but —" She moved her shoulders negatingly. "I guess I didn't have time for that and hockey."

We continued to look into each other's eyes and in hers I saw the same flicker of awareness I felt careening through my body.

Silently we both drank in each other, our bodies, our features, our memories. Eons later Chrissie moved, reached out and touched my cheek in much the same way she'd done when I was sixteen and had had the breath knocked out of me during the hockey game. And I felt just as winded. I gulped a shaky breath but it didn't steady me much.

"Are you okay?" Chrissie asked, her voice low and heavy and electrifying.

I felt that same earth-stopping wonder I'd felt all

those years ago and I smiled. I wasn't going to wait and worry another sixteen years.

"I am now," I said softly and there, right in the middle of the bookshop, with old Mr. Craigie still dozing in his chair, I kissed those wonderful, velvety lips again.

She Shoots, She Scores

Tracey Richardson

Corrie Martin sipped the last drops of beer from her mug, licked her lips in frothy enjoyment, then settled into a full-lipped pout in the hope one of her teammates would take pity on her.

"Hey, Marty, your best friend just die?"

"No, just my beer," Corrie answered sullenly, eyes downcast for full effect.

"Aw, poor baby. You gotta make it last. Don't you ever learn, girl?"

Corrie smiled dispiritedly at her team's goalie, Brenda Smith, and wished for once the coach would relax her rule of only one drink the night before a game. Corrie's eyes lit up playfully. "Hey, Smitty, you aren't really going to drink that entire glass of beer, are you?"

Brenda laughed, shook her head. "Marty, you're cute. But you think I want to get in trouble with the coach for getting you half pissed the night before the opening game?"

"Look, Smitty," Corrie whined plaintively. "I'm not gonna get drunk on a couple of glasses, for Christ's sake. I just want to have a good time. I'll even compensate you."

Brenda frowned skeptically. "Well, go on."

Corrie's grin was sly. "I'll introduce you to some cute dyke here and tell her how great you are."

Brenda shook her head, still frowning. "The only cute dykes here — no offense — are from the other teams, and Coach Kershaw would have a fit if she caught us fraternizing with the enemy."

Corrie rolled her eyes. "She would not. And besides, it *is* the pre-tournament get-to-know-you shindig. Aren't we supposed to fraternize?"

Brenda sighed out of boredom. "We're only here because the tournament organizers insisted all the teams show up and rub elbows with the sponsors."

Hooking her thumbs through the belt loops of her Guess jeans, Corrie leaned into the wall and scanned the room. It was full of women. She smiled, thought this surely must be heaven, except that come tomorrow, she'd be trying to score *against* most of them, not score *with* them. *Too bad.*

She straightened, squinted through the crowd at

the most delicious-looking woman she'd seen in a long time. "Hey, Smitty, isn't that Shannon Murphy?"

Brenda looked in the direction Corrie was drooling in. "So it is."

"God, I am such a fan of hers. I think she's the greatest, don't you?"

"*Was* the greatest maybe, but she's kind of old now. I'd say her best years are behind her. Hell, she'll be lucky if she makes the national team next year."

"Of course she will!" Corrie gasped. "She's only been on the national team like forever. And she's still great."

"Yeah, yeah, that's just your hormones talking."

Corrie grinned, her voice low. "Yeah, well, my hormones could have a great conversation with her hormones."

Indeed, Shannon Murphy was hot. Wavy dark hair glanced off her shoulders. Her eyes were as big and blue as the Atlantic Ocean, her nose long and straight, her mouth supple yet delicate. And her body was to die for. Tall, lean, but shapely in her button-fly, low-hipped jeans.

"I gotta go talk to her," Corrie said. "I've wanted to meet her since I was a kid and used to watch her on TV."

"Hold on there a minute. Meet who?" It was their team captain, Jessie O'Sullivan. Her teammates called her Bones because she was so tall and wiry.

"Just thought I'd go say hi to Shannon Murphy," Corrie replied defensively.

"Forget it, Marty. We're playing her team

tomorrow afternoon. Time to put on our game faces. Once we're the national champs, you can be friendly all you want."

Corrie scowled. Maybe Bones had a point. She should be concentrating on the tournament at hand, not on girls. And she needed to have a good tournament to impress the coaches and scouts if she was to make her first national team next year. She leaned into the wall again. This time her pout was for real.

Corrie reefed on her skate lace, tied it tightly, then reached for her Team Alberta jersey. She had been ignoring the grumpy players in the locker room; she couldn't be bothered listening to them complain. Some of them had gotten 6 A.M. anonymous phone calls in their rooms and they swore it was their imminent opponents trying to throw them off their game. Bones was not to be placated.

"Listen girls, this means war." Bones leveled an ominous gaze around the room. "When we go out there, we're going to make them pay."

Corrie sighed; she wanted to roll her eyes but didn't dare. Though she was one of the bigger women on her team, scoring goals and flying around the ice was why she played hockey. Throwing her body around and flattening other players wasn't her thing and she wanted none of it.

When they took to the ice, Corrie knew that as soon as the game-starting whistle blew, bodies would fly. She squared off in the face-off circle against her idol, Shannon Murphy, and tried not to think about those long legs and narrow waist, those aqua eyes.

The puck dropped. With her superior upper body, Corrie quickly blocked her opponent and kicked the puck back to her teammate, then untangled herself from Shannon Murphy and made a break for open ice.

Behind her, the boards reverberated as two players crashed into the wall, her teammate landing atop the British Columbia player. Like moths to a flame, the players on the ice from both teams hovered, jawing and shoving. Corrie skated to the periphery to make a show of support, but had no intention of jumping into the fray.

Shannon Murphy skated up to Corrie and they stood side by side, both ready to take each other on if duty called and things got really ugly. Corrie winked at her idol, nodded hello, then grinned when Shannon did a double take at the unexpected show of friendliness.

Over the rest of the period, more bodies flew, the penalty box a revolving door. The intermission did nothing to cool tempers, but Corrie concentrated on the game and on scoring another goal.

The blade of her stick collected the pass with a feather touch and she guided it into enemy territory, skating and deking with lightning quickness, leaving her opponents inanimate pylons. Her brown eyes giving nothing away, she skated to the net. Just one player — Shannon Murphy — was all that remained between her and the goalie.

Corrie deked again, but Shannon wasn't so easily fooled. Lowering her shoulder, Corrie barreled straight on, spinning the lighter Shannon around and right off her skates. No one in the way now, Corrie faked a shot, then flicked her wrist, burying the puck in the top shelf.

The whistle blew, the ref frantically waving off the goal and indicating a roughing penalty to Corrie. Her heart pounding, Corrie saw red as the blood rushed to her ears.

"Fuck you!" she yelled at the ref as Bones began pulling her away before she got herself into more trouble. It was then she noticed Shannon Murphy writhing around on the ice in obvious pain, her teammates bending over her.

"Aww, shit," Corrie said.

Corrie lay on her bed, feeling like shit. She hadn't meant to hurt Shannon Murphy. Now it would be her fault if Shannon's broken ankle ended her hockey career. Winning the game and her teammates' offer of beer had failed to console her.

She swung her legs over the side of her bed. The only thing would that make her feel better would be to apologize to the hockey legend, to let her know it wasn't intentional.

All the teams were lodged in the same hotel, so, still in her stocking feet, Corrie took the elevator up two floors to Team B.C. territory. She briskly knocked on the door before she had a chance to change her mind.

Shannon opened the door, a pair of crutches under her armpits. Her stomach somersaulting, Corrie

sucked in her breath at the long-legged beauty before
her.

"Ah, hi," she finally managed.

Shannon frowned sourly, leaning on a crutch for
support.

"I, ah, wanted to apologize," Corrie uttered,
hoping she didn't sound like the dork she felt. "I
really didn't mean to hurt you and I feel like such a
shit, I —"

"Look kid —"

Kid? Shit. So I'm a kid to her?

"— I don't want your apology, okay?"

"But . . ." Corrie wasn't expecting this. Just what
was she expecting, she chastised herself, a big kiss on
the lips to thank her for being so chivalrous? She
wanted to kick herself, knew now this was a mistake.

"Your team was looking to kick our ass any way
you could, even if it meant maiming us," Shannon
said acidly.

Corrie shook her head lightly, her eyebrows
knotting in protest. "But, wait, that's —"

The door slammed shut and Corrie stood there,
her hands still jammed in her pockets. She stood
another minute, shifting from foot to foot, hoping the
door would miraculously open again.

Corrie knew she was Public Enemy Number One,
having taken out the renowned Shannon Murphy. Her
gut ached as she laced up her skates for the second
game against Shannon Murphy's team. It was a
double knockout tournament and they could finish off

Team B.C. with another victory. But winning was the last thing on her mind. She just wanted to survive.

Corrie kept her head up and tried to lay low every time her blades touched the ice. But then she found the puck on her stick just as two opponents hurtled toward her. She swore to herself, clutched her stick with all her strength to protect the puck. It was herself that needed protecting.

Corrie was sandwiched like a tuna and thudded heavily to the ice, pain searing her arm like a hot poker. "Fuck!" she screamed as she curled into a fetal position, her left wrist flopping uselessly beside her. She bit her lip until it bled and considered the bleak possibility that she might never breathe again as her teammates uttered unheard words of consolation.

Corrie's wrist was broken, relegating her to cheer-leader for the rest of the national championships. Now that she could drink all the beer she wanted, she was in no mood to. She just wanted to lick her wounds and fantasize about the MVP award she might have earned. She shunned her teammates and wandered aimlessly around the arena, lost in a haze of jaundiced self-pity. No one or nothing could console her. Hockey was her lifeblood.

She watched her team go through their practice drills, listened dejectedly to them chatter in the locker room.

"Smitty," she whispered as the players began to stream out, discussing plans for dinner. "Will you help me put on my skates?"

Brenda's eyebrows shot up in curious amusement. "Why? What are you up to?"

"Nothing. I just want to skate a few laps."

"All right, but you better be careful."

"It's my wrist, not my legs. And don't worry, I won't do anything stupid."

Skates snugly on her feet, Corrie stepped onto the ice, feeling free and untethered for the first time since her injury. She glided slowly at first, building up speed as she rounded the end of the rink. She loved the feel of the cool air ruffling her short hair, the faint smell of Zamboni exhaust, the swooshing sound of her metal blades cutting into the ice. She loved everything about arenas, about ice.

Focusing on her stride, she didn't notice the figure hobble into the penalty box from a door beneath the grandstands.

"Corrie," the figure called out, the voice echoing across the empty, dimly lit arena.

Corrie rounded the rink and slowed at the sight of Shannon Murphy leaning on her crutches in the penalty box. She braked in front of her, relief and bitterness battling for supremacy. She had no idea which would win out if and when she opened her mouth.

"Hey, kid, I'm —"

"I'm not a kid," Corrie spat.

Shannon's lips curled into a slow smile; she gave a slight nod of acknowledgment. "I just wanted to say I'm sorry about what happened to you, Corrie."

It was Corrie's turn to be sore. "Just save it, okay? Obviously you told your team to have a field day with me."

Corrie skated off before Shannon could answer. She'd told her, all right, showed her she wasn't some naive "kid." Shannon could stick it up her ass, for all she cared. Shannon hadn't shown her any forgiveness earlier, so why should she be any more charitable?

She skated a lap, and when she reached the penalty box again, Shannon opened the gate and hopped tentatively onto the ice.

"Look, you want me to chase you down and knock some sense into you with these crutches?"

Corrie stopped, spun around, and tried to restrain a smile as she envisioned a crazed but beautiful hockey player waving a crutch over her head. She sheepishly skated back to Shannon.

"I did not tell my team to do anything to you," Shannon said, her eyes, her mouth so serious that Corrie wanted to kiss a smile back onto her.

"In fact, after I got hurt," she continued, "I specifically told them not to retaliate."

Corrie followed Shannon back into the penalty box and sat down with a heavy sigh. "I'm sorry. I'm just pissed off about not playing, okay? I know it's not your fault."

Shannon sat down beside her, tossing her crutches to the floor. "Hey, I know what it's like, believe me. I was pretty pissed off at you at first, but I know you didn't hurt me intentionally. I was just too upset about being out of the tournament to see that."

Corrie shrugged. "It's all right."

"No, it's not all right, the way I acted with you. It took guts for you to come and apologize. I was a jerk."

"Yeah, well, so was I just now, so I guess we're even."

Corrie took a deep breath, turned to face the woman she had admired from afar for years. In an instant, she forgot about her wrist and the tournament. She smiled shyly. "I think you're the greatest player women's hockey has ever seen."

Shannon's laugh erupted deep from her throat. "I think that's just a tad overdramatic." Her smoky blue gaze slid up and down Corrie like a tight glove. "But not a bad pickup line."

Corrie felt her face flush and her tongue lock up. Her mouth dropped open, then closed again.

Shannon grinned a mouthful of perfect white teeth. "I guess it's my turn to try a line. How's this? I think you're the hottest young thing on skates I've seen in years. And I'm not just talking about your scoring abilities." She ran the tip of her tongue over her teeth in agonizingly slow fashion. "But then again, maybe I am." She smiled, gave that look again. "So, are you a good scorer or what?"

Corrie blushed even more and for the life of her, she couldn't get any words out. Was the woman whose poster had adorned her teenage bedroom wall really trying to hit on her, or was this some cruel joke?

"I saw you watching me at the banquet the other night," Shannon persisted, her raised eyebrows posing a challenge.

Corrie nodded, swallowed and mentally kicked herself off the bench and into the game. She knew the score here. After all, she was an offensive player herself, aggressive with an aptitude for great bursts of scoring initiative.

"Yeah, I was." Corrie smiled in a calmness that belied the churning in her guts. "I think you're incredible and I want to get to know you better."

Shannon grabbed a fistful of Corrie's sweater and pulled her to her, her lips firm, demanding, against Corrie's. Her hand touched the back of Corrie's neck to ensure that Corrie wasn't going anywhere, while her insatiable mouth told Corrie there was no escape.

They kissed for a long time, their tongues hungrily exploring each other's mouths, until Corrie thought for sure she'd melt into a puddle on the ice. She moaned softly and was surprised when Shannon took it as a cue to go further.

"Here?" Corrie panted in astonishment as Shannon's hand slipped beneath her sweater, then her bra. Corrie shuddered at the gentle yet firm massaging of her erect nipple, shuddered again at the throbbing wetness between her legs that was growing by monumental proportions.

Shannon's lips caressed Corrie's constricted throat, her hands pushing Corrie to a prone position on the bench. A kaleidoscope of moving hands, parted legs and discarded jeans was all the answer Corrie needed to her earlier question. Her back arched in pure, wanton pleasure as Shannon's tongue teasingly snaked its way into her, Shannon's mouth and Corrie's hips locked into a delicious, clandestine dance.

Corrie lost all track of time and space as the volcano of arousal knotted inside her, swelling and surging with each fiery stroke of Shannon's tongue.

When she could no longer contain it, Corrie took one final breath before she burst out, hot liquid dampening her legs, sweat turning cold on her forehead, her body convulsing.

Wary of their respective injuries, Shannon gingerly crawled up and kissed the tip of Corrie's nose.

Corrie smiled back, collecting her breath. Now it was *her* turn to score, to even the count. Oh, and she was good at comeback situations, at evening the score. Her grin was wide, conspiratorial. "Why don't we continue this back at my room?"

DriveTime

Therese Szymanski

As I stood behind the couch, delivering a line that had gotten huge belly laughs from the audience every night the show played, I glanced about the theater with a slight grin on my face, and that's when I noticed her . . .

Our eyes locked for a moment, and under the heat of the powerful stage lights I felt a jolt of energy even greater than the adrenaline I was already experiencing.

Anyone watching would've thought I was merely waiting for the laughing to subside before continuing with my next line, but she and I both knew the truth: I was locked into those gorgeous green orbs, locked in time and place. A slow smile eased its way across her face, and then I knew for sure that she knew, and that she was here for that very reason.

I suddenly realized the laughter had stopped and everyone was hanging on for my next line. I brought my focus back to the stage, and tried to pull my thumping heart back into character . . .

The first time I heard her voice was during the kind of God-awful freezing rainstorm only a Michigan winter can provide. The sort that has your wheels spinning in circles while cars all around you fishtail into curbs, one another, and anything else they can find.

Her voice that day, as she narrated the traffic situation on WGLT, was that deep pitch you feel right in the pit of your stomach — y'know the type I mean, the voice that makes you believe she's thinking of sex. But there was something else to it — an edge of taunting clarity, a certain cockiness, something that makes you know she's as sure of herself as a redneck at a tractor pull.

Since that day three years ago, I've followed her as she moved up the ladder of the Detroit radio market — first a traffic reporter, then her own late-night and weekend shows as a deejay, jumping from one station to another, with me always hot on her tail. Now she was back on mornings, during the coveted early-morning drive in to work. Who needs coffee when you've got that velvety smooth voice to greet you in the morning?

Because I work in advertising it's never been difficult for me to find her when she moved from one station to another; that information has always been right at my fingertips. So was the location of her very first remote, which I attended, as well as almost every one since. Sometimes I just pop in for a quick doughnut and glance if she's at a restaurant in the morning, or I pretend to actually go shop if I'm in the mood for a longer look at those beautiful legs, slender build and long curly red hair that frames her face so perfectly.

She first caught me with her voice, then got me in deeper with her looks, but of late it's become something more . . .

Going to all these remotes I've gotten to know her, the real her, not just her radio personality. I like her sense of humor on the radio, when she's teasing the other deejays or playing with a caller, but in real life it's apparent she really does like people and interacting with them, and I love watching her at it. I love watching her smile when she picks up a baby, seeing her tousle some gangling youth's hair, reach out and lead someone by the arm up to the microphone, play tough guy to some asshole's snarl.

One day I was following her into a mall and a book dropped from her purse. *Wuthering Heights.* Another day I watched her seat an old woman in the audience; I later discovered that was her grandmother. In all the rumor mills in this town's ad community I've never heard one negative word about Erika Hill, not one.

One of the few things halting the flames of my crush was that I had no reason to even remotely suspect that she was a lesbian, none until now, that is . . .

Erika Hill hit the button on the control panel, letting out Fred Flintstone's "Yabba Dabba Doo" all over the city's airwaves. "It's quittin' time in the Motor City," she purred into the mike. "And we're here to jam you all the way home on our all-request drive at five." She hit another button, setting a CD to play yet another song while she checked the settings for the next commercial block. She never should've agreed to take the afternoon drive, but someone had to cover while the regular deejay, or "personality," as he insisted on being called, took a vacation.

She glanced down at the folded newspaper sitting on the chair next to her and grinned. Miss Shawn Donnelly was in for a surprise tonight, that was for sure. If she could ever get out of here and over to the theater on time.

She had first noticed the cocky little butch just over a year ago at a remote she did for a new grocery store. It was one of those chain megastore things, although she couldn't remember just which one anymore. Through her few years in radio, all the remotes were blending together so she couldn't remember one from another.

The one thing she could remember was that drop-dead gorgeous woman. Those dark eyes, the snarling little smile, the short hair neatly brushed back over her ears. Sometimes the eyes, which had first caught Erika's attention, were hidden behind the black lenses of expensive Ray-Bans, and sometimes the slender yet obviously muscular frame was clad in a suit jacket, whereas other times she donned black leather and jeans.

Erika could imagine the woman pinning her down, holding her in strong arms while she ripped open Erika's shirt and popped the buttons on her jeans. She could also imagine wrapping her arms around those strong shoulders and biting that tanned neck, exposed in a neckless white silk or, better yet, black silk pirate shirt.

Erika sat back in her chair, lightly running her tongue over her lips. It had been far too long — far too many days of flirting with guys, pretending to be something other than what she was — selling her soul to the devil for a job, for a way up the ranks to her own morning show. Soon she would be there. That was what she kept telling herself. But surely she could permit herself this one little distraction. After all, what was this woman but a two-bit actress? A gorgeous, absolutely edible one at that, but she was working out of some little theater regardless.

Erika took another glance at the article in the *Detroit News* about local queer theater, which contained a photo from one of the plays currently going on. The photo had a group of five people, and in it was her little mystery butch with her arms wrapped around another woman. The play was that night at eight.

The lights went down and the curtain music, Sister Sledge doing "We Are Family," came up. Joan and I quickly rushed to kneel upstage of the couch, out of sight of the audience, and waited as the other actors cleared out and the stage lights came back up. The others entered, two by two, and went downstage to take their bows, and then it was time. Joan and I walked to the center of the line the others had formed and bowed, then grasped the hands of the others and, as a single unit, bowed again.

I tried to spot her but the bright stage lights were right in my eyes, blinding me. Suddenly, I felt someone touch my leg, and I looked down.

Erika Hill stood there with a dozen red roses.

I suddenly felt as if the stalker had become the stalked.

Erika glanced at her watch. Ten-thirty. She was usually in bed by this time. And she wouldn't mind being in bed sometime soon, as long as it wasn't to sleep.

Working the morning drive meant she had to be at the station by six A.M., but it wasn't as if her tightly secured closet left much room for a social life anyway.

Shawn Donnelly was obviously a woman used to being in control — her eyes expressed her amazement at being handed the roses. Erika could either let Shawn reclaim her control, and play into it, or give the woman a bit more of a challenge. In fact, right now, she felt like being aggressive, taking charge. But first, Shawn had to come back out.

She sipped her soda and joined a group that was deep in discussion about the play. Making sure that she could see the door she supposed the actors would come out of when they were done changing costumes, she half-heartedly joined in the discussion of whether the play was a comedy or a farce.

"Well, the first act didn't really even have any farcical elements to it . . ." one woman began.

"But you've got to admit, the second act was over the top," another woman countered.

"It seems to me it was two one-act plays, with a common theme and characters," Erika said.

The first woman stopped and looked at me. "Y'know, I know I don't know you, but your voice sounds so familiar."

Erika knew things weren't as bad as they once were — after all, WDRQ had an openly gay drag queen on their morning show — but still, anyone in the public eye had to be careful. "I don't get out much, so tell me, is that the replacement for 'What's your sign?'"

Fortunately, before the woman could give any sort of outraged reply, Shawn appeared. She came striding across the stage in Doc Martens, ripped blue jeans, and a T-shirt that was torn at the collar just enough to reveal a bit of her collarbone. The roses were in

one hand while the other held a simple black leather
jacket tossed over her shoulder. The overall effect was
of someone who didn't give a damn.

Erika felt a surge of heat rush through her body.

When she noticed me coming at her, her big
green eyes belied the cockiness she had exhibited just
a few minutes earlier. I had rushed in getting my
costume off and dressing in my civvies again, hoping
against hope that I wouldn't be too late, that she
would still be there when I went back out.

One look into those eyes told me I had nothing to
worry about.

I had her. Voice and all. Now I just had to reel
her in.

I stopped at the edge of the stage, which stood
just three feet over the theater's floor, and looked
down at her. I leaned toward my left, with my thumb
hooked into my pocket, and then realized that that
probably looked kinda stupid, what with the flowers
in my hand. So I jumped down off the stage and
walked up to her.

She was a bit taller in person, standing next to
me and all. A bit taller than me, in fact.

"Thanks for the flowers," I said with a slight
grin, turning on the charm.

"Your performance was wonderful."

Her smell was intoxicating. A light airy scent that
hinted at a thought not quite remembered. Her smile
was fabulous, but now it was beyond a doubt that

she was wasted on the radio. She needed to be where people could see her. See those long legs, that beautiful hair, slender figure, penetrating eyes, and . . .

"I've noticed you at some of my remotes . . ."

. . . and hear that incredible voice. "Just a few of them. I guess you could call me a fan."

Several of the women Erika had been talking with gathered around me, asking questions and congratulating me on my performance. She stood back with her arms crossed as I spoke briefly with each of them. Her tight blue jeans clung to her shapely legs and tight ass, leaving little to the imagination.

Fortunately, as an actor, I have a bloody wonderful imagination.

Her top was just loose enough to outline her breasts and arms. The open collar revealed a nice cut of her collarbone and showed off a tiny labrys necklace lying on the soft skin just above her cleavage.

I love collarbones, especially the sort that jut out just enough to be defined — pictures that show too much aren't anywhere near as much of a turn-on as something that just hints and leaves me to fill in the blanks. A woman in an off-the-shoulder dress can just about make me come with a simple smoldering gaze. The softness of her skin, the hints of the full breasts that lie just beyond the top of the dress . . .

Full soft breasts, hard nipples, trim belly, skin as soft and smooth as the well-cared-for leather of a beat-up old biker jacket . . .

Someone was asking me something — whether the

play was a comedy or a farce — but all I knew was that Erika Hill was just a few feet from me, staring right into my eyes . . .

Erika leaned back against the wall, trying to remember how to flirt, how to be a femme fatale. Trying to remember the days before she got into radio, when she was still free.

Shawn obviously had no trouble flirting. She probably didn't even notice the way the women were looking at her. Didn't know the effect she had on them, was clueless as to how she was flirting back with them: she was who she was, didn't hide it and didn't care.

Erika envied that. Envied and admired it . . . She enjoyed watching the women around Shawn, enjoyed watching all the women still hanging around the theater, flocked around the cast. There were even some boys flirting with the male cast members, but it was the women who interested her, especially the women around Shawn.

It was obvious that Shawn was becoming as impatient with these hangers-on as she was, for she kept looking up at Erika, looking deep inside her with those mysterious, dark eyes.

Their gazes met, and Shawn winked at her before flipping a cocky smile.

Erika allowed her gaze to slowly work its way down Shawn's lean muscular body, from velveteen brown eyes down to polished black boots, pausing at critical places along the way.

It seemed like ages later, but was probably less than fifteen minutes, that she and Shawn were the only ones left in the theater. Erika had a vague recollection of people talking about going out to the bar, and Shawn's saying she'd lock up the theater, and then it was just the two of them, standing a dozen or so feet from each other. Shawn's back was to the theater door, which she had just locked behind her, and Erika's back was to the wall — she was leaning against it, with a foot propped up.

My heart was racing; my breath was shallow. I was trying to keep my cool, keep my composure, but I was sure I was gonna lose it.

Here was Erika Hill, the woman I had been listening to for years. And she had just given me roses, and sultry looks all evening long. I couldn't count the number of times I'd been driving down the road, listening to her voice, and considered unzipping my pants and slipping my fingers inside, to caress myself to those tones, to that voice that was already caressing me so much like a touch itself.

She was sizing me up, just like she had been doing all night long. Taking me in in a slow glance, from boots up my legs, pausing at my crotch, up over my tight stomach, resting at my shoulders, examining my hands, probably imagining how they'd touch her . . .

I advanced on her, the adrenaline from the show, from being on stage, only increasing with our proximity. I knew I was still a bit sweaty from the heat of the stage lights, from the anxiety of the performance. And I had a feeling she liked it.

Sometimes you know words will only kill the mood. Stop what should happen. I had never before seen her in a gay bar, never heard a single rumor about her, never gotten a single indication in any way that she was gay, but everything about her said that she wanted me — from her body language and the way she approached me, to the tone of her voice and the fact she hadn't protested when I locked the two of us alone together in the theater.

As much as I wanted to hear her voice while I did her, I knew that wasn't possible.

She took a step toward me. I stayed glued to the wall, wanting to go to her but unable to.

Her lips were against mine, her tongue in my mouth, every inch of her body pressed tightly against mine. I wrapped my legs around her strong waist while she carried me with those strong, rippled arms across the theater to the stage as if I were simply a prop, some piece of paper she'd use on stage.

I groaned, and she put a finger against my lips.

"Don't say a word," she ordered. I wrapped my lips around the finger. She put my ass down on the couch then leapt to her feet. "Stay right there."

With a few easy strides she crossed the theater and climbed the ladder to the lighting booth, quickly playing with the switches till the theater was filled with total darkness and the hard beats of Prince until, out of the darkness, bright lights filled the stage, centering on the couch where I sat.

She came back to me, emerging from the darkness like some sort of ethereal visage, a goddess emerging from the mists of Avalon . . .

She pushed my legs apart, stretching them wide so she could kneel on the floor between them. I leaned forward while she grabbed both my wrists in one hand, holding them tight behind my back while her mouth blazed a trail from my mouth, down my cheek and chin and down into my shirt, burning wherever it touched.

I groaned, needing more, so much more, and squirmed under her grasp, struggling to free my hands. She roughly opened my shirt, then my bra, almost ripping my clothes off.

She wouldn't let me get any of her clothes off, but then, I was naked, stripped down, lying on the couch with her crouched next to me. Her lips were on mine, her hands burning a trail across my breasts, down my stomach, teasing between my legs.

I was arching up, trying to entice her to take me, to use me. Those dark eyes were watching me, staring at me, taking in every piece and particle of my body under the heat of the bright stage lights.

A slight grin touched her lips. I stretched out, planting one naked foot on the floor and tossing the other leg up over the back of the couch, laying my arms up over my head, knowing she was enjoying my body and liking the fact.

The lights left nothing hidden; every inch of my body was open and exposed to her. Her fingers went down between my thighs while her teeth clamped onto my nipple.

I knew I was wet. I knew I was greedy, but I couldn't help it. Her strong arms and fingers just went where they pleased and I gave up even trying to fight against it. I knew there was no use trying to be coy or playing hard to get. She could take what she wanted and do what she wanted to me.

And I wanted her to do whatever she wanted to.

She arched up, her legs spread as wide as she could get them spread. She couldn't have been spread better if I'd tied her down. I knelt between her legs and pushed them just a little wider, leaning over her, trailing my tongue down her breasts, over her belly and right into her cunt, which she shoved up into my mouth.

I pulled away from her as she groaned. She reached up and grabbed me by my leather, pulling me down on top of her.

What she didn't know was that when I had changed out of my costume I'd put on a little something extra for her . . . And now I unzipped my pants to let her see the little gift I had wrapped just for her.

At first she pulled away, her eyes very large, but I grabbed her by the hips and pulled her back onto me, onto it, and I pushed it in all the way.

"Oh, God, Shawn!" she screamed as she took it all. I pulled her onto my lap, my hands on her hips as she rode my cock, as we pushed it in and pulled it out, my mouth clamped onto her breast, whipping my tongue over it. My hands went down to her cunt, rubbing it gently as the tool went in and out and my fingers toyed with her wet pussy, her swollen clit.

"Oh, God, Shawn, please, Shawn!" she screamed as she came. I relished every syllable as it came out of her mouth, passing through those luscious red lips. Loving how my name sounded riding her waves of passion.

I knew that whatever reason or motive kept her closeted so thoroughly entrenched in secrecy, wouldn't allow her ever to see me again, so I had to commit each moment of this to memory: the texture of the couch caressing our bodies, the lights that left no secrets, the pounding music that futilely attempted to cover any thoughts except of action. The look of ecstasy on her face as she screamed, the way her hair draped across her features in reckless abandon, the pitch her sensuous voice took as she toppled over the edge of forever ... Each detail lodged itself in my brain, even as my mind's eye saw her in each moment of our past, and the two became melded as one.

I couldn't get enough — first her fingers and her mouth, then the dildo, then her mouth again before she used her fist. We went on and on, all night long, throughout the theater. This was surely what a one-night stand was meant to be.

I used her, needed her, for hours on end. Then, finally, as the dawn began to break, with the taste of her still on my lips, she pulled me up into her strong arms and held me. As I rested my head on her breast I was comfortable for the first time in years.

We began to doze off, but I suddenly knew that I couldn't fall asleep with her. I leaned up, looking at the eyes that had watched me all night, the aristocratic nose that was perhaps a little too big, the mouth that was turned up slightly in a smile.

I looked into those deep eyes, relaxed now, and thought of all the times I had looked into them in the past, remembered how they had first drawn me in, led me on, brought me here, and I knew that if we spoke or slept together, I wouldn't be able to leave, not ever.

I left.

I was more relaxed than I had ever been before. I had no idea how wound up I'd been. I almost wished I had given her some way of getting back in touch with me again, for yet another night, but that night, under the stage lights, had to remain a fantasy — far removed from anything in my normal life.

Monday morning, after the show, I still had a grin on my face, even though it was off to another unending meeting with yet another ad agency, trying to help our salespeople sell more time to more advertisers ... And I was Erika Hill, the morning-drive, heterosexual personality again, flirting with all the boys as we walked into the high chrome-and-glass building and took the elevator up to the media department on the fifth floor ...

We entered the conference room, filled with a dozen or so account and media types, all in their nice, professional suits, ties, heels, makeup and uptight smiles . . .

And looking worse than any drag queen that even Harvey Fierstein could create was Shawn Donnelly, without her leather or T-shirt, but with that grin I knew so well slowly spreading across her face, as our eyes met . . .

The Journal
Kaye Davis

Some people say cops and baseball players are the most superstitious people in America. It's not true. Twenty-two years on the force and I don't believe in luck, although bad luck can be a tempting crutch, an excuse for failure. Bad luck. That's what they said last week when they jerked the funding on the Lindsey Martin task force — just our bad luck that we didn't catch a child killer. That's when I exploded, losing a shouting match with the chief. It earned me a free counseling session with the department shrink and orders to keep this fucking journal. They say it'll assist me in "controlling my anger and channeling my aggression." Of course they promised no one will read it and encouraged me to write anything I want. Yeah, I believe that one. Watch the lawyers line up at the courthouse to get subpoenas if I'm involved in a controversial shooting. It'll be a race to see if the department gets it before the bad guy does. Hope they're not surprised when I surrender ashes.

Kim slammed down her pen and pushed back her desk chair. God, she couldn't believe she was actually writing in the damned thing. Angrily, she tossed ice cubes into a tumbler, filled it with Crown Royal and added a splash of Coke. They hadn't even sent her to a psychiatrist after her partner was killed in 'seventy-nine. Those were different times, but she remembered them like yesterday. An elderly black woman had flagged down their squad car and mumbled something about a shooting at the Circle Bar D Grill.

Jake had laughed. "Maybe we'll grab a little breakfast while we're there." His black face broke into a grin. "A growing boy like me needs his protein."

Back then the unwanted, blacks and women — especially women who weren't married or fucking other cops and, therefore, might be queer — were partnered. Despite the sorry system, she'd lucked into the best partner in the department and he'd died in the doorway of the Circle Bar D. Screams, flashes of faces, colors, distorted images — total bedlam — greeted her when she stepped over him into the restaurant. Later she found out the gunman had already systematically executed nine customers. Witnesses say a dozen more would surely have died if she hadn't killed him. How his shots missed her, she'd never know. But hers didn't miss.

Destiny, a friend told her. Luck, a crusty twenty-year man grumbled. Not your time, her sergeant said. The blood bath bought her a special distinction in the department. She, Kim Coleman, was only the third person to be placed on the Wall of Honor while still living. The last time was in 1965 and he was dead three years later — a suicide. She was the only woman on the Wall, living or dead, and she'd spent the last nineteen years trying to live up to her reputation and the honor that had both helped and hurt her career.

That's why she didn't think they'd go against her and cancel the task force. But they called her bluff and threatened to pull her off the case entirely if she didn't control her obsession — their words, not hers. She called it dedication to duty. Sipping her drink, she returned to her desk and began to write.

I passed her house on my way to work and saw her running to the car, dressed in a bright, pretty dress and clutching a doll while her beautiful, well-dressed mother chased after her. The child always looked up giggling wherever her mother caught her hand. I'd enjoyed watching their game and had wondered many times why it was just the two of them. Why couldn't I have been at that corner on that morning?

Wednesday, September 17, 1997, was a clear day with temperatures in the mid-eighties. Lindsey's mother, Julia, had taken a day off from work and the two of them had peanut butter and jelly sandwiches for lunch at their backyard picnic table. A glass of milk slipped from Lindsey's four-year-old, jelly-stained hands. Julia went inside for more milk and left Lindsey coloring in her Little Mermaid *coloring book. She swore she was gone for less than five minutes. I believed her — all the officers did. We know how little time it takes to steal a child. If only there'd been a dog or the gate had been locked. Or it'd been raining.*

An elderly neighbor saw a white male carrying the little girl to a dingy beige van. Lindsey sucked her thumb and clutched a red Crayola in her other hand. He carried the coloring book. The neighbor sensed nothing amiss. The little girl's father, she assumed. Then, like smoke in a thunderstorm, the child and kidnapper were gone. They're still gone.

I avoided talking about him — what he might . . . would be doing to her. Her mother asked me constantly, at first, if Lindsey was alive. I'd spout the standard line — the longer she's gone, the less likely . . . but I knew she was dead within hours. We haven't found the body yet, but Julia doesn't ask anymore. Thankfully, she doesn't make accusations or point fingers, but I know she thinks I — the whole department — have failed. She's right.

She closed the book and made another Crown and Coke. Standing at the back door, she whistled for her German shepherd, Browning. She bounded to the door but ducked her head reluctantly when Kim beckoned for her to come inside. A cold front, the first of the season, was moving in and the dog was

restless. Leaving her outside, Kim turned off the
lights and opened the drapes to the picture window
overlooking the backyard. Moonlight and the glow of
the yard lamp softly illuminated the room. She
dropped into her recliner.

Everything important in her life seemed to happen
in September. Jake was killed on the twenty-second
in 'seventy-nine. Karen left her two weeks before
Lindsey disappeared, but that might have been a
blessing in disguise. There'd always been signs of
their incompatibility. They'd been together two years
before Karen discovered that Browning was named
for the gun manufacturer and not the poet. That's
how well Karen had known her. They should have
ended it sooner while there was still some warmth
left.

Only on nights like this did she feel the
loneliness. Six months ago, on the Saturday night
following a particularly tough week, she'd uncharac-
teristically picked up a woman at the bar. The
encounter left her depressed and she'd sworn not to
pick up strangers again. Her last real date was four
months ago when she'd gone out twice with Denise,
whom she'd actually known for two years. She and
Karen had first met Denise and her ex through
mutual friends and frequently ran into them at
parties. From the beginning, she'd been drawn to her
and was secretly pleased when she heard she was
also single. Both dates had been to dinner followed
by a movie. Each time, she'd cut the evening short to
chase fruitless hot tips after a page from the task
force duty officer. Denise told her not to call until
things settled down and she had more time. Since

then she'd thought often of the tall brunette with her flashing brown eyes and captivating smile.

The ringing telephone startled her as she swallowed the last of her drink. "I called to remind you about Cindy's birthday dinner tomorrow night," Stephanie said.

Shit, she couldn't believe she'd forgotten. Cindy was her oldest friend, the only other lesbian in her small east Texas high school. They'd always done something for her birthday with Stephanie, Cindy's lover, joining the tradition six years ago. Yet she found herself making excuses. "I don't know, Steph. Tomorrow we're officially disbanding the Lindsey Martin task force. I have to tell her mother in the morning and hold a press conference at noon."

"Well, I hope you'll come. We haven't seen you in ages. Cindy chose steak . . . again. The Dallas Cattle Company on Knox."

"I'll try to make it."

"Promise?"

"Promise."

"Denise will be there."

"Not matchmaking again, are you?" Kim smiled. Stephanie was known for setting up unsuspecting singles.

"Of course not. I just thought you'd like to know she's not seeing anyone right now."

She was surprised at the relief she felt when she hung up the phone. She'd figured that by now there'd be someone else.

* * * * *

Kim arrived at the steakhouse early, grabbed a stool at the bar and ordered a Bud Lite. The television suspended above the mirror and rows of liquor bottles was tuned to the channel eight news. She was dreading the replays of the noon press conference. Cindy and Stephanie approached bubbling with excitement. They hugged her, ordered drinks and wandered away to welcome others in their party. She drained her first beer quickly and was tempted to switch to Crown but instead she ordered another Bud Lite. Walking around, she greeted other arrivals and fended off their questions about the investigation. When the news conference came on, she retreated back to the barstool. Seeing herself on the tube was a shock. The harsh television lights accentuated the gray sprinkled throughout her dark brown hair and emphasized the lines of tension etched around her eyes and lips. She jumped when Denise's cool fingertips brushed her forearm.

Catching the bartender's attention, Denise said, "Can we switch to ESPN or something?" She ordered a glass of white wine and leaned back against the mahogany bar with a confident elegance. With a flick of her hand, she tossed back her thick, dark hair and smiled. "You handled the press conference well."

"The reporters were easy compared to telling Lindsey's mother."

Denise's dimples flashed and disappeared and she frowned sympathetically. "But you're still investigating the case?" she asked.

"Nelson and I are on it full time. It's not over yet."

"I know." Denise gripped her forearm and leaned closer. "I've missed you. Maybe I was unfair . . . about telling you not to call."

Kim felt herself relaxing. "No, you weren't." Tearing at the label on her beer, she said, "I fought like hell to keep them from closing the task force."

Leaning closer, Denise whispered, "You'll catch him. It's your destiny."

"The table is ready," Stephanie announced. Winking at Kim, she whispered, "Aren't you glad you came?"

"Sometimes destiny has a helping hand," Kim said, smiling as she took Denise's arm and escorted her to the table.

Sitting on her left, Denise pressed against her with an implied intimacy whenever someone said something she enjoyed, and Kim felt the first flicker of arousal. Watching Denise throughout dinner, she found herself spellbound by every smooth, graceful movement — even the way she held her fork, buttered her roll and lifted her wineglass. Her fingers were long, supple, and her hands, unlike Kim's, bore no scars, no crooked fingers, no weathered creases. Fueled by a sudden hunger, Kim devoured her T-bone and half of Stephanie's grilled chicken. After a couple of brief comments about the press conference, no one mentioned the Lindsey Martin case. Instead they teased Cindy and made plans to go dancing after dinner.

Denise cocked her head to one side. "You up to it?"

"Only if you're going. Otherwise, I'd rather go somewhere quiet where we can . . . talk."

She smiled. "My place is close. You do remember how to get there?"

Kim stood and reached for Denise's hand. "I thought you'd never ask."

Denise lived in a condominium on McKinney Avenue not more than ten minutes from the restaurant. Once they were inside, Denise slipped off her blazer and turned to hang it on a nearby doorknob. "Want something to drink?" she asked.

"No, thanks." Stepping toward her, she drew Denise close and kissed her. "All I ever think about is Lindsey Martin and you."

Denise wiggled out of Kim's embrace and squeezed her hand. "Come with me," she said, leading her down the hallway.

"Nothing's changed. I'll work on this case as long as it takes. Today, tomorrow, five years from now . . . even after I retire."

"I know."

"And I'll have other cases —"

"I know." She left Kim in the doorway while she turned on the lamp on the bedside table. Smiling, she kicked off her heels and pulled the turtleneck over her head.

"You have the sexiest dimples," Kim said.

In reply, Denise grinned, unhooked her bra and

let it fall to the floor. Kim tossed her jacket on a nearby chair and unbuckled her belt. Hastily she removed the pancake-style leather holster with her Colt .45 Lightweight Commander and placed it near the lamp.

Denise lay back on the bed and opened her arms invitingly. Kim couldn't finish undressing fast enough. She pointed at the light to see if she wanted it off and Denise whispered, "No."

Kim fell into her arms and felt Denise run her hands through her hair, down her neck and across her shoulders. Embracing her, Kim traced small circles in Denise's lower back urging her closer as she pressed against her. She kissed her and caressed her lustrous hair. Inhaling her subtle perfume, she nuzzled her neck.

Denise moaned and whispered, "I've wanted this a long time."

"I thought, by now, there'd be —"

She touched Kim's lips. "Not now."

Kim slipped a hand between Denise's legs and her fingers gently found their way inside. Denise rocked against her and dug her nails into Kim's shoulder. Reluctant to leave her arms, Kim shook herself free and kissed her way down Denise's stomach. She used her tongue while moving in and out until Denise called out her name and clamped her legs tightly around her.

Hours later when they were both exhausted, Denise nestled against her and said, "Why did we waste all of that time going to the movies?"

Kim laughed. "Because I'd have shot the guy who paged me away from this."

It's September again. After leaving Cindy's birthday party early, Denise and I are celebrating our one-year anniversary.

Kim smiled down at Denise who lay curled against her as she leaned against the headboard writing in her journal. Throughout the year, she'd kept it sporadically. Her last entry was in July after a couple of kids found Lindsey's remains in an empty field in the southwest corner of Dallas county. She'd been wrapped tightly in a blanket and discarded like so much trash underneath a tattered sofa. The preliminary identification was based on the remnants of her clothing and shoes. Telling Julia, Lindsey's mother, was the kind of thing she hoped she'd never have to do again. When new evidence discovered in and around the sofa looked promising, at least the chief had immediately reassigned two detectives to the case to help her and Nelson.

Her German shepherd rose from her favorite spot near the closet and stretched. Coming to the side of the bed, Browning nuzzled her with a damp nose. Kim rubbed her broad head, scratched her ears and told her to go back to sleep. Smiling, she returned to her journal.

We're getting so close to this bastard that I bet he can feel us breathing down his neck. We're going to make an arrest soon and when we do, I know he'll still have Lindsey's coloring book and her red Crayola. They'll be the final nails in his coffin. And someday, I'll stand in the prison at Hunstville to watch when they put him down by lethal injection. I'll welcome the results but despise the method. You put a faithful dog to sleep when he's too sick or too old to go on living. It's too kind for a fucking child-killer.

Then, when it's over ... when he's burning in hell, I'm going to torch this journal.

Denise stirred against her and touched her arm. She slammed the journal shut and dropped it to the floor. She caught Denise's hand and kissed it.

Le Baron

Barbara Johnson

I watched through parted curtains as Carrie drove
up in her new Chrysler Le Baron. She'd told me
about it the other night on the phone, and I could
hear the pride in her voice. I had to admit, it was a
beautiful car. Cherry red and sparkling like a ruby in
the bright sun. The top was down, of course, and I
could see the interior was cream-colored leather.
Carrie parked parallel like a pro. I half expected her
to leap over the closed door to get out, but she
opened it and unfolded her long, lanky body in the
conventional way.

We'd been dating almost a year, but the sight of Carrie still gave me a thrill. I remembered well the first time I saw her in the dim light of a downtown lesbian hangout. I was sitting at the bar feeling sorry for myself, and lonely. As I glanced around the room, she emerged from the heavy smoke surrounding the pool table, like Nessie coming up through the mists of Loch Ness. Her long-limbed body strode purposefully toward me. I noted with pleasure the richly embroidered black vest over a white cotton shirt open at the throat, tight black jeans and black leather cowboy boots. She carried a black cowboy hat, and as she got closer I saw big hands with strong fingers. On her right ring finger she wore what appeared to be a class ring.

Long. Everything about her was long. Throat. Legs. Arms. Body. Everything, that is, except her hair. The rich dark curls framed her head like a cloud. As she walked under a light, they shone like polished wood. Auburn. My favorite.

I tried not to stare, but I was mesmerized. She approached the bar, squeezing in between two women who leaned against it. Suddenly she looked straight at me, as if she sensed my eyes on her. I should have looked away, but I couldn't. She held me captive. I smiled. She smiled back. I was smitten. She got her beer and disappeared to the back of the bar, through the smoke and into the darkness.

I noticed the curtain moving in the window as I drove up. I knew then that I had to park the car on my first try, and without any mistakes. I wouldn't want Erika to think I didn't know what I was doing.

The new car handled like a dream. I'd always wanted a Chrysler Le Baron. I'd see people driving down the road in one and be envious. And now I was a proud owner myself. My first new car too. It proved that I was finally successful as a carpenter. It had been hard to break into the male-dominated profession, but my folks had always told me I was the most stubborn person they'd ever known. I proved them right time and again.

I'd bought a red car because I knew it was Erika's favorite color. We'd been dating about a year now, and I intended to ask her to live with me. I wanted to wait until I had something to offer — stability. Not living together right away kept our relationship fresh and new. I wasn't worried it would become stagnant when we moved in together. Erika was much too exciting for that.

As I walked up her walkway, I couldn't help but remember the first time I'd seen Erika. I'd been at the bar with a woman who turned out to be the date from hell. The only thing that made the evening bearable was frequent trips to the bar for beer, something I knew wasn't a good idea but did anyway.

It was really smoky that night. My date and I sat in the back behind the pool table. I got up to get another beer. It was crowded at the bar. I had to squeeze between two women who didn't move one inch to let me in. As I waited for my beer, I'd suddenly felt someone's eyes on me. It was such an intense feeling, one that gave me prickles on the back of my neck. I looked up and saw her right away.

She was dressed in red. Some kind of sundress — an unusual sight in this particular bar — that left her shoulders bare. She appeared to be tall, with long, shapely legs dangling from the bar stool and crossed at the ankles. Blonde hair shimmered down her back, and when she turned slightly I could see it reached her waist — a real-life Rapunzel. She picked up a glass of pale pink wine. Her delicate hands had long fingers topped with crimson nails.

Though I was expecting it, I jumped when the doorbell rang. My heart was beating fast, and I felt butterflies in my stomach. It was almost as if Carrie and I were about to go on our first date. I opened the door and smiled. She was dressed, as always, in jeans and a cotton shirt. Blue jeans this time, with a red plaid shirt. Its open collar showed she wore the gold chain necklace I'd given her. She'd traded her cowboy boots for Nikes that were obviously new. When she took off her Ray-Bans and smiled back at me, I felt my heart drop to my knees.

"Hello, Carrie," I said, almost breathlessly. "Nice car."

"You like it?"

She leaned forward to kiss me. I backed into the house and closed the door before I let her lips touch mine. It was electrifying. The tingle swept up and down my body as her kiss deepened. I was lost once again. I felt her big hands grab hold of my arms as she pulled me close to her. We were practically the same height, though she was an inch or two taller. I reached up and wrapped my arms around her broad shoulders, letting my fingers caress her long neck the way I knew she liked it. Not too soft, but letting my nails prick her just the littlest bit. It made her kiss me harder, her tongue thrusting deeply into my mouth. I heard myself moan. My body melted against hers, my knees beginning to go weak. She held me tight.

Carrie pushed me away, breathing heavily. "If we don't stop, we won't make it out for our drive."

"My housemates have all gone for the day," I said suggestively. I glanced at the stairs leading to my room. Her dark eyes smoldered with restrained passion.

She caressed my cheek. "I want to show off my new car. Maybe we'll find a secluded spot somewhere?"

I smiled. There was no "maybe" about it. Carrie had someplace in mind. She knew the surrounding countryside like her own backyard. The trunk of that cherry red Le Baron probably held a picnic basket and a blanket or two.

"I brought along a picnic basket," she confirmed. I smiled wider. "Thought we might go down to the river."

"That sounds wonderful." I grabbed the hand that caressed my cheek and kissed each fingertip one by one. Then I took her index and middle fingers in my mouth. I closed my eyes as I sucked her fingers, then opened my eyes slowly. Carrie was breathing with her mouth open. Her eyes glittered dangerously. I licked her fingers one last time, kissed her mouth lightly, and turned away to grab a sweater. It might be cold in the car with the top down and the wind blowing.

Erika looked stunning. She wore faded blue jeans like me, tight ones that molded to her rounded hips and firm ass. A snug red T-shirt showed off full breasts. I could tell she wasn't wearing a bra and felt my own nipples harden at the thought. She'd bound her sun-kissed blonde hair into a loose ponytail, tied with a red and white ribbon. Her hazel eyes looked more green than light brown today. And those beautiful lips glistened with what I knew was berry-flavored lip gloss.

I tried to kiss her in the doorway, but she backed into the house. Though she lived in a lesbian group house, she was still paranoid about the neighbors. It drove me crazy sometimes. I lived in a more gay neighborhood, and when she moved in with me, as I hoped she would, I believed she'd be more comfortable.

The kiss was worth the wait. As she teased me with her nails against my sensitive neck, I grabbed her arms, ready to throw her to the floor and ravish her right then and there. My breath was ragged. I felt like I'd just run a marathon. I pushed her away, reluctantly.

She tried to entice me to her room, but I had a special treat planned. I'd packed a picnic basket and wanted to take her for a drive to the river. I'd found a pretty and secluded spot the other day in my explorations. It was about a 20-minute walk from where I'd park the convertible. A little path through the trees led to higher ground and a miniature waterfall. I'd always found the sound of gurgling water to be sensual and erotic. I could almost visualize the clear water flowing over Erika's naked body. The idea of her nipples hardened by the chill of the water made me instantly wet.

She grabbed a sweater and we headed to the car.

*Even though I'd bought it only a week ago, I'd
washed it until it shone like a polished apple. I
opened the passenger door with a flourish and helped
her inside. She leaned back against the leather seat,
her mouth slightly parted, the tip of her tongue
licking her top lip. I felt my resolve failing. It would
be so easy to return to the house and spend the
afternoon in the cozy warmth of her tiny room.*

*"Don't tease me," I warned, keeping my voice low
the way I knew she liked it.*

*She brought her hand to her breast and let it rest,
knowing that my eyes would be drawn there. Her
nipples poked against the tight shirt. I felt my knees
grow weak. I'd been with many women, but none had
affected me the way Erika did. She had a playfulness
mixed with raw sexuality that our year-long
relationship hadn't diminished. I'd known in six
months that this was the woman I wanted to spend
the rest of my life with, but I needed to be sure I'd
succeed in my chosen profession. With my promotion
to foreman just three weeks before I bought the car, I
finally had that confidence.*

*It was a spectacular day for a drive — sunny and
warm and not a cloud in sight. I shifted into gear
and pulled away from the curb. I could feel the wind
blowing my hair and was glad I kept it short. I
glanced at Erika. The ponytail kept the hair off her
face, but it whipped behind her like ribbons in a fan.
The sun on her face made her even more lovely.*

I couldn't help but notice Carrie's hands as she
confidently gripped the steering wheel. It was one of
the features I liked most about her. Those hands and

fingers had brought me to ecstasy more times than I could count. They were firm hands, powerful hands. They could be soft or hard, but I liked it best when they were hard. Sometimes they would leave little bruises on my body, which made me smile with secret remembrance each time I noticed a new one. And when she thrust those long fingers deep inside me, my thoughts would go all hazy, my body reacting with a primal response that left me as limp as a newborn kitten. Just the thought of it now made me squirm in my seat.

"So, where exactly are we going?" I asked to take my mind off her hands and what they could do to me.

Carrie didn't take her eyes off the road. I watched her strong profile, noting the incredibly long eyelashes behind the sunglasses, her slightly pointed nose and the firm chin with the little cleft in it. Her auburn curls danced in the wind. I reached over and placed a hand on her muscled thigh. She put her hand over mine only briefly, then back on the steering wheel.

"I took the car out the other day when I finished a job early," she said. "If we go along the river for about five miles, we'll get to one of those scenic overlook-type places. I found a little spot about a mile's walking distance."

"Sounds romantic. And private."

She reached for my hand and brought it to her lips for a quick kiss. "I thought so. I sat and relaxed there for about two hours, and no one came by. If we're lucky, it'll be the same today."

I was glad I'd brought my sweater. Though the

day was warm, the wind as we drove chilled me. I knew my nipples strained against my shirt. I'd deliberately not worn a bra. I smiled as I saw her glance at my chest more than once. When the corner of her mouth twitched, I knew she was having trouble concentrating on her driving.

We exited onto the highway. I watched her wonderfully strong hand move the gear shift. She gripped it firmly, like when she held me tight. Back on the steering wheel, her long fingers rested easily along the round form, almost like she caressed a woman. I pulled my sweater close and let the sun kiss my eyelids.

I couldn't help but glance over at Erika. Her nipples straining against the red T-shirt grabbed my attention like a beacon. I began to wonder if we'd ever get to the river. It seemed much farther than I remembered. Her hand rested lightly against her jean-clad thigh, her blood-red nails matching her shirt. There is something so sexy about a woman with long red nails.

I finally pulled off the highway and sped down the country road to the river. I managed to find the same place to park and quickly leapt out of the car to open Erika's door. I debated whether to take the time to put the top up on the Le Baron, but one look from Erika and the invitation in those hazel eyes had me impatiently pulling the picnic basket and blankets from the trunk. I took Erika's hand and led her down the path. She'd never looked more delectable, and when she untied that red and white ribbon and sent her glorious blonde hair cascading down her back, I almost took her then and there. She looked at me through half-closed eyes. I could feel the blood surge through my veins.

As we walked deeper into the woods, the green-filtered light made me feel like I was floating under water. Erika's hand in mine felt soft; her fingers curled into my palm, her nails against my skin making my scalp tingle. Not a moment too soon, I heard the waterfall. I was pleased to see Erika's expression as I pushed aside some bushes to reveal my secret hideaway. A little slice of river gurgled and bubbled over dark rocks, the sun glinting like diamonds in its transparent blue depths. I spread the blankets on a moss-covered rock and started to unpack the picnic.

When I turned to give Erika a glass of champagne, I felt such a rush of blood to my face that I almost felt dizzy. She lay stretched out on the blanket, completely naked. She'd draped her long resplendent hair over her body in all the strategic places. She ran her hands lightly down her chest, over her belly, down her thighs and then back up again. I noticed my hands trembling as I placed the champagne glasses carefully out of the way.

I knelt beside her and brushed her hair away, letting my mouth close around one erect nipple as she arched up against me. She moaned deeply as her hands grasped my head, pulling me closer still. I rose up to kiss her mouth, letting my fingers walk down her body to the river that flowed between her legs.

I didn't think Carrie would ever get to where she was bringing me, but she finally pulled off the highway and onto an unpaved road. I was so hungry for her by the time we stopped, I was tempted to have her pull the convertible top up and make love right there, but she leapt out of the car too fast.

The woods were lovely. The soft light coming through the trees brought a warmth that surrounded us like a silken shawl. It was quiet but for our footfalls; not even a bird twittered. She held my hand gently at first, but when I tickled her palm with my nails her grip tightened. I stole a look at her and she caught me. Her dark brown eyes made promises that set my pulse racing.

Carrie's secret spot was every bit as beautiful as she'd said it would be. I hoped it would also be as private as she thought, for I already had plans of my own. I'd always liked the sound of water, and the river with accompanying waterfall both soothed and excited me. I could sense the sexual tension in Carrie's body, see the way it made her muscles tight. Her movements were precise and quick. She spread the blanket, and when she turned away from me to the picnic basket, I knew I'd have to work quickly. By the time the champagne cork popped, I'd stripped off my clothes and stretched across the blanket, arranging my long hair in ways to cover yet not hide the intimate places on my body. The smoldering blaze in Carrie's eyes ignited when she turned and saw me. I ran my hands lightly down my body.

She held two glasses of golden champagne, which she placed carefully on the ground. She knelt beside me, looking down with the gaze that made my whole body tense with anticipation. Her big, strong hands made goosebumps rise on my skin as she brushed my hair from my breasts, her mouth hot against my nipple. I felt the moan rise from deep within my body as her fingers spread my legs and found what waited for her there.

She kissed me deeply, her tongue both teasing and insistent. I'd wanted her from the moment I saw her drive up in her new Le Baron, and now I was ready. I pushed against her hand, urging her fingers inside. She laughed softly against my neck, her breath tickling me before she kissed me again on the mouth. Just as I thought I'd die from want, Carrie's long fingers found their mark.

I'd always liked the way Erika's smooth body responded to my touch, and today was no exception. I knew her so well. She was wet and ready for me, but I didn't want to rush. I kissed her, letting my tongue gently torment her. My fingers teased her skin; she squirmed beneath my touch, unwilling to wait. I laughed as her hips thrust against my hand. I knew what she wanted. She liked my fingers to go hard and deep. Sometimes I surprised her with a dildo, but today I'd decided to let my fingers do the walking.

I cradled Erika's head and neck with one arm. I could feel the heat from her body through my clothes. I usually preferred to feel her nakedness against my own, but sometimes I liked the feeling of total control that staying fully clothed gave me. I only hoped the buttons from my jeans wouldn't give her tiny bruises, even though she seemed to like those reminders of our passion.

My free hand traveled the length of her body. I gazed upon her face, watching the different emotions that played across it. Her eyes were closed, the long pale lashes splayed across her skin. Her lips were parted, and I smiled as the tip of her tongue peeked out every so often. Her hair was spread beneath her like a nest of spun gold. I took some strands and let them flow through my fingers and across her hips and thighs.

She whimpered softly and suddenly opened her eyes. Those hazel depths implored me, and I answered her plea with a long, deep thrust of my fingers. She was so wet, they slid in easily. Not all of them, just two or three. I would make her wait for the rest.

But for the water, the silence around us was so deep, I could sense Erika's struggle to keep quiet. I liked it when she was loud, but she buried her face in my shoulder whenever she moaned, sometimes biting me gently. There was only one way to stop that. I carefully released her head from the crook of my arm and let my mouth burn kisses down her body. She sweated a little, and the salty taste made me again think of the sea.

Her legs opened wide for me as I removed my fingers and let my mouth and tongue take over. Erika's loud answering moan made me smile. Her hands grabbed my hair as my hands held her hips. I thought I heard the bushes rustling, but I could only concentrate on Erika. Her shuddering release was answered by my own as she grabbed the collar of my shirt and pulled with all her might, not to make me stop, but to prevent her from pulling my hair. I'd told her before I liked it, but she worried about hurting me.

"Oh, God, Carrie," she said finally, "you were wonderful."

She usually said that very same thing, but I never tired of hearing it, especially when she spoke in that low, breathless voice. When she tugged on my shirt this time, I kissed her once more and let her pull me up. Her skin was flushed, her nipples hard. Her chest moved with rapid breaths that slowed as I held her tight.

I kissed her lightly on the forehead. "I want you to move in with me," I said.

She didn't answer, but merely smiled and took my hand. She nodded each time she kissed one of my fingers.

"Was that five yeses?" I asked.

"Uh-huh, and here are five more," she answered as she took my other hand to kiss each finger before lacing them with hers, her nails glinting cherry ripe in the sun.

Games Night Orange

Penny Hayes

Toni had spent many evenings in Sidney's company, but irritating as hell to Toni, it was never without a pile of people around, and tonight would be no different.

Once a month, "Games Night" was held at someone's home. Word-of-mouth and e-mail invariably drew new people each time, everyone joining in, playing one table game or another, or just talking and laughing uproariously with whoever wasn't into games that evening. The simple event was fun, organized only to the point of somebody new volunteering to host each time and providing some not-too-costly fruit, munchies and drinks.

This month Toni had offered her modestly furnished, two-bedroom apartment. A good number of women had shown up, but the warmth of the logs blazing in the fireplace before which she stood with Sidney and Pat couldn't have melted the ice. Throughout the living room and kitchen, women conversed in rigid, little clusters of twos or threes, quietly talking. A few lounged on the sofa and chairs; others who'd arrived alone stood shyly off by themselves. Too many new people at once, Toni suspected.

Sidney laughed musically, distracting Toni from her concerns, something she did easily.

Sidney, a tall, strong woman always on the go, always doing something, was seldom inert for long. She purposely sought out new conversations, making new friends while carefully maintaining the old. She was known as a woman of great fun and before long, had people in stitches fully enjoying themselves.

Toni, not outgoing at all, jealously envied Sidney her people skills. She watched Sidney's restless, green eyes scanning the room, the women, the action, giving Toni and Pat only half her attention.

Sidney declared, "This boat is dead in the water tonight." Abruptly she left them, walked over to a fruit bowl and selected two oranges. With one hand she held them high in the air and moved to the living room's center.

"Okay, everybody. Two lines, right here and here." Her deep voice was commanding but full of mischief.

Thank God for Sidney, Toni thought. It wasn't by accident that she'd made sure the woman would be here tonight.

"Come on, folks," Sidney encouraged. She smiled big, flashing white teeth albeit a little crooked from getting hit in the mouth by a fast-pitched softball once and by a catcher's face mask another time. "I want two lines right here. Equal length." With her free hand, she slashed the air along each side of her body.

There were grateful, relieved looks as twenty unsure women dressed in jeans and casual tops obediently broke into two equal lines, falling into place like well-trained seventh-grade schoolgirls in PE class.

"Anybody here who's co-dependent better get over it right now," Sidney decreed, initiating the group's first small chuckle.

A diminutive, dark-eyed woman began doing jumping jacks. "One, two, one, two, one, two," she counted as her sizeable breasts bounced along in rhythm. Laughing, a couple of others followed suit. The ice in the room cracked, and Spring Thaw began.

"Okay here's the deal." Sidney waited until the two still-juggling lines settled as she casually tossed an orange several inches into the air before catching it, never looking at it, never dropping it. Toni would have had to go get two more by now. The others would have been pulp at her feet. "Okay, gang, we're going to pass this orange" — again Sidney held the sphere aloft — "from one person to the next."

"Sounds easy enough," someone muttered.

"If you drop it, your team starts over. First line to reach the opposite end without dropping their orange, wins."

Toni looked down at the floor as did several others. She remembered this game, remembered it from kindergarten. It was a muscular development thing to increase dexterity and strength in a five-year-old's hand. *Borrrrrring.* She thought about suggesting using eggs instead of oranges to add some interest and life to the game. But then, what if somebody dropped an egg? She'd just had these carpets cleaned.

As smiles faded and folks started eyeballing Monopoly, Waterworks, Scattergories and other recently ignored games, Sidney said, "Here's how you do it. Pat, come and stand in front of me." Toni thought Sid should have chosen her. *She* was the hostess here, tonight.

Sidney set aside one of the oranges as Pat planted herself three feet before Sidney. "Now what?"

"Come closer." Pat obeyed with a big grin. The waiting lines grew quiet, expectant.

Both women, the same height at five-ten, looked straight into each other's eyes. Toni didn't like that one bit.

"I call this game 'Look Ma, No Hands,' " Sidney said to them, "because the one rule is that you can never touch the orange with your hands when you pass it. Anything else goes."

There was a collective "Ohhh" as the contestants caught on, and another of soft, unsure —Is this going to be okay with my partner? — laughs.

Sidney anchored her hair behind her ears, then

tucked the fruit beneath her chin. "Okay, now watch. Pat, grab the orange with your chin."

Sidney tipped her upper body to the left as Pat tilted slightly in the opposite direction. She pushed her throat against the orange, pulling Sidney close to her and captured it. Her hold was tenuous, but she was successful and that's what counted. She stepped back letting the fruit drop to her hand before handing it to Sidney and returning triumphantly amongst cheers and hoots to her place in line.

"Got it?" Sidney asked everybody.

They got it as the oranges were positioned and ready.

It's not an easy task passing an orange from throat to throat without using hands, and at the conclusion of the first contest, more than plain old ice had been broken. A whole city could have been flooded out, taking buildings and all. And the women howled with laughter.

By the time Toni had successfully passed her produce to Sidney (and wasn't it kind of Sidney to again support Toni's hostessing duties by muscling her way into line to stand next to her?) she had been pulled so close that there had been zero space between them, thighs pressed together, chests mashed flat, their very bones seeming to merge.

Toni's short brown do didn't get in their way. But Sidney's long, blazing copper-colored hair hanging loose, flapping around their faces, was considerably more distracting. So were those great breasts of Sid's pressing into Toni's upper chest while her pelvis hit Toni just below the bellybutton, a good- sized chunk of heaven-sent hail assailing her.

She would have been permanently mortified, never again showing her face in the community, if she hadn't watched others passing the orange in like manner. "Here's a perfect example of positive co-dependency," she said, laughing, nearly dropping the orange as she pressed harder than ever against Sidney's chest and throat and God knew what else.

Because Toni was much shorter, at five feet, four inches, there was considerable adjusting and bending occurring between her and Sidney. During their struggle — and that's exactly what it was — Toni considered purposely dropping the orange just before Sidney grabbed it so they'd have to begin again. But she'd have been found out for sure. Besides, Sidney had never shown an interest in Toni. No sense in overdoing it.

Groping, clutching, fighting laughter all the way, Sidney turned and passed on the orange. Once freed of the fruit she whispered in Toni's ear, "Practice."

"Uh, well, it's good to keep fit." Sidney the jock looked practiced and altogether *too* skilled at passing off the orange while breathing down somebody else's neck besides Toni's.

Later, after her apartment had cleared out and half-empty soda cans and smeared plates of dip and chips had been emptied and ignored, after the echos of laughter had died away, Sidney still sat on the couch. One long leg lay across a knee and an arm rested lazily along the back of the couch.

"What's up?" Toni asked. Why hadn't Sidney left with the others as she routinely did?

Sidney settled further into the soft cushions. "I

want to pass the orange to you one more time before
I go."

Now, didn't that cause steam to rise from around
Toni's shirt collar? "It did get things moving around
here, didn't it? Thanks for the help." Better that she
begin cleaning up the place.

"I don't know where your head is at, Toni. A
couple of years have gone by now, and I still don't
know how to approach you. I've tried humor; I've
tried acting lonesome and depressed. I've even sent
you flowers lately, and you still don't get it."

Sidney had sent those roses? Why no card?

"So I'm going to have to come right out and tell
you that I want to pass you the orange again."

For the first time, Toni questioned Sidney's
mental stability. After all, the woman did have two
doctorates and a full professorship at Cornell. That
had to put pressure on a person's mind, even that of
a very bright person. "Good Lord, Sidney, if I'd
known it meant that much to you, I'd have let you
do it a long time ago." *Repeatedly, Sidney, repeatedly.*

"It's an excuse."

"For?" Toni wished her head wasn't suddenly
throbbing so hard, feeling ready to explode. She
wished her knees weren't shaking and that sweat
wasn't suddenly popping out all over her body. Her
heart hammered insanely against her ribs, as if
fighting to leap free of its confining cage.

"Getting close to you."

Nada! Not big, tough, independent Sidney who
never let anybody get close to her and, other than at
occasional socials, barely had time to.

"But I've noticed that you're rather blind to that sort of thing," Sidney continued.

Only because Toni had never wanted anyone in her life but Sidney, and therefore who else was there to notice? Toni remained mute, blank-faced, unable to speak, fearing to hope.

Sidney rose, stretching her long frame. She picked up her coat and headed toward the door. "I apologize. I think I've said too much."

Toni looked at her. "You have, Sidney. Nothing but talk and jokes coming out of you all the time. Do you really believe you need to use a stupid piece of fruit to get next to me?" She picked up the last orange and went to her bedroom, but not before tucking the citrus beneath her chin and turning to take one look at Sidney.

Sidney dropped her coat at the door and followed Toni, who waited by the bed. "Okay, Toni." She stopped a few inches before her. "It's Games Night, right? Let's play a real game."

Sidney didn't go for the orange that couldn't be touched with her hands. She went for the buttons on Toni's blue flannel shirt, freeing each one as Toni, unable to raise her head because of the orange, watched. Sidney's long fingers moved to Toni's jeans, popping the snap, unzipping the zipper, kneeling as she drew them and Toni's pink briefs to her ankles. The last to go were Toni's sneakers and socks. She stepped out of them and waited.

It was difficult for Toni to breathe and more to the point, pant, with her head tucked so tightly and her throat so moist with sweat that extra effort was needed to keep the fruit in place, but resolutely she clung to it.

Sidney slipped the shirt from Toni's shoulders, unhooked her bra and pulled it off. "Toni, let go of the damned orange," Sidney told her in a husky voice. Her nearness was inebriating.

"Never." If she had to drive a fingernail file through it, straight into her throat to keep it there, she would not drop the thing.

In seconds, Sidney had stripped too. "You were warned."

Sidney crouched, accommodating Toni's shorter height, her stiffened nipples dragging along Toni's chest, her skin burning wherever Sidney touched her. There were no groping, heavy-handed clutches now. Sidney's touch was light, painfully pleasurable. Toni could have fallen to her knees.

But she might drop the orange.

Sidney wedged a thigh between Toni's legs, and Toni's breath caught raggedly. She lost her grip on the fruit, managing to stop its fall between their breasts by pulling Sidney closer.

"We're going to have to start over, Toni, if it hits the floor." Sidney's voice had become a raspy thing as her hips arched against Toni's in their cooperative effort in winning against the orange. She spoke between clenched teeth, "You are so beautiful, Toni."

Forget the frickin' orange, Toni told herself. Take this woman to your bed, *now!*

Sidney pressed her hips more firmly against Toni,

allowing the orange to fall even farther, stopping it with her belly. "I bet I could roll this thing right down to your —"

"Sidney." It was a breathless whisper, since Toni could barely speak at all right now. Gasps were big things for her at the moment.

Cleverly, Sidney lowered herself to her knees, controlling the orange until she had positioned the fruit in the triangle of Toni's thick, brown hair.

Toni shuddered. "How can an orange feel this good?"

Sidney grabbed the orange and rose to her feet.

"I can't stand long enough to start again, Sidney." Toni was very near collapse.

"Neither can I."

They yielded to the more comfortable bed and lay down. "You touched the orange," Toni playfully accused.

"We'll start over." Sidney gazed into Toni's brown eyes. It was then that they first kissed. Long, deep — for keeps. Backing away, Sidney said, "I'll put the orange here and grab it. No hands."

Toni jumped as the fruit pressed against her pelvis. "Sidney!"

"I promise I won't use my hands, Toni."

Sidney placed the orange between Toni's thighs, then turned and lay in the opposite direction. Toni felt the orange roll to her feet as Sidney butted it aside with her head. "You dropped it already, Sidney." She was going to reach for it until Sidney used her mouth.

Toni cried out at the sharp, rocking pleasure of Sidney's tongue. There was a sensation of being fully clasped as Toni gasped, "That is *not* the orange, Sidney," and damned glad that it wasn't as she clutched at Sidney's legs.

Sidney encircled Toni's thighs, gently moving them farther apart. There was a brilliant, orange flash as Toni's body slammed upward colliding against Sidney's tongue. Entire orange groves of thousands of green trees heavily laden with millions of big, juicy oranges, sprang up and surrounded her. Birds trilled "The Orange Blossom Special."

The song and vision slowly faded as she came back to herself. "Sidney," was all she could manage. "Sidney."

Minutes slid by while Sidney held Toni in her arms, whispering to her, promising her anything on earth that she might want.

Toni thought about that. "Just give me that orange down there, Sidney. And, honey, I won't be needing my hands either."

Manicure
Julia Watts

It's the fourth day of the big snow. Teresa sits in the recliner, playing with the remote control, surfing through the barren wasteland that is daytime TV. On one channel, a scrawny, mustachioed man rants about someone named Crystal while the live studio audience oohs and gasps in shock. *"My girlfriend's a ho'"* was printed on the screen under the man's face. On another channel, a perfectly made-up woman lying in a hospital bed opens her eyes, slowly looks down at her body in horror and exclaims, "I can't feel my legs." Seconds later, a woman in a commercial proudly proclaims, "If you don't believe me, you can just ring my doorbell and smell my toilet." Disgusted, Teresa clicks off the TV.

Without the TV's drone, Teresa can hear Ann's phone conversation in the kitchen. She's laughing, saying, "Yeah, well, I bet you're not half as sick of truck-stop food as I am of my own cooking." She laughs again, then says, "Maybe they'll get the interstate opened up tomorrow."

Teresa has been staying at Ann's since the snowstorm got bad. Ann's husband, a long-distance trucker, is snowed in in Cincinnati, and Teresa's boyfriend, Dave, is stranded in his apartment on the other side of town, which, in this weather, might as well be as far away as Cincinnati. The two women figured that if they stayed together, they could consolidate their food and keep each other from going stir-crazy. "It'll be fun," Ann had said when she made the invitation. "Like a grown-up slumber party."

It has turned into the longest slumber party on record: three days, going on four. But it hasn't been that bad, really, taking a vacation from the men, sitting around in sweatsuits with no makeup on, their hair just snatched back in ponytails, not worrying about how many cookies they eat. No wonder walruses are so fat, Teresa thinks. They're snowed in all the time.

From the kitchen, Teresa hears Ann say, "Okay, honey. I love you, too. Bye-bye." When she comes back into the living room, she says, "You want some hot chocolate or something?"

"No, thanks. I'm still full from lunch."

Ann grins again. "Well, come to think of it, I guess we did just eat an hour ago." She flops down on the couch. "Nothing on TV, huh?"

"Not a thing."

Ann sighs. "You know, I wasn't kidding when I told Roy I was sick of my own cooking. You know what I'd like for supper tonight?"

"What?"

"A Quarter Pounder with cheese."

"I'm more of a Big Mac girl myself," Teresa says. "I'll tell you what. I'll cook tonight."

"That'd be great." Ann grins. "You wouldn't happen to be able to sling together a pepperoni and mushroom pizza, would you?"

"I'll see what I can do."

Teresa and Ann both work at the Piggly Wiggly. Technically, Ann is Teresa's supervisor, but she's not the type to pull rank — not like Mr. Callahan, the balding assistant manager, who seems to think of the Pig as some type of military organization. When Ann's working the cash register and Teresa's bagging, they cut up and have a great time. Even though she's a supervisor, Ann will still make fun of customers and other supervisors just like a regular employee. She calls Mr. Callahan the Patton of the Pig.

"You wanna play another game of Monopoly?" Ann asks.

"What, and have you beat me to a pulp again?" Teresa laughs. "No way."

"Wanna pop *Sleepless in Seattle* in the VCR?"

"We watched it day before yesterday."

Suddenly Ann's eyes light up. "Hey, I know! I can't believe I didn't think of this before." She disappears into the bedroom and returns carrying what looks like a pink plastic version of the box Dave uses for his fishing tackle. "We can give each other manicures."

"Manicures?" Teresa looks down at her grubby, nondescript fingernails. She doesn't bite them, and she trims them when she gets a hangnail or something, but that's about as close to manicuring as she gets.

"Sure. I give a great manicure. I used to go to beauty school, did you know that?"

Teresa shakes her head no and watches as Ann sits cross-legged, opens the box and begins arranging various files, sticks and bottles on the floor.

"Come down here and sit by me," she says.

Teresa slides out of the recliner and onto the floor.

"Give me your hand."

Teresa puts her left hand in Ann's, feeling self-conscious for some reason she can't quite put her finger on.

"First, we start with a massage." Ann squirts out some lotion, warms it in her own hand and begins smoothing it over Teresa's hand's back, palm and fingers. Her winter-dry skin drinks up the lotion like a dry garden soaking up rain.

Ann rubs on more lotion, starting to knead the muscles in Teresa's hand — the muscles that get so tired from pecking on the cash register and bagging groceries. Ann leans over Teresa's hand with a look of pure concentration, as though nothing else in the world matters but making Teresa feel good.

Teresa tries to remember if Dave has ever touched her hands. Maybe he held her hand, once, on the first date, but that was just a test to see if she'd let him touch her, let him move on to touch other parts of her. It's always like that with guys, Teresa thinks. It's like, okay, she let me hold her hand; now will she let me kiss her? She let me kiss her. Now will she let me feel her up? And so on and so forth on down the line — it's all about getting from point A to point B to point C. There's so little touching like what Ann's doing, touching another person just to make her feel good.

Ann is massaging Teresa's cuticles now, softening them up. One night when he and Teresa had a date, Dave brought over a porno video. She just laughed when she saw its sleazy cover, thinking she should've known better than to tell him to pick out a movie to bring. She had watched with her usual amount of disinterest at the Malibu Barbie look-alike women and the squat, hairy men.

Until one scene. At that point in the movie, two of the women ended up in bed together, touching each other and kissing. Teresa had gotten interested all of a sudden — really interested — until one of the hairy-butted men came back, and the women started paying attention to him instead of to each other.

That night, in bed, with the image of those two women in her mind, Teresa had been more ready to make love than she had been in months. But, as usual, it was over in five minutes. Before she could even get into the rhythm of it, Dave was already snoring.

Ann is massaging her right hand now, kneading all the tension away. Teresa wonders what it would be like if the two of them did the same things as the two women in the movie. It would be so much better than in the movie, though, because they wouldn't be two silicon Barbies wallowing around together, but real women with real bodies. Real friends, touching each other, not to get from point A to point B, but to make each other feel good.

Teresa closes her eyes, thinking of Ann's lotioned hands moving not just over her own hands but over her shoulders, her belly, her breasts. Her face heats up as she thinks of Ann kissing her, wonders if Ann would use her mouth on her the way Dave refuses to. Now, really, she tells herself, you've got to stop this. It's the snow, it's making you crazy.

The snow. Outside, the snow is piled against the trailer in huge drifts. The temperature hasn't risen a degree in four days. The interstate is closed, so there's no way Ann's husband can make it back from Cincinnati today. And Dave's all the way across town, the parking lot of his apartment building a solid sheet of ice. Teresa lets her hand close around Ann's for just a second. If it happened just once, no one would ever know. The snow would hide their secret.

"Teresa?"

Teresa's eyes snap open. "What?"

Ann is holding two bottles of nail polish. "I was asking which you wanted, the Midnight Mauve or the Carnation Crème."

"Oh. The Midnight Mauve, I guess."

Ann smiles. "I like that color, too. Put your hand here." Ann places Teresa's outstretched hand on her thigh, opens the bottle of Midnight Mauve and starts to paint.

Fire and Ice
Diana Braund

It had been four days of uninterrupted and unrelenting ice. The sleet against the window sounded like tips of razor blades scratching glass; raspy and nasty. The bitter chill wind shrieked, and the one-hundred-year-old New England farmhouse groaned. Tree limbs entombed in thick shells of ice sagged, and branches cracked under the weight. A blackness walled in the night.

"Yes, I am fine, Miki." Jackie shifted the telephone to her left hand. She could visualize her friend on the other end. Long legs propped up on her desk, her chair pushed back as far as it would go. "I lost power about four days ago and my telephone here in the house about three hours ago. I told the office to call me on my cellular phone. Let's hope nothing happens to the towers or I will be completely without a phone. Thank God I'm not on call tonight. Hopefully this weather will keep everyone at home. How are you guys doing?" Jackie sipped her glass of wine as she listened. "Look, if you need me, call me on this number." Jackie smiled. "Great, I just guess we'll do what Mainers have been doing for hundreds of years, hunker down and wait for it to blow over."

As she punched the clear button and laid the cellular phone on the table, Jackie sighed and for a microsecond envied Miki and her newfound love. It had been five years since Marianne died, and at times like this she longed for the touch of a woman's hand to help keep loneliness away.

She picked up the hurricane lamp that had belonged to her grandmother, tucked her book under her arm and had started toward the kitchen when she heard a knock.

With the lamp held in front of her, she walked through the entryway and opened the front door.

"Hi, I'm sorry to bother you," the woman said. Her long black hair was stuck to the sides of her face and water dripped off the end of her nose. She had pulled her coat collar tight up around her neck, but water rolled down the side of her face and onto her shoulders. She wiped at it with a wet glove. Ice clung to her hat and coat and stayed there like the beginnings of a glacier. "I am sorry to bother you," she said again. "I live up the road, and I don't have a telephone. Haven't had one for days, but I understand some people still have phones. I'd like to call my parents, let them know I'm okay."

Jackie studied the woman. There was a nagging familiarity. "As a matter of fact I do have a telephone that works. My regular phone is out, but my cell phone is working. Come in. You're soaked." Jackie stepped aside to let the woman enter.

"Thanks. Only in Maine would someone let a stranger into their house."

"You're right." Jackie shook her head. "I guess it will be that way until something bad happens. Most people around here don't even lock their doors."

"I know. After I moved back here, I had a guy doing some work on my parents' house." The woman pulled her hat off and unbuttoned her coat. "When I suggested I should be there while he did the work, he looked hurt, as though I didn't trust him."

Jackie liked her gigawatt smile. "Where's your car?"

"I was afraid to drive. The road looks like the ice skating pond at Hadley Lake."

Jackie smiled as she recalled those years when as a child she carried ice skates over her shoulder and walked the four miles to the lake. "You must be local. I'm sorry I —"

"Didn't recognize me?" the woman finished. There was an amused expression on her face. "I'm not surprised. I've been in New York for a lot of years. You used to pal around with my sister, Mavis. I'm Dana, Dana Bradley." Dana wiped her wet hand on her jeans before extending it to Jackie.

Jackie took the hand. "Of course. I knew there

was something familiar about you. I'm sorry, I should have remembered. It's been how long?"

"Very long," Dana agreed. "I've been gone for years. In fact I've only been back a few weeks." She looked down at her boots. The warmth in the room was melting the snow on her coat and a small puddle had formed around her feet. "I'm sorry —"

"Here, let me take your coat." Jackie set the hurricane lamp on the alcove table and reached for Dana's coat as she slipped out of it. "Come over to the stove and get warm. Your hand feels like ice." Dana followed Jackie into the living room. She walked to the wood stove and extended both hands toward it, letting the warmth caress her skin. Jackie watched her.

"I have a wood stove at the house, and that has been a real source of comfort. Any idea how long this power outage is going to last?" Dana turned back toward her.

"I didn't expect it to last this long. But the weather folks keep referring to this as the hundred-year ice storm. So I guess it's anyone's guess."

Dana pushed her hands into her jeans pockets. She looked at Jackie. "I remember the last time I saw you, it was the year you graduated from medical school. You came back here for a visit."

"I remember. And I remember you had just turned ten. Your parents and Mavis were planning a surprise party for you."

"Very good, but I had reached the old age of eleven." Dana laughed.

"Eleven." Jackie shook her head.

"I know. Sometimes I think back to that time,

and it seems as though those years belonged to someone else and I was just an observer."

"Believe me, when you get to be my age, it's worse. Eleven seems like a lifetime ago."

"Not so old," Dana said quietly, her cobalt eyes taking Jackie in.

Jackie smiled. "Some days, yeah, that old." Jackie suddenly felt shy. She reached for the telephone on the table and handed it to her. "Here, this is still working."

"Thanks. I haven't been able to call my folks for several days, and I know they are worried. They're part of the contingent of snow bunnies who head for Florida at the first sign of snow." Dana's smile was provocative like her sister's. Jackie remembered Mavis's cobalt eyes, her long and slender face. Jackie wondered why it had taken her so long to recognize Dana. She was a younger version of her sister.

"Would you like something to drink? Coffee? Wine? Hot cocoa?"

"Hot cocoa?" Dana laughed. "I haven't had that since I was a kid. Are you sure it's not too much trouble?"

"I fix it all the time. It's an essential food group in Maine. Make your call, and I'll be in the kitchen."

Jackie left the hurricane lamp for Dana, picked up the flashlight next to her chair and went into the kitchen. She reached for a farmer's match and struck it on the side of the matchbox. She lifted the glass chimney on the hurricane lamp on the table and touched the flame to the wick then set the glass shade back in place. The single flame cast uneven shadows on the walls and floor.

As she reached for a pan and two cups and get milk out on the countertop, she could hear Dana's soft voice in the other room. Jackie thought back to the last time she had seen Mavis. It had been last year's class reunion. Jackie smiled. Mavis had been a walking family album with dozens of pictures of her grandchildren and of her son Jack, a Navy commander, and her daughter Joanne, an attorney in Boston.

"I really appreciate this." Dana stood in the doorway.

"I appreciate the company. The first, second and even the third day of a storm, you love the solitude. I finished four books. By the fourth day, it's kind of lonely." Jackie poured the steaming hot cocoa into the cups. "Marshmallows?"

"Absolutely." Dana reached for the cup Jackie offered her.

"Come on, the living room is the warmest room in the house." Dana followed her back across the hallway. "Sit anywhere," she gestured around the room. Jackie set her hot cocoa on the table next to her couch and walked over to the wood stove. She reached for a log, opened the cast iron door and tossed in the log. The bark on the white birch caught fire, and curled into blue and yellow flames. "Are you living here year-round?"

"I haven't made a decision about year-round yet. I need to make some career decisions first."

"What do you do?" Jackie brushed the wood fragments off her hands. She picked up her drink and stirred it.

"I'm a photographer." Dana sat on one end of the couch. She used her spoon to stir the semi-melted marshmallows into the hot cocoa. She watched as they melted down to create uneven patterns in the dark liquid. She blew on the hot cocoa and then tasted it. "This is wonderful."

"I'm glad you like it." Jackie sat down on the other side of the couch. "Now I remember. Mavis told me you had been all over the world."

Dana laughed. "Umm. I'm a photojournalist — *Newsweek, Time.* I can pretty much live anywhere as long as there is an airport nearby. I am trying it out here for a few months. If I like it then I think I might buy a house. It's funny. I've been all over the world, yet I found I really missed Bailey's Point. It is always home to me."

"I understand. I took my residency in Boston, and I got a job offer at Massachusetts General, but I turned it down."

"I know. Mavis told me." Dana studied Jackie. "She loved seeing you at the class reunion. Said it was a hoot."

"God, rekindling the past." Jackie smiled as she recalled that weekend. "And Mavis sure seems happy. I couldn't believe anyone could carry that many pictures in one purse."

"Knowing Mavis, that's probably all she had in there."

"But no picture of you."

"No, I'm always on the other side of the camera," Dana said after a vivid instant of a smile added a glow to her face.

Jackie frowned as she tried to recall something long since buried in her memory. "Tagalong, that's what Mavis used to call you."

"Umm. We were fifteen years apart. I was the accident," Dana said, rolling her eyes. "All I heard growing up was how I ruined her social life." Dana's demeanor was warm, comforting. "Today, we're very close. But not when we were younger. Mavis was mad at my parents. She wanted a puppy and instead got what she used to call the blue-light special. She got the idea from one of those discount stores where a voice over the loudspeaker advised people to follow the blue light to aisle such-and-such for a last-minute bargain. Mavis always said I was a last-minute bargain."

Jackie's laugh was involuntary. "I remember that little kid."

"Not so little anymore," Dana said quietly.

"Wait a minute, I remember now. Your parents bought you a camera one year for Christmas."

"That's right," Dana said, clearly surprised that Jackie had remembered.

"You used to drive Mavis mad. The endless pictures of her. She said she didn't think she ever had a private moment, said you even snuck into her room early one morning and took pictures of her sleeping."

"I did." Dana shook her head. "My parents grounded me. Took the camera away for a whole week." She paused and then looked over at her fondly. "I even have pictures of you."

"Me?"

"A particularly nice one of you and Mavis sitting on the front stoop talking."

Jackie shook her head. "Don't show it to me. I even destroyed my high school pictures. I was a gangly geek."

"Not such a geek," Dana said softly.

Jackie blushed. She had always felt uncomfortable talking about herself. "Your life must be very exciting." She shifted on the couch and reached for her own cup; it felt like safer ground.

"It has had its moments." Dana turned on the couch to face Jackie. She tucked her legs under her and rested her cup on her knee. "Mostly it seems it has been one endless deadline. And of course it has been. But hopefully that will change. I'd like to settle in one area, work maybe six months of the year on assignments and spend the other six months on my book."

"A book?"

"Umm. Something incorporating some of the pictures I've taken over the years." Dana pushed dark hair off her forehead and Jackie watched as long fingers held the hair away from her face then let it drop gently onto her cheek. Jackie caught her breath as she realized how erotic and exotic Dana's hands were. "I don't know. At times I think of it as an endless dream, or maybe just an ego trip."

"It sounds exciting." Jackie felt the muscles in her throat constrict and found it difficult to swallow. She shifted on the couch. Stay focused, she told herself. She knew she was reacting only to the moment and to the loneliness she had felt earlier.

She did a mental shake of her head and refocused on what Dana was saying.

Dana leaned forward. "That's how I feel, yet I have this dissonance. One side says gamble on the book. The practical side says stick with what you know. Sometimes I fear my practical side will win. Anyway, the next few weeks will tell." Dana set her cup on the table.

"What would the book encompass?"

Jackie listened as Dana described her book and watched Dana's hands sketch pictures in the air. Dana's eyes snapped like a camera lens as she described each picture, and Jackie felt drawn into her swirling energy.

Ah, to be thirty again, Jackie thought. Dana's enthusiasm seemed to have subdued the outside night. The sleet had stopped.

Dana suddenly looked embarrassed. "I'm sorry. Sometimes I have this unabridged enthusiasm that runs on its own."

"Don't apologize. I've enjoyed it. Please tell me more."

Dana held up both hands as if putting a period at the end of a thought. "First tell me about you. What has Dr. Jackie's life been like?"

"Well, not much to tell. I've been a country doctor it seems like forever. And I stay pretty much right here doctoring or walking on the beach. I do get away to the occasional medical conference, but I like it here."

Jackie stopped as she felt the loneliness descend

like a giant wreath around her heart. She couldn't look into Dana's eyes, nor could she suppress the pensiveness that had been building for the past few days. She had trained herself to ignore it, but now with this woman sitting so close it reminded her of other nights and another woman. Those stormy nights when she and Marianne had sat on the couch, reading books or talking. Or making love. It had been five years since Marianne's death, yet the raw and naked gash in her heart continued to ooze pain.

Dana reached across the back of the couch and touched Jackie's fingers. She leaned over and set Jackie's cup on the table. "Mavis told me what happened. I was so sorry." Dana's voice was soft, her eyes a window into which Jackie viewed a kinship for her sorrow. Jackie felt a seismic vibration in her heart. She swallowed. She had forgotten what pleasure there was in the touch of a woman's hand. She remembered telling Marianne that touches were lifelines.

Jackie looked at Dana's long fingers, her hands a picture of stark and timeless beauty. It had been so long since any woman's touch had been so electrifying. She stomped on the image. Dana was a child. Fifteen years younger. Her old friend's baby sister.

"I wish I had known her."

"Marianne was a woman's woman." Jackie's voice was a whisper. "Funny, that's the first time I've ever described her that way. It sounds strange, almost something a man would say, but I don't mean that."

Jackie hesitated and looked over at the fire. She was playing solitaire with her memories. "She was that rare blend — secure in who she was, but so much a part of a partnership." Jackie sighed. "The only thing —" She stopped as she tried to put words on what she was feeling. "The only reason I continue to put one foot in front of the other is that I can keep the memory of her alive in me." Jackie stopped again. She looked at the fingers that gently held hers. "I'm sorry, I didn't mean to talk about this."

"Don't be sorry." Dana eased across the couch. "You loved her so much." She touched Jackie's face. Jackie felt another shock travel through her body.

Jackie leaned forward and gently pulled Dana toward her. Her mouth sought comfort, her body sought release. Her lips found Dana's neck and she felt the low rumble in Dana's throat even before the sound reached her ears.

Dana kissed Jackie's eyes. Her tongue traced a circle on the outside of her ear. "I've had a crush on you forever," she whispered. Her lips again sought Jackie's.

Jackie felt long-suppressed emotions, a whirlpool ready to burst violently to the surface. She pulled Dana down on top of her and her mouth and tongue sought lips so passionate she could barely breathe. She felt a shudder begin at her toes when Dana touched her hand.

Dana pulled up Jackie's shirt and her tongue traced first one and then the other nipple. Jackie gasped as Dana's hand trailed down Jackie's side to her running pants and then inside to touch her thighs. Her fingers sought the heat of Jackie's passion and Dana groaned. Jackie's fingers closed around her shoulders as the first spasm of orgasm engulfed her.

The wind whirled outside. "This is what I have always wanted," Dana said as she again touched Jackie with her fingertips.

Salt

Laura Adams

When I cry over you, I give up the two most precious chemicals in my body: water and salt. Tears are not as salty as the ocean and they are less salty than sweat.

Salt is created when a metal reacts with a non-metal.

I have sweated over you, but that was different. That was joyous exhilaration. That was muscles straining, my heart singing. I sweated for pleasure. Do you remember that trip to Mexico when we made love so often that the margaritas never seemed salty enough to replenish us? I never got enough of you.

Salt was once more precious than diamonds. When I cry over you my tears are diamonds for you. But you are drowning in the gem of a new love. I hate her because she's with you. No, I can't be big about it.

At least let me cry. Let the hot tears spill down my cheeks; they're for you. They're over you. I'm not over you. Did you have to introduce us? Did you have to touch my cheek in that fond way? You're over me; that's what your touch said. Of course you are.

She's lovely.

I'm not Medusa.

There are some women interested in me, now that I'm single again. Some of your old friends, as a matter of fact. I could be with one of them right now. I don't turn them to stone. But I look back, and I cry over you. I am slowly turning into a pillar of salt. What's it to you? Nothing.

If I cry me a river, would it flow to your shore? The ocean refuses no river, but you refuse me. If I cry me an ocean, I would float on the buoyant saltwater of my tears. I can still see you stretched out on that beach chair in Hawaii. You said you loved the ocean.

You said you loved me. You've taken up snow skiing.

If I cried you an ocean you still wouldn't love me. I really shouldn't be crying. These tears aren't for me. I get nothing from them except splotches and an ache from my throat to the top of my head. And the salt in my wounds, of course.

It's ironic that the most essential chemicals in my body are the ones I give up under extreme emotion and yet you care nothing for them. I cried the first time we made love. I cried when you told me you loved me. I cried when you left me. I'm crying now because she's lovely and you're over me. I'm crying because I can.

I'm entitled to a good cry. More than one. What's the proper ratio? One good cry for every year we were together? I'm closing in on one good cry for every time we had sex. I may eventually reach one good cry for every smile you gave me. You asked for all your gifts back, but you can't have the smiles.

I feel as if I'll never stop crying now. I'm going to cry forever. Every day since you left is forever. Did you really think I'd make nice-nice with her, with your wrapping your arm around her tiny waist? I'm sure she tells you how much she loves the snow, and how much she loves you. Someday the snow will weep and so will you.

Tears are pathetic. Tears are a part of grief. Tears are anger, and uselessness and frustration. Crying over you is weak and pointless.

But if I couldn't cry over the loss of your love, what kind of person would that make me? Everyone says you're not worth crying over. They didn't lose your love. I'm glad I can cry. I'm so glad I can cry, I could just cry.

But when she leaves you, I'll laugh. She will discover you salted your mine with diamonds and rust, not love. I'll laugh until I cry, and that will be more tears for you, tears you don't value, but I'll treasure them again.

Can I taste salt without thinking of you? Memory of you is as common as salt. When I met you I should have thrown salt over my shoulder. I do wish we had never met. So now I know what love is. So now I know what love isn't. What I didn't want to learn was how to cry like this.

You are water, too—the memory of you intrudes when I bathe, when I drink. Particularly when I drop an ice cube into water. You are the ice. Salted ice freezes.

I smell the salt of you on my fingers and I feel faint. I have no smelling salts, only you. I reach for water, but it tastes like the ocean. I am surrounded by my ocean of tears and so thirsty for you that nothing else could sate me.

Salt is a preservative. As the water evaporates from my cheeks, the salt remains, just as you remain. I could scrub with tissues and soap, and salt would still cling to me. I scrub your memory with acid and lye and your memory clings ever harder, biting into my sleep, ravaging my future and feasting on my past.

When something is preserved with salt, it's called "cured." With so much salt on my skin you'd think I would be. I would be the salt of your earth, but salted earth grows nothing. Salt flats are the purest form of desolation.

You said you loved me and yet you could tell her that we've remained friends. Love does not dissolve to friendship. My love for you will never mellow to something else. I wonder if you ever loved me. I will never react with you until I'm neutral. Our chemistry will always create salt, my heart throwing itself against yours.

Salt and water. Water is the universal solvent. Long ago, you dissolved my defenses and then you left. I'm still vulnerable to you, to the touch of your hand, to the casual welcome of your lips.

Your cool surface reflects like a mirror. I see myself and all the tears. You should look at yourself. You should look at her. You smile at me the way she smiles at you. You are crying, but you don't know it yet.

Enough Said

Laura DeHart Young

She had forgotten how to flirt. That's how long it had been. Work was all she had known for the past two years. The transfer from New York to Chicago in 1996. And then, only six months ago — another transfer — from Chicago to Atlanta. No time to meet people. No time for a lover. But Atlanta seemed permanent and, finally, her life had some stability — if only in the mere fact that she could remember her home address — and repeat her phone number without digging out a scrap of paper.

The living room she stood in was large and open

with black leather furniture and a contemporary decor that reminded her of New York City's Museum of Modern Art. Two skylights directly above her cast a shadow of sunlight across gray carpeting. The house belonged to a co-worker, and the event was a party to celebrate her fortieth birthday. As soon as she caught a glimpse of the woman across the room, thoughts of flirting, and the lack of practice she had in executing this skill, flooded her brain like sun from the windows above.

She scanned the room, looking for her co-worker so she might wangle a personal introduction. Unfortunately, Theresa was nowhere in sight. She was on her own, but that was nothing new. The woman's back was to her. Sipping her drink, she took a few steps closer, trying to get a better look. The woman was about five-foot-three with short dark hair and skin the color of a southern pecan. She was wearing a black cocktail dress, cut low in the back. The dress revealed the soft lines and curves of her small frame. Kate watched the woman's head turn from person to person, obviously very much interested in the conversation. When her head turned far enough, Kate caught the smile — bright and warm.

Approaching the woman from behind, she tried desperately to think of a "line." God, she hated that. Why not just say hello and be real about it? The few people the woman had been listening to started to move toward the buffet table for dinner. Before the woman had a chance to follow them, Kate leaned

forward and asked, "How do you know Theresa?" No
answer. Not even a glimpse back over her shoulder to
acknowledge that anyone had spoken to her. "Excuse
me, how do you know Theresa?" The woman,
continuing to ignore her, stepped toward the buffet
table, picked up a plate and got into line. Kate
stayed glued to her original spot, frozen in disbelief.

"Hey, Kate. Thanks for stopping by tonight. Get
any food yet?"

Kate spun on her heel, still stung by the rebuff.
"Happy birthday, Theresa. Nice party."

Theresa glanced around the room. "Yeah, it
turned out okay. Glad you're enjoying it."

"Can I ask a question?"

With a flip of her hand, Theresa's auburn hair
flew back over her shoulder. "Sure."

"Who's the woman in the black dress by the
buffet table?"

Craning her neck past Kate, Theresa smiled and
said, "Oh, that's Casmin Johnson. Pretty, isn't she?
She's an old friend from college. Want to meet her?"

"I tried."

"Tried?"

Kate put her hands on her hips. "Yeah, I spoke to
her and she ignored me. Can you believe that?"

"Why, Kate, you must be losing that infamous
charm." Theresa twirled a mostly empty wineglass in
her hand. She raised her eyebrows and shrugged.
"But, maybe there was a communication problem."

"I walked right up behind her, said hello — and
she didn't even turn around to acknowledge my

greeting." Kate folded her arms in front of her. "Pretty straightforward communication, if you ask me."

Theresa grabbed Kate by the elbow. "Come with me. You need to be introduced."

Kate reluctantly followed Theresa to the buffet table, not really keen on being snubbed again. Theresa put her hand on Casmin's shoulder. Her friend turned and smiled warmly. She put down her dinner plate and threw her arms around Theresa's neck. Kate stood impatiently, still annoyed, shifting her weight from one foot to the other. Suddenly, as she watched the two women interact, she wanted to be anywhere else on earth. Feelings of intense embarrassment shot to the core of her as Theresa signed to Casmin. Casmin was deaf. Theresa made some quick motions with her hands and extended her arm, signaling Kate to step closer. Kate smiled meekly, her face flushed with humiliation. How could she be so stupid?

"Casmin can lip-read, but I'll sign anyway," Theresa said to Kate. "Casmin, this is Kate Fields. She works with me as a consultant in our communications division."

Kate grimaced. "Yeah, I'm an expert on communication."

Theresa directed a smirk toward Kate and signed the words to Casmin.

Kate nodded hello. "Nice to meet you."

"My pleasure, Kate," Casmin said haltingly, shaking hands. Her words were muffled and hard to understand.

Theresa continued signing as she talked. "Casmin

lives in Sandy Springs, just north of the city. She's a computer programmer for an engineering firm."

Kate found herself drawn into Casmin's eyes — deep, brown pools that reflected an inner sweetness she was finding irresistible. "I live south of the city, near the airport."

"Do you travel a lot?" Casmin asked.

Kate carefully processed the sounds made by Casmin's voice, struggling with each word. She looked at Theresa. "Do I travel?"

Theresa nodded yes.

"Oh, yeah. Some here and there. I just live near the airport 'cause no one else wants to."

Casmin smiled and Theresa laughed. "Well, why don't we all get something to eat?" Theresa suggested. As Casmin returned to the buffet table, Theresa teased Kate. "Nice going, my friend. Not like you to jump to conclusions."

Kate picked up a set of silverware. She held the knife to her throat and made a slicing motion. "I feel like an idiot. Everyone should have to feel this way at least once. The world would be a helluva lot more humble."

Theresa leaned into her ear. "You like her, don't you? I can tell."

"There's something about her — I mean, besides being attractive."

"Casmin's a super person. She's smart, successful, has a great sense of humor. And, she's also available."

Kate shook her head in disgust. "Yeah, and she'd think I was a first-class jerk if she knew what I just did."

"I'll keep your secret for you."

"Thanks."

"Well, Kate, this will sure be a challenge for you. She's black, you're white. She's hearing-impaired, you're not."

"I think I'm the one who's impaired. Hopefully, it's something I can work on."

Six weeks later, Kate was standing in her kitchen, head inside the refrigerator. "Well, I've got beer, wine, diet soda, spring water and orange juice. What can I get for you?" Kate shoved the orange juice carton aside and grabbed a beer for herself. "Casmin?" Kate freed herself from the bowels of the refrigerator. Casmin was leaning up against the kitchen counter reading *Southern Voice*, Atlanta's gay and lesbian newspaper. Kate smacked her hand against her forehead. "God, I will learn. Truly I will." Kate stomped her foot on the floor — a trick she learned from Theresa. Casmin felt the vibrations and looked up. "Casmin, what would you like to drink?"

"What do you have?"

Kate laughed and repeated the contents of the refrigerator.

"A glass of wine, please."

"No problem."

In the six weeks she and Casmin had been dating, Kate had gone through a crash-course in sign language. It still took her a long time to complete a sentence, but she was determined to master yet another form of communication.. In social situations, she found herself exasperated for Casmin. Even though her lip-reading skills were excellent, it was difficult for Casmin to follow conversations with groups of people. People tended to talk over one another and didn't always face Casmin when they spoke. Kate tried to repeat things but often gave up and felt guilty about it. The process was tiring and frustrating. She was often angry with herself for her own impatience — and with others for their indifference. Through it all, Casmin remained unfazed — at least on the surface.

But Kate had also discovered that underneath the calm exterior, Casmin was hurt when people avoided talking with her because they decided it was too much damned trouble. And she was very self-conscious about her speech. She knew she was difficult to understand. There were times she wanted to say things but didn't. It was easier not to. Inside, the sweetness that Kate had first perceived was sometimes overshadowed by sheer frustration. Casmin would retreat into herself, content to let the world go on without her. Kate had learned to barge in.

"I want to know what you're thinking," Kate had told her as they walked hand-in-hand along a small rise of trees in Piedmont Park. "Please don't push me away. Be patient with me, okay?" Kate squeezed Casmin's hand. "Even when I seem impatient with you. I have a lot to learn."

"I won't shut you out. Promise."

"Good. And when you really do want to sit and be quiet, just tell me to shut up."

Casmin laughed. "Shut up." She grabbed Kate's other hand and pulled her to the grass. "Shut up and kiss me." Casmin's arms wrapped themselves around Kate's back. "Mary Chapin Carpenter."

Kate laughed. "You know the song?"

"Yes. More importantly, I know how to shut up and kiss."

Kate sat on the sofa facing Casmin who was signing a mile a minute. Kate was struggling to keep up with the story about Casmin's day at work and another job offer she was considering. The hand movements were making her dizzy. Casmin finished the story by asking Kate what she thought.

"I think you're stunningly beautiful," Kate painstakingly signed.

Casmin smiled and looked away.

Kate touched Casmin's cheek lightly and mouthed, "Would you mind if we talked later? I really want to hold you."

Casmin melted into her arms like some missing piece of herself she had never found. Suddenly, Kate remembered again how a touch could say so much more than words — no matter how the words were communicated. Maybe they were both trying too hard.

* * * * *

The bedroom walls reflected the soft shadows of candlelight. Kate watched as Casmin's dark skin pressed against the creamy-white of her own. There were many differences between them — and yet the connection was deep and undeniable. Kate ran her hands through the tight curls of Casmin's hair, kissing her until her breaths came in quick gasps.

Kate rolled over. As Casmin lay beneath her, she kissed her again. Her tongue rolled over Casmin's, caressing the inside of her mouth, the softness of Casmin's face warm against her own. Her hands slid down to Casmin's breasts, cupping the softness of them. Nipples hardened between her fingers and, with a deep sigh, Casmin's head turned toward the pillow. Casmin put her hand to her face and moaned, her eyes closing slowly as her other hand caressed the back of Kate's head. Kate teased a nipple with her tongue, then took it between her teeth and tugged softly. Casmin's hips rose slightly from the bed. The hand at the back of Kate's head pulled her closer until Kate's mouth surrounded the nipple, sucking it inside as deeply as she could. Kate ran the palm of her hand over the other nipple until Casmin's thighs opened beneath her and she could feel their wetness against her own skin.

Making love to Casmin was like having a wonderfully erotic dream. It was dreamlike because of the joy she felt when this woman came in her arms, and she came, too, giving what she had given. Kate kissed away the tiny beads of sweat from Casmin's forehead, swept up the tears with her tongue. Leaving her hand inside Casmin, she laid her head on Casmin's chest. Her fingers could still feel the last moments of Casmin's orgasm ebbing away.

Some minutes later, as they remained in each other's arms, Casmin spoke. Kate heard the words clearly, because she had learned to listen with her heart.

"I love you, Kate."

Kate smiled and wiped away her own tears. No matter how it was said — with words, with sign language, with the movement of lips or bodies intertwined — it was always enough.

Missed Opportunities

Peggy J. Herring

Tacey finished installing her new watch battery and went to check the dryer again to see if her shirt was ready yet. The house had a warm, savory smell from the chicken that Maria had placed in the crockpot earlier. As Tacey went about her morning routine she had a fleeting flash of brilliance about the money that could be made if someone would just come up with a new potpourri scent called "Crockpot Chicken." She'd certainly be one of the first to try it.

She took her shirt out of the dryer and gave it a few shakes to cool it off, then found the morning paper that Maria had left neatly folded on the end of the sofa for her. Maria was a good friend and a thoughtful roommate; their new living arrangements were working out better than Tacey had expected. They were both recovering from breakups that had left them emotionally and financially at a disadvantage. Somewhere along the way these similarities had sparked a close friendship that eventually led to rent sharing and a grass-mowing schedule.

Tacey glanced at her watch again and then stuck the newspaper under her arm. It was her turn to open the gourmet coffee shop at the Rivercenter Mall and she didn't want to be late. Maybe she'd get a chance to talk to that cute paramedic who came by every day at eleven. Just the thought of seeing her again made Tacey smile.

"What did you say to her today?" Maria asked as she set the table later that evening.

"Nothing," Tacey said, the disappointment still a vivid part of her bad mood. The lunch rush had come and gone without a sign of the paramedic. It really surprised her how much she'd been looking forward to those precious few seconds with a total stranger. "There's a rumor that she's probably off on Wednesdays and Thursdays." Tacey set a steaming bowl of cauliflower on the table and went to get the salad from the refrigerator. "So tomorrow shouldn't be any fun either. I feel like I did the day my big brother told me there wasn't a Santa Claus."

"Ah, what a mean thing to do," Maria said. "How old were you? Fourteen? Fifteen?"

"Five," Tacey said over her friend's laughter.

"Tell me again about this mystery woman of yours," Maria said. "It always cheers you up to talk about her."

"It would only depress me tonight," Tacey said.

"I bet it wouldn't once you got started. I like seeing that little gleam in your eye when you talk about how good she looks in her uniform," Maria teased. "Go ahead. Describe her to me again."

"Jesus. All that *starch*," Tacey said dreamily. "I can just see myself sliding my hands up and down the front of her shirt." She opened her eyes and discovered Maria grinning at her. Heat spread up into her face, and Tacey knew she was blushing.

"How do we find out if she's a lesbian?" Maria asked after a moment. "What's your gaydar telling you?"

"It definitely goes off whenever she's around," Tacey said. "As a matter of fact, my *every*thing starts going off when she's around."

"Good sign."

Tacey shook her head. "I guess my real question is, how do I find out whether or not she's single? I've never been very good at that."

"You should just ask her," Maria said. Her dark brown hair still had a touch of curl in it from the hot rollers she'd used that morning.

"At the most I've got fifteen seconds to talk to her. That's not a lot of time for chitchat."

"Take time," Maria said. "Life is nothing more than a series of missed opportunities, my friend. What if she's *the one* and you let her get away?"

"A series of missed opportunities," Tacey repeated thoughtfully. "Whoa. That's deep."

"Make a move the first chance you get," Maria suggested. "Life's too short to be waiting around for something to happen."

"Listen to you!" Tacey said. " 'Missed opportunities . . . life's too short . . .' You sound like a fortune cookie."

"It's good advice, kiddo."

At work the next day Tacey made sure she was up front at the register at ten forty-five, just in case the paramedic arrived early. She knew the woman's routine by heart: she would have a small box of popcorn under her left arm, a Schlotsky's sandwich bag in her hand and a book on some sort of tropical fish that she'd be reading while she waited in line for her large decaf café mocha. Tacey made it a point to be the one to take her order every day. Once the woman got her café mocha, she was off to find an empty table outside near the Riverwalk where she would then eat her sandwich and feed the popcorn to the pigeons. Tacey had discovered all this by watching her at every available opportunity. At eleven-thirty sharp the woman would always stuff the Schlotsky's bag and the coffee cup into the empty popcorn box and then throw it away before leaving. If a convention was in town, then the Food Court could easily have hundreds of people jockeying for tables, so keeping this dark-haired beauty in sight wasn't always easy. But yesterday the woman hadn't shown up for her mocha, and today it wasn't until after two o'clock that Tacey finally stopped looking for her.

When she got home later Maria tried to talk her into going to the bar for steak night where she was meeting other friends, but Tacey didn't want to go.

"Let me guess," Maria said. "You didn't see her today. Which means you'll probably see her tomorrow for sure. Come on. I've got an extra steak here. I think you should go. I'll even help you plan some new strategy."

Tacey could hear Annie Lennox at a reasonable volume as soon as they arrived at the bar, but as the night wore on she knew everyone would be yelling in order to hear one another. Arms began waving on the other side of the huge, dimly lit club as Maria's friends spotted them.

"There they are," Maria said.

Tacey felt suddenly shy. "I'd better get the steaks on or we'll be here all night waiting to eat."

She got in line behind twenty or so other women and waited her turn to hand their steaks over to the cook. By the time she got back to the table, Maria was already a beer ahead of her and engaged in conversation about hot tubs. Maria pulled a chair out for her and just as Tacey began to sit down she noticed another group of women several tables over. And the woman on the end just so happened to be the paramedic Tacey had been lusting after for weeks now.

"She's here," Tacey whispered urgently.

"Who's here?" Maria asked.

"My paramedic. Jesus, she looks good."

"Really? She's *here*? Where? Point her out but don't be obvious."

Tacey explained which table the woman was sitting at and where she was at the table. "The blue and white striped shirt," Tacey said. "Goodness. Check out that starch, will you?"

Maria asked the other women at their table if they knew who she was, but no one was any help.

"This is what you do," Maria said. "You grab your chest and sort of roll to the floor. She'll rush over here and offer to help save you, and once those lips are close you take it from there."

Tacey eyed her skeptically. "Hey, with my luck that chunky straight guy over there is a doctor and I'd end up with *his* lips all over me. No thanks. Bad idea."

"Then go ask her to dance," Maria suggested.

"They're playing eating music, not dancing music," Tacey said. "And besides. What if she's *with* someone?"

"You're right. I didn't think about that." Squinting through the dim light, Maria said, "I count five people at the table. What're the chances that she's the odd one out?"

"Not very good," Tacey said. "Look at her. She's gorgeous. No way is she here alone."

Maria picked up her glass and took a sip of beer. "So what are you gonna do?"

"Nothing," Tacey replied.

Maria rolled her eyes. *"That'll* sure get her attention."

"This has already gotten way too complicated," Tacey said. "But at least now I know she's gay." As she continued stealing glances at her, Tacey's confidence began to dwindle. "But then just because she's at a lesbian bar doesn't really mean anything, I guess. Does it?"

"I say ask her to dance," Maria repeated. "Or buy her a drink. I'll even deliver it for you. But sitting here drooling over her certainly isn't accomplishing anything."

The whole table got quiet as the paramedic and the woman sitting beside her got up and went to the bar. Tacey watched her every move, the way she shook her long dark hair away from her face, her easy laughter as she ambled through the crowd. And her khaki shorts with the blue and white striped shirt neatly tucked in — both impeccably starched and wrinkle-free.

Starch, Tacey thought as she took it all in. *Why am I suddenly so hung up on starch?*

"She's worth your attention," Maria said. "Definitely worth your attention."

As the two women came back from the bar with a round of drinks for their table, Tacey couldn't help but continue to stare at her. The woman looked more relaxed tonight . . . more relaxed and casual than Tacey had ever seen her before. The woman glanced up and noticed Tacey looking at her, then did a double take and smiled.

"Hi," she said as she came over. "This is so strange. We were talking about you earlier."

Tacey was speechless, and utterly amazed when a word actually squeaked out of her mouth. "Really?"

"I was telling my friends where to find the best café mocha in town." As she smiled again Tacey could feel herself melting. "But they've got Starbucks on the brain. It's like there's no place else that can make a cup of coffee."

The woman she had gone to the bar with had set down the drinks that she'd been carrying and then returned for the other two that the paramedic held. She surrendered them easily without ever taking her eyes from Tacey's.

Think fast, kid, Tacey mused. *You need to make the most of this.* She then blurted out, "I have a question for you," and to her immense relief, Maria politely suggested that the woman sit down.

"I have a question for you too," she said as she took the chair next to Tacey's. "But you go first."

"It's about the popcorn," Tacey said as she struggled for clarity and something semi-coherent to say. "I've seen you feed the pigeons every day. I was wondering if you ever eat any of it or if you just buy it for them."

That sounded like gushing, she thought with a cringe.

Their eyes met and it seemed as though the woman was actually looking at her for the first time.

Tacey's whole body began to tingle under her warm gaze.

"I don't even know your name," Tacey finally managed to say.

"Erica," the woman said, her piercing brown eyes still studying her. "And your name always makes me think there's a typo on your name tag. Like maybe the *r* fell out of Tracey or something."

Tacey laughed and was relieved that she hadn't made a bumbling fool of herself yet.

"And no," Erica said. "I don't eat any of the popcorn. I buy it for them."

Their eyes met again, and Tacey could feel her heart begin to race. "And you had a question for me," she reminded her.

"Yes, I do," Erica said.

"Ask away."

Erica glanced around the table and then leaned over and said, "Are you here with friends or with someone special?"

"Is that your question?"

Erica laughed. "No."

"I'm here with friends. And your question is?"

Erica took a deep breath and nervously cleared her throat. "I've often wondered what your hair smells like at the end of the day. Does it smell like fresh-ground coffee? Hazelnut? Amaretto? Breakfast Blend?"

Tacey laughed. "How often have you wondered that?"

"I don't know," Erica said with a shrug. "Lots, I guess. So what does it smell like?"

"Right now it probably smells like smoke." Tacey

met those brown eyes again and added, "But feel free to give it a sniff if you like."

Erica chuckled and slowly reached over and touched Tacey's hair. "Would you dance with me?"

Tacey turned around and checked out the empty dance floor just as "Nights in White Satin" began to play. If anyone else but Erica had suggested a dance on an empty dance floor she wouldn't have agreed, but this wasn't just anyone.

"Sure," she said as she took Erica's hand and led the way.

The wall-to-wall mirrors surrounding them once they were there made it seem as though several couples were dancing instead of just one. Erica insisted on leading and held her close.

"Let me get this one thing over with so I can concentrate on what we're doing, okay?" Tacey said. She placed her palms on Erica's upper chest and ran her hands over the stiff shirt several times.

Erica looked down at her with a crooked grin. "Need any help with that?"

"No, thanks," Tacey said. "Just a little fantasy check. All better now."

They continued dancing, and after a moment Tacey inquired about her hair and what it smelled like.

Erica's cheek brushed the side of Tacey's head. "Cinnamon mostly. Very much the way I thought it would."

She's thought about my hair, Tacey mused. *Jesus. I don't believe this.*

Erica lightly kissed the top of Tacey's head as their feet continued to move to the music, and occasionally Erica would sink her nose into the side of Tacey's neck, no doubt searching for more cinnamon.

"Such a great song," Erica said. Her lips brushed Tacey's ear and sent a shiver down her spine. "I think this is where you're supposed to kiss me," she said, and without waiting for a response from her, Erica leaned over and gently touched her lips to Tacey's. Their feet stopped moving and their arms tightened around each other. The kiss was deep and exhilarating, with Erica's tongue dancing in Tacey's mouth. They kissed this way for several minutes, forgetting where they were and who they were, and when Erica finally broke away from her, she whispered, "I live two blocks from here. Come home with me."

Tacey took her hand and led her off the dance floor and out the door, stopping only long enough to tell Maria that she'd see her whenever.

They kissed in the parking lot until the windows in Erica's car steamed up, and they kissed again at a stop sign and then through two changes of a red light on the corner. Tacey was squirmy with anticipation as Erica drove with one hand and slipped the other inside Tacey's shirt to rub her breasts.

Once they arrived at Erica's house, they were out of the car and quickly into the living room, where Tacey immediately heard the gurgling of aquariums. Erica pulled her into her arms and kissed her again deeply. Her tongue was curious and demanding, and continued to offer hints of things to come.

"You have the softest mouth," Erica whispered a while later. She unzipped Tacey's shorts and buried her face in her neck and hair. Tacey's hands slid up and down the front of Erica's shirt all on their own until finally Tacey's desire to feel warm, soft skin became greater than her need to feel starch.

"I could kiss you all night," Erica said in a breathless rush. "But then we'd never get to the good part."

Tacey maneuvered them to the sofa and eventually ended up on top of her. "The good part's closer than you think."

They scrambled out of their clothes despite their lips being welded together. The atmosphere they were operating under was surprisingly romantic, with the lights from several aquariums casting a soft glow throughout the room, and Erica's low moans and heavy breathing enhancing Tacey's arousal meter.

The sofa, however, wasn't nearly big enough for what Tacey had in mind, but she managed to improvise quite nicely. She helped slide Erica's bikini underwear off and managed to prop one of Erica's legs on a nearby coffee table while the other was flung helplessly over the back of the sofa.

"Oh, God!" Erica panted the moment Tacey's mouth found her throbbing center. She grabbed Tacey's head and started moving her hips to the rhythm Tacey had started. Erica came fast and loud, shrieking her pleasure and frantically grinding herself against Tacey's very willing mouth and tongue.

When it was over, Erica lay spent, with her legs limp and her fingers gently rubbing Tacey's hair. "Hot damn," she mumbled weakly.

Tacey kissed Erica's glistening center, then rose up on her arms and teased her further by brushing a hard nipple into total wetness.

"Are your neighbors home?" Tacey whispered as she moved up and lowered herself between Erica's still opened legs. "They probably thought someone was killing a cat over here."

Erica giggled and then whispered, "You haven't heard anything yet, doll." She took Tacey's face in her hands and kissed her hungrily as they began to move against each other. "It's always better for me the second time."

Immediately Tacey could feel how good it would be for both of them just by the way Erica was moving and holding her. And at the same time so many things began flashing in her head all at once: popcorn, pigeons, a Schlotsky's bag and cinnamon coffee. As the heat between her thighs increased and Erica's moaning began again, Tacey's thoughts drifted back to the coffee shop and chocolate syrup, whipped cream and warm milk frothed to perfection. Then seconds later it also occurred to her that she'd never made love in front of fish before.

Erica grabbed her and pulled her closer as they thrashed around on the sofa in mutually intense pleasure. They rubbed against each other until there was nothing left but racing hearts and throbbing pelvises.

Erica hugged her after a moment and then buried

her nose in Tacey's hair once more. "Cinnamon," she whispered. "I'll never feel the same about cinnamon again."

Tacey rested her head on Erica's shoulder and slowly ran the palm of her hand along soft, sweaty skin. *Starch,* she thought. *I wonder if she'd mind slipping that shirt on again just for a minute . . .*

My Brother's Keeper
Marianne K. Martin

In their early years she never thought of him as particularly sensitive. He was smart and fun and as annoying as younger siblings often are. But she never thought about his being sensitive. Not until they stood before the caskets, his hand refusing to leave hers for even a second. Until the innocence of his eight-year-old face lifted pools of dark syrup to look into her eyes and spilled his sadness and fear over his cheeks. She knew then, even at twelve, the depth of the pain they shared. She held him tightly while huge droplets splashed onto his bark-brown head and

177

promised him she would never leave him alone. It was a promise meant for a lifetime.

Trevor wrapped sun-toasted arms around his girlfriend. "Not bad for a 'girl movie,' " he said, winking at his sister.

"They're important training tools — like anniversary celebrations and Valentine's Day." Jenna gave him her most captivating pill-in-the-peanut-butter smile and planted a kiss on Trevor's cheek.

Tami, her swimmer's legs draping the end of the coffee table, stretched her arms lazily up the back of the futon they shared. "How do you think we keep you guys from swinging on vines and dragging women off by their hair, dear brother?"

"It has nothing to do with training. We're an evolved species with highly sophisticated means of seduction."

Jenna laughed as she rose from his embrace. "Yeah? Like what, for instance?"

"Well . . ." He leaned into the soft back of the futon and rubbed the palm of his hand over the surfer's wave on his T-shirt. "Like holding you during a sentimental movie, and like picking up a bottle of Merlot on our way to your place." He smiled, watching his sister and girlfriend pick up the dishes.

Jenna dumped the unpopped kernels from the popcorn bowl into the garbage and nudged Tami's shoulder. "God, it's a shame to let all those years of evolution go to waste, but I've got to open the store in the morning."

"You'd have to kick him out early in the morning anyway," Tami added. "We've got the Harolson job tomorrow. Five huge beds to plant. I picked up all except the palmettos today." She directed her words toward the other room.

Trevor groaned. "When was the last time we took a Saturday off?"

"I vote we all go to Cocoa tomorrow night," Jenna offered, whisking glasses through a stream of hot water and placing them in the strainer. "We'll eat oysters on the beach and listen to the jazz band at Coconuts."

He didn't have to tell her when something was wrong; it showed up in other ways. Routine became locked in stone. He ate the same thing for breakfast day after day, listened to the news every night at 11:00 no matter how tired he was, parked in the same space in the parking lot even when there was a closer one open. Tami pulled the pickup past Trevor's red Jeep. He hadn't forgotten to put the sunshade on the windshield in over two weeks. The signs had been there for at least that long.

"Hey, Tam," Trevor greeted. "You're late. Jenna's meeting us at Coconuts in a half an hour."

"You go ahead," she said, tossing her keys on the counter. "I'm tired."

"Ah, come on. We've worked overtime all week to catch up. You need a break."

"Laura's been bugging me to see some movie with her. If I don't fall asleep, maybe I'll call her later."

She tugged the tie-back from her sandy-brown tresses and disappeared into her bedroom. "Besides," she called, "if my instincts are on line, you and Jenna need some time alone."

He appeared in the open doorway, his face minus its usual boyish grin. "I figured if I said anything you'd sabotage whatever you have going with Laura."

"What are you talking about?"

"You've done it before... My relationship fails and suddenly you're Dr. K."

"Coincidences, Trevor. Nothing I did on purpose... What do you mean, failed?"

He remained in the doorway, hands in the pockets of his favorite blue Dockers. He dropped his gaze to the floor and said nothing.

"What's going on, T.?"

He shrugged his shoulders. "I was thinking rings, and vows, and baby surfers, but... Jenna's not."

"Are you sure? Maybe she's just not ready yet."

"I'm sure."

The sun had long since set against the palm-studded skyline. Tami returned home alone. As was her habit, she slapped the center pull of the wind chime hanging just outside the apartment door. The brass tubes sang their melodic tune but alerted no one tonight; the apartment was empty. Without turning on a light she made her way through the shadows and the sliding glass door, and settled into the papasan chair on the balcony.

She hadn't been able to shake thoughts of Trevor and Jenna all evening. They had clung like fine threads of a web around dinner, and the movie, and her entire conversation with Laura. Sometimes, like tonight, Laura sounded almost objective enough to be right. "He knows you'll always be there; you always have been," she said. "He's twenty-five. He'll find the right woman; give him time. Meanwhile, you've got to stop sacrificing chances for your own happiness." All true. She wasn't disputing her deductions. But what Laura didn't understand was that she wasn't really sacrificing. The emotional support, the bond that had brought them through the shuffle from distant relative to relative, from state to state, was there for her, too. Brother and sister had done whatever was necessary to stay out of foster care and stay together. It had always been that way. Together they could get through anything. Together they were "T-n-T," a force to be reckoned with.

Understandably there were no off-the-rack girlfriends who could ready-wear themselves into their "family," as unconventional as it was. But when Jenna came along with her contagious laugh, her zeal, her love of the ocean, their family of two very naturally became three. There was no doubt in either of their minds that she was the right one for Trevor. How could she leave now, after all they had shared, and leave them with still another loss? Maybe, she thought, Trevor was wrong.

Suddenly, the door of the apartment banged loudly against the wall. "Tami!" Trevor called, thudding into the wall with his load.

Tami raced into the apartment and snapped on the light as Trevor struggled to hold Jenna upright against the wall. "Is she all right? What's wrong?"

"Yeah. She's just drunk. Help me get her to the couch."

"Looks like you've had a few yourself."

They staggered through the room, bumping their knees into one another and into the edges of the furniture, while Tami tightly held Jenna's waist and tried to hold the balance for the three of them. They stumbled over the corner of the futon, and Trevor lost his balance. Jenna tumbled down on top of him, nearly pulling Tami onto the heap.

Eyes the color of the ocean at midday opened and focused hazily in Trevor's direction. "T.," Jenna mumbled. "I'm sorry."

He kissed the side of her face, then rose unsteadily. "Tam?"

"I know." Tami grinned. "You don't look much better than she does. Go to bed. I'll get her settled out here."

Jenna muttered and struggled to lift her head, wedged between the pillows and the back of the futon. ". . . goin' on home." Her focus wandered about without connection as Tami returned with a washcloth and a clean T-shirt.

"I see where that last daiquiri ended up." Tami grinned, removing the shirt with its pink sticky front and wiping the washcloth over Jenna's face and chest. "Good thing, too. One more and you just might've been drunk."

Jenna replied with an indecipherable mumble and with surprising dexterity pulled her bra up over her breasts before Tami could get the T-shirt over her head.

"Leave it on, Jen," she said, tugging the bra back into place over the soft vanilla mounds. But she had barely drawn the shirt over Jenna's head, and the bra was nearly off again. This time Tami relented and pulled it the rest of the way off. "Shit, Jen," she said, continuing to dress the less-than-cooperative ragdoll. "This is not Sister Mary here working on sainthood."

"T., I'm sorry," droned Jenna, grabbing Tami's neck and pulling her over her.

"And I'm not T." She tried freeing herself, but Jenna clung to her neck like a new chimp to her mother, and all Tami could do was brace herself. "Okay. Let go now . . . You're all right." Then the tears began to flow from blurry blue eyes to the shoulder of Tami's shirt. "Shhh, it's all right. Shhh . . . okay. Come on." Tami shifted her position, slipped her arm around Jenna and held her. "It's all right," she said softly as she stroked the baby-fine hair. "Things will look better tomorrow."

Tami was dismissing the words herself as they echoed unconvincingly in the silence when Jenna lifted her head. Without warning, lips meant for Trevor touched her own. She turned quickly from their softness, excused the mistake automatically. But Jenna clutched her tightly and rubbed tear-streaked cheeks across Tami's face to find her lips once again. Insistent, they denied each attempt to move away from them. They pressed and parted and persisted — until they got their way. Tami yielded momentarily, pressing her lips back into warm temptation, while

her conscience fought to excise the twinges of
pleasure she felt and scrambled thoughts sought
justification.

But there could be no justification — not for the
excitement stealing from her senses, not for the
simmering of heat beginning its descent, and certainly
not for what she was about to do.

She took Jenna into her arms and kissed her like
a lover — deeply, openly — exploring the wetness,
tasting the alcohol and the sweetness that was Jenna.
And with that kiss came a feeling, swelled to flood
level, that suddenly overwhelmed its banks and
rushed free. Where it came from she wasn't sure. She
only knew she was unprepared for the need that
came with it.

There was a soft moan as Jenna's body, naked
and pliant beneath the loose material, moved against
Tami's chest and suddenly there was only the feel of
Jenna's tongue filling her mouth — and Tami's
accepting it, wanting it. Wanting her — enough not to
stop. She let the kisses continue, knowing Jenna was
too drunk to remember tomorrow, knowing she
thought it was Trevor.

She found herself beginning the long caress down
Jenna's back. The natural beginning to an intimacy
beyond any hope of exoneration. She was able to stop
her hand short, but not the thought of it. It
continued — down the curve of her spine, over
quivering buttocks, to the silky skin of her thighs
parting to her touch. Challenging a rule high on her
own list of commandments: Thou shalt never covet
thy brother's girlfriend. A rule set in stone and
strictly adhered to — a rule broken.

It was her last shred of conscience that kept the thought of touching her mouth to the tender warm flesh of her breasts, of moving her lips from warmth to heat and tasting the heat of warm silk only a thought. Without it she would surely have teased the trembling desire until Jenna moaned with excitement. She would have grasped the pleading hips, slid her thigh into their wet center and let the rhythm of Jenna's need drive her feverishly toward orgasm. She would have stroked with her tongue all the tender flesh while Jenna gasped for release, and slid her fingers through the wetness — slowly, so slowly — until the writhing hips stopped in the beginning shudder of orgasm. She would have entered only then, using the last slow stroke to send her into convulsive ecstasy. She would have told her that she loved her.

Instead, she cradled Jenna in her arms and whispered warnings to herself to quiet the turbulence in her chest. She'd hold her until she slept peacefully. Then tomorrow she'd begin searching for her own peace, and for some way to replace the loneliness they were each about to face.

It took only a couple of days for the reality of forever to drop its veil. No matter how busy the sunlit days or how beautiful the sunset-painted nights, they could not hide the fact that Jenna was no longer in her life. Tami had already begun to realize that grieving was not reserved for death when Jenna walked through the apartment door.

"T.'s still loading the truck for tomorrow," Tami managed over a sudden surge of hopefulness. "He'll be home in less than half an hour."

Jenna nodded and dropped a folded T-shirt on the kitchen table. "I just wanted to bring this back . . . and apologize for getting so tanked last weekend."

Tami handed her a Dr. Pepper from the refrigerator and avoided the eyes that, given a chance, might guess her secret.

Perched lightly on the edge of the chair, and looking as if ready for flight at the slightest noise, Jenna asked, "What has Trevor told you?"

"What I guess I already sensed," she said, settling in the chair across the table. Tami finally made eye contact. "You know I am going to hire someone part-time to take the load off the weekends. You would have more time together."

"It's not that, Tam." She watched Tami carefully picking loose the seam of the Twister label. "We tried. It isn't meant to be."

"It's so hard after all this time."

Jenna filled her end of the resulting silence staring at the way the geometric pattern on the floor changed from flat to three-dimensional.

Tami's eyes never left her own fingers. "I guess I thought, at this point, there wouldn't be anything that couldn't be worked out."

"There's someone else, Tam."

The fingers suddenly ripped the label clear and shoved the bottle spinning to the middle of the table. "How, Jenna?" she snapped, aiming her look of perplexed shock directly into the wide blue of Jenna's gaze. "My God, you're here ninety percent of the time." She stared into Jenna's eyes while the realization crashed its thunderous wave against the walls of her heart. "Oh, God," she gasped, then dropped her head heavily into the palm of her hand.

"I've been hiding it for months." She appeared quietly, kneeling beside Tami's chair and taking the work-worn hand in her own.

"Don't say any more." *Don't say out loud what isn't possible anyway.*

Jenna stared in silence for a moment, holding tightly to the reluctant hand. "I know you would never do anything to hurt Trevor. And neither would I." She reached for the hand supporting Tami's head. "I wasn't going to come back."

The hand finally gave way and Tami turned downcast eyes on Jenna's face. The tears she saw in the penitent blue looking up at her brought a tightness to her throat. She caught an impending tear with her thumb before it spilled down Jenna's cheek and felt as if her heart would break once more.

"With all you know of Trevor's needs," Jenna said softly, "you know so little of your own . . . He knew before you did — he knew before *I* did." She squeezed Tami's hand. "*He* made me come back here."

His love, like a wave rushing to shore, washed over her guilt and sadness and left her heart as smooth as an unwalked beach. Tami gathered Jenna in her arms and held her tightly to her chest.

"I was so sure, so afraid," she said through tears of relief, "that you would tell me to leave."

The Singing Heart
Karin Kallmaker

It had taken nearly an hour for Matt's plane to disappear into the distance, but Leslie wouldn't leave the airport until it did. Sarah waited patiently. She was used to waiting. To date, their courtship had had plenty of waiting.

First they'd spent a pointless six months denying the attraction, and all the while Sarah had been foolishly involved with someone else. It wasn't until she had been unceremoniously dumped by Melissa that Sarah had really appreciated the friendship Leslie offered. They had spent last Christmas together, platonically, but Sarah had glimpsed behind Leslie's affection and seen passion waiting for her, when she was ready.

She was ready. Man, oh man, she was ready.

After fiddling about for a couple of months having "get-togethers" (never dates), not saying what needed to be said, they had come to an understanding. Part of the delay had been Leslie's need to know that Matt, her son, liked Sarah and wouldn't mind her being a part of their lives.

"What did Matt say?" Leslie turned from the window with a smile that unsuccessfully hid her sadness at Matt's departure.

"Oh." Matt had beckoned to Sarah just as he went up the jetway. "He said he wanted me to be here when he got back. I still have to teach him to use the longbow. He keeps growing like he has been and he'll be able to use mine." It was scary how quickly Matt had shot up.

They walked through the terminal with their shoulders just brushing. Sarah could smell Leslie's shampoo.

She'd never dated a woman with a kid before. It really put the skids on renting a U-Haul. Maybe that wasn't so bad. Leslie's need to protect Matt's welfare was natural, but his presence also added a logistical hurdle.

"He's at that age," Leslie had finally managed to say over coffee in her office, "where he's ready to start fooling around. If we, well, if it's noticeable, well, I'd think he would think it was permission. I mean, I've told him sex is okay, but I'm not ready for him . . ." She had blushed beet red. "Do you get this at all?"

Sarah had said yes, she did get it. Matt was old enough to know exactly what was going on if Sarah was there when he woke up in the morning. And Leslie would not leave him alone at night to come to Sarah's. They didn't talk about it very much, only enough to assure each other of their understanding — when Matt went to his dad's for his next visit, they'd get to know each other very, very thoroughly.

When they reached the parking lot Leslie started the car, then turned to Sarah. "So where is this surprise dinner?"

The fragrance of Leslie's fabric softener teased Sarah's nose. "The Fairmont. I made reservations."

"Ooh. That sounds delicious. And romantic." She half-backed out of the space, then pulled in again. "Only . . ."

"Only?" Sarah watched Leslie's fingers moving through curly hair.

"Well, a heavy meal puts me to sleep."

Sarah blinked, then laughed. "Come to think of it, it does me, too." She felt her cheeks stain with color.

"Maybe we could go tomorrow night."

"Maybe that would be best."

"Do you have a Plan B?"

"No, I hadn't really . . . except for, well, after — you know." *A babbling idiot, I'm a babbling idiot.* She didn't look at Leslie. If she did she'd scream, "I want to have sex! Lots and lots! Now!"

"Sarah?"

"Mm-hmm?" She studied the door lock.

"Sarah, you know I lived in a commune once upon a time."

"Yes." Leslie's colorful past was very dear to Sarah. She'd never met anyone like her.

"We don't have to wait until after dark, you know. I learned that in my free love days."

Leslie was laughing at her. She did that a lot. "I've had sex during the day," Sarah said peevishly.

"So what are we waiting for?"

"Well, here and now is okay by me, but I'm going to wipe out my knee on the gear shift."

Leslie chuckled. "Let's just go home. My place. Okay?"

"Okay. No, wait." Sarah lifted Leslie's hand before she could put the car in gear. "I just want to do this."

She heard Leslie's breath catch as she kissed Leslie's palm. She nuzzled her lips against Leslie's fingers. Blood pounded in her ears as she flicked the tip of her tongue on Leslie's index finger, then blew softly on it.

Leslie had the hands of a mother/executive. Rough in a few places, but mostly soft. Not manicured, nails short for convenience. The brush of Leslie's fingertips against her mouth made Sarah ache; her entire body began to throb deliciously.

She rubbed Leslie's hand against her throat, and her eyes closed. Her own fingertips brushed Leslie's as they stroked her neck, a confusion of sensations that increased her pulse further.

"Sarah, give me my hand back so I can drive us home."

She blushed and let go. "Sorry."

"I'm not sorry. I just want to get home. Very soon."

They emerged from the parking lot into the brilliance of an early spring afternoon. Yesterday's rain had left the sky electric blue and the hills shimmering green. "Let's go to the beach tomorrow," Sarah said. "That would a great way to spend the first day of our vacation."

"Maybe in the afternoon," Leslie answered.

Sarah looked at her inquiringly.

"I don't plan on getting up early. I'm going to keep you in bed as long as I can."

Sarah swallowed. "You'll have no objections from me."

Leslie maneuvered to the fast lane and then stroked Sarah's knee. "I'm out of practice, you know. Really." She kept her eyes on the road.

Sarah watched Leslie's hand slowly move from her knee to her thigh. She could feel the heat of it through her jeans. She shifted in her seat, trying not to be obvious about parting her thighs. "Bicycle," she managed to say.

"Hmm, probably. I think it may all be coming back to me," Leslie murmured. Her hand rubbed Sarah's inner thigh.

Sarah's lower lip trembled. She couldn't breathe. She raised her hips slightly, her legs opening farther.

The car swerved slightly and Leslie took her hand away. "Sorry. I think I should just concentrate on driving."

Sarah watched Leslie's hands as she drove. It was

so easy now to imagine those hands on her body. She didn't dare look at Leslie's mouth — that would be the end of any ability to think.

She realized that Leslie was wearing the soft chambray shirt she'd had on when she had comforted Sarah after Melissa's abrupt departure. Sarah had cried her eyes out on that shirt. She remembered the way it had felt against her cheek.

Careful to not interfere with Leslie's driving, Sarah reached over to undo the top button on Leslie's shirt.

"What are you doing?"

"You're still decent," Sarah said. She continued for two more buttons. "I just wanted to . . ." Her fingertip found its way under the shirt, encountering soft voluptuousness that made her dizzy.

"Sarah, we're gonna die if you don't stop."

I'll die if I stop, Sarah thought. She settled back in her seat, turned so she could look at the curves she had uncovered. It was sexier than if Leslie had been naked. Her mouth watered.

"New Year's Eve," Leslie said.

Sarah blinked. "What about it?"

"In my misspent youth we would make a big deal out of New Year's Eve. We were too holistic for alcohol, you understand." Her mouth quirked. "However, we saved our pennies to procure the best pot available. We looked forward to New Year's Eve for weeks, more than any other holiday."

Not sure where this was going, Sarah said, "And?"

"We got loaded by ten, ate all the food by eleven

and fell asleep before midnight. New Year's Eve never lived up to my expectations . . ."

Comprehension dawned. "Oh. Well."

"I'm just saying, well." It was Leslie's turn to blush. She did it quite attractively.

"I've been looking forward to this," Sarah said over the hum of the engine. "But I'm looking forward to waking up with you tomorrow morning almost as much. I'm looking forward to eating ice cream on hot summer nights, going camping with Matt and kissing the tip of your nose."

"Matt likes you."

"I like him. You did good. Look, I am really looking forward to . . . you know. But that's just one of the steps on what I hope is a staircase we build together."

"For a lawyer you can be poetic."

"I'm Welsh," Sarah said. "Being Welsh means you make everything in life into poetry and song. Even coal mining can be poetic if you're Welsh."

"And here I am just a plain ol' American girl."

"I've got enough for both of us," Sarah said. She trailed one finger along Leslie's jean-clad knee. "If mining can be poetry you can imagine what other things will be like."

"My imagination is running overtime." Leslie neatly cut over two lanes for the exit.

On impulse, Sarah reached over to run her finger along the top of Leslie's ear. Soft, slightly fuzzy skin tickled her fingertip. How strange and wonderful that the sensation made her smile, and how quickly the smile changed to longing when she brushed Leslie's cheek.

A touch to Leslie's shoulder and Sarah was content to settle into her seat. Her stomach rumbled, reminding her of her hurried, inadequate lunch.

Leslie was already turning into a drive-through. "I have to have something to eat, for energy." She grinned.

"Sure this isn't a delaying tactic?"

"My stomach says it's not."

"So does mine."

Sarah hadn't quite finished her chocolate shake when they pulled into Leslie's driveway.

"Want to start in the hot tub?" Sarah drained the last of her shake as Leslie shut the door behind them.

"I want to start right here."

Leslie's voice, suddenly husky and taut, made Sarah turn in surprise. As Leslie advanced on her she felt a rush of terror, like a doe confronted by a tigress. But that was ridiculous — there was no reason to be afraid. Except she was.

Leslie took the empty milkshake cup out of her hand, then unbuttoned Sarah's shirt. "I don't think I've gotten a good night's sleep since I met you." She kissed the hollow of Sarah's throat.

Sarah reeled, but Leslie caught her, pinning her to the wall. She could get lost in Leslie's sudden strength, let Leslie tumble her to the ground . . . it would be welcome surrender after all the months of waiting. Surrendering at this moment would be easy;

Leslie's mouth was persuasive. Easy, and familiar, and yet she wanted to resist the impulse. This time needed to be different if her life with Leslie was going to be different from every other relationship in her life.

Leslie's arms were around her waist. Sarah captured Leslie's head in her hands and tried to draw the demanding lips up to her own, but her knees were buckling. Leslie steadied her, but they were both losing their balance.

The floor knocked the air out of Sarah's lungs, but she managed a choked laugh. Leslie groaned next to her, then sat up, rubbing her elbow.

They stared at each other for a few moments, then said at the same time, "So much for —"

"You first," Leslie said.

"No, you. I can't breathe."

"I was going to say, so much for my attempt at macho."

Sarah chortled. "That's *exactly* what I was going to say."

"I may have lived in a commune, but I'm really an old-fashioned girl." Leslie got to her feet. "Let's just go to bed, okay? Meet you in the middle. Last one there is a rotten egg!"

Sarah scrambled to her hands and feet, trying to block Leslie's escape, but it was no use. Leslie nimbly danced around her and up the stairs to the master bedroom.

Sarah followed, feeling more lighthearted than she would have thought possible.

Leslie was shimmying out of the last of her clothes when Sarah entered, then she slid between the sheets. "You're a rotten egg."

"Cheater." Sarah disrobed in record time and with a giggle joined Leslie in the middle of the bed.

The sheets were cool and the press of Leslie's warm skin against Sarah's made her shiver, and laughter fled. "Let's get serious," she murmured, then Leslie kissed her.

It was so sweet that Sarah sighed. It felt like coming home after a long absence, to a warm fire or a good book. She smiled against Leslie's mouth. This felt like a happy ending.

"No laughing," Leslie whispered.

"I'll laugh if I want to."

"Laugh later." Leslie's warm fingers slipped between Sarah's thighs.

Leslie's gasp was an echo of Sarah's. Answering the pressure of Leslie's hand, Sarah straddled Leslie's waist and rested her forehead on the headboard. Leslie was paying delicious attention to her breasts and Sarah ground her hips toward the welcome heat of Leslie's fingers.

It was too much to bear in silence. She stuttered, "There, there, there," then a taut cry of exhilaration escaped her.

Below her Leslie gasped.

Even as Sarah stammered, "More," she was beyond needing it. Her body shook with release as she crumpled on top of Leslie. Their mouths met again with hunger, but Sarah was startled to taste tears.

She held Leslie tight and whispered in Leslie's

ear, "I thought I was the one who was supposed to cry."

Leslie sniffled. "I love you, you big dope."

"You tell me this just to insult me?"

"Can I go on?"

"Insulting me?"

"No." Leslie seemed caught between laughter and tears. "Loving you."

Sarah said softly, "There's an old Welsh story about a singing heart. If you search for it you'll never find it, but when you stop looking its music will lead you to your true love. I didn't understand until now what a singing heart was."

"That's so sweet. Kiss me."

"I love you, too."

"Kiss me."

"I'll do more than that." Sarah shinnied under the covers. The sheets were warm now, and Leslie's thighs against her cheeks even hotter. She groaned while Leslie twisted against her, calves tangling arms, knees bumping shoulders, and they rolled in a dizzying coil of silken skin and slick passion.

"So how is New Year's Eve so far?" Sarah reached over Leslie for the carton of ice cream.

"I think I'm staying up until midnight this year. Give me that back."

"You've had more than half," Sarah protested, but she surrendered the spoon and carton.

"You really do love me," Leslie said in mock surprise.

"Romance is sharing the ice cream." Sarah snuggled her head into the shelter between Leslie's arm and ribs. She was suddenly sleepy — small wonder.

The downy hair on Leslie's arm tickled Sarah's eyelashes. She smiled on her way to sleep, aware that Leslie's breathing had slowed, as aware as if it were her own. She felt Leslie's pulse under her cheek, and the rhythm was a lullaby to her singing heart.

Author's Note: *I wrote this vignette for the readers who wanted that "final" moment with Leslie and Sarah from* Embrace in Motion. *To those of you who wrote or e-mailed — I promised, and here it is!*

Bow and Arrows

The Real Story of Cupid and Psyche

PART ONE:
In Which Psyche Receives Visitors

So it's settled?" Bitchiana asked her sister Psyche, tossing her long golden tresses back over a plump, rounded shoulder. "You're going to go through with it?" she said with a smile, batting those long lashes over huge blue eyes.

At her side, Foolissima, sister to both Psyche and Bitchiana, leaned over, her skinny frame squeezed awkwardly on the sand between the two other girls. "Yes, tonight. You'll do it tonight, won't you?" Frizzy brown hair fell down into her eyes, and she pushed the curls away with a sharp jab of her long fingers.

Psyche sighed and put down the sandwich she'd rustled up from the depths of the basket. Cool, fresh sea breezes swept over the little picnic she'd put together for her sisters. The sun was bright; the ocean whispered and sang at their side, the sand warm beneath them. A perfect day for an outing, especially when it was the first time in over a year that she'd seen her sisters. Over a year since she'd seen any of her family, actually — not since the day she'd been wedded to the Snake from Hell.

So it was hard to refuse her sisters now, even though they were the ones who'd gotten her into this in the first place. "But — but I promised him —"

"That doesn't count!" Bitchiana spat the words out. "Good grief, Psyche, haven't you learned anything about men yet?" She turned aside from her own reflection, mirrored in a pool of seawater, and adjusted once more the three gold bracelets Psyche had just presented her with — a token of affection to her long-lost sister. As she admired the way the buttery-yellow circles set off her plump rosy skin, Bitchiana went on, "You always were an innocent little fool, Psyche."

"Don't forget — she's married to a snake, not a man." Foolissima shuddered and closed her eyes in horror. Her skinny fingers rested for a moment from counting for the fifth time the pile of gold coins heaped in a silk bag Psyche had given her earlier in the day — Psyche's generous offering to another long-lost sister. "Talk about gross!" she whispered in horror, carefully closing and tying the strings on the bag before she put it in her lap.

Psyche, all appetite completely gone now, watched her sisters as they plowed again through the picnic basket. It had been so long since she'd seen Bitchiana and Foolissima — not since they'd persuaded her to sacrifice herself in marriage to the Snake from Hell.

"After all, it's for the family," they'd chorused at her, over and over. "You don't want Venus to punish us forever, do you?"

"No, but —" Psyche had tried to protest, but what was a girl to do, when her family had a jealous goddess on their case all the time? "But it's not my fault," she said lamely, in a feeble attempt to stand up for herself. "I can't help it if Venus thinks I'm competition. I couldn't care less about all those shepherds and kings and gods that she finds so irresistible, anyway."

"Then why wouldn't you go ahead and marry that rich old man Daddy found for you?" That was Bitchiana, who stood with round arms folded over her plump breasts, her body threatening to burst out of its too-tight tunic.

"Yeah, he would have been a good match. Better than mine," Foolissima muttered. She stood behind Bitchiana, her tall thin body looming up, crow-like, to tower over both her sisters. "Better than Bitchiana's, too."

Seeing all the trouble her family was put to — the blight that Venus sent to the crops year after year, the strange disease that continuously swept through the flocks of sheep, the itches and scratches suffered by every member of the family — Psyche almost gave in and married the old geezer. But his grizzled and gloomy face, which was perhaps a foretaste of the rest of his anatomy, revolted Psyche so much that she'd fled from her prospective groom practically at the altar.

Her reverie was cut short by a glimpse of her own face, reflected in a small pool of seawater trapped in the hollows of the rock next to where they'd laid out their picnic. In spite of what everyone said, and what Venus seemed to believe, Psyche knew she was not beautiful. She was small and square and solid, and her tunics never fit quite right. Yes, it was the same face looking back up at her from the small circle of water — the same high brow and plain brown cap of hair, the same straight no-nonsense mouth. Only the eyes, she decided, revealed any kind of liveliness. They were brown, like her hair, but sparkled and gleamed as if they contained some hilarious secret that she, Psyche, couldn't wait to share. So what the hell was Venus so worked up about, anyway?

"Psyche, have you heard anything we've said?"

"There she goes, daydreaming again."

Bitchiana and Foolissima looked at each other, then, pityingly, at their younger sister. They shook their heads in unison.

"Sorry," Psyche muttered. "You wanted me to try to get a look at him, right?"

"Not only that — you have to defend yourself.

Show her, Foolissima." While Bitchiana looked on, Foolissima drew something long and shiny from the folds of her tunic.

"You have to use this, Psyche," Foolissima whispered, handing Psyche the dagger. "Your husband is a snake, right? That's what the oracle said would marry you when we left you on that mountain, remember?"

"A snake!" Bitchiana hissed at her as Psyche took the blade from her sister. "Imagine — having a snake make love to you! Gross!"

"But he's been absolutely wonderful to me!" Psyche cried out, confused. "He makes sure everything I need is right there in the castle, and I don't have to even clean the house, and we just got our satellite dish!" She tossed the dagger into the sand, where it flashed in the sun as it tumbled away from the picnic basket. "I don't want to kill him!"

"And quit calling it 'him,' " Bitchiana said as she struggled up from the sand and chased after the dagger. "It's a damn snake, all right? Jeez, it's like you really liked it or something."

"Besides," Foolissima said, "it'll kill you and eat you the minute you have its baby." She glared down at Psyche and took the dagger from Bitchiana. "Come on, you wuss. You have to kill it before it kills you."

The dagger's sharp edges blurred and shimmered as Psyche's eyes filled with tears. Could her sisters possibly be right? Could the snake who'd saved her from the mountain, brought her to the castle and made love to her every night actually want her dead?

Foolissima laid the dagger across Psyche's outstretched hands. "Then, as soon as you've killed it, we'll all come to the castle."

"All?" Psyche asked, clutching the dagger carefully with both hands.

Bitchiana nodded. "Oh, yes, that place is far too big just for you by yourself. Foolissima and I and our kids and husbands will join you there. Won't that be fun?"

"You have all these nieces and nephews you haven't even seen yet!" Foolissima said, her thin shoulders shaking with laughter. "They'll love the place — although I doubt it will look as nice once they get finished with it."

"Oh, and now that you have that satellite dish, our husbands can watch the Monday night arena games," Bitchiana added, her eyes aglow. "Mine's been too cheap all this time to get it for us, but that won't matter."

"No," Foolissima chimed in. "Not once you kill that disgusting creature."

Psyche looked up at her sisters. She'd already done so much for the family by agreeing to obey the oracle's pronouncement that she must give herself up to the Snake from Hell in order to save her family. Lying up there in the dark and lonely forest, waiting in the howling winds and cold rain for some horrible creature to ravish her, Psyche had shivered and sobbed, terrified and certain she'd meet her death. Then, just when Psyche was sure she was doomed, the soft wind had gently lifted her over the storm, through the clouds, and slowly lowered her down into the castle by the sea.

And now it seemed her family — her sisters whom she hadn't seen in such a long time, whom she'd missed so much — needed yet another sacrifice.

"Oh, yes," Bitchiana said to Foolissima, smiling broadly. "I think we've convinced her, don't you?"

Foolissima nodded. "It's the Psyche we used to know. Now I recognize my sister again."

Together Bitchiana and Foolissima embraced Psyche, who stood trembling in their arms, the dagger fallen to the warm sand at her feet.

PART TWO:
*In Which Psyche Receives a Different Kind
of Visitor*

Oh, great! Now what are we going to do?"

Psyche stared in amazement and horror. In one hand the dagger gleamed and blazed silver bright. In the other, an oil lamp dripped hot liquid onto the shoulder of her husband.

The all-too-human shoulder of her husband. Her husband, who tossed covers off to reveal two small perfect breasts, a thatch of dark hair between her legs and nothing in the least resembling a snake on her body anywhere.

It had been so very easy, after all — hiding the dagger beneath her pillow, and the tinder box and oil lamp just below her side of the bed. Psyche had waited until she'd heard snores rising up from the tangle of furs and coverlets before she'd slipped the blade out and fumbled cautiously for the lamp. Now she shuddered to think that, if she hadn't leaned over too far and dripped hot oil onto the bed, she might have killed this woman who glared up at her from the bed. How horrible, if she'd killed the wrong person! But then —

"Wait a minute!" Psyche cried out as the dagger clanged, unheeded, onto the stone floor of the bedchamber. "Who the hell are you? And where is the Snake from Hell?"

The woman in the bed winced and twisted around so that she could see the small circle of burned skin, where hot oil from the lamp still glistened. Psyche was taken aback at the sight of her small, firm breasts, her well-developed arms and shoulders, the way her neck curved gracefully, the huge soft brown eyes that blinked back tears of pain —

No, no, this wouldn't do. "Who are you? Where's my husband?"

"Look — Ouch! Jeez, that hurts." The stranger gingerly touched at the burn on her shoulder and squinted up at Psyche. "Could you move that lamp a little? I can't see anything with the light in my eyes!" As Psyche took a step back, the woman sighed. "Thanks. Okay, okay — I'm sorry about the whole Snake from Hell thing. I get a little carried away with all the camp stuff, you know? Like the whole bow-and-arrows thing." Psyche couldn't be sure, but she thought the woman was grinning. "And I didn't know how else to get close to you."

Realization fell over Psyche like a cold shower. "Oh, my Goddess! You're — you're my husband?" She nearly dropped the lamp. It slipped in her hand and sloshed more hot oil onto the floor.

Now the woman was grinning sheepishly, and she pulled the sheet back up over her breasts. "Guilty. Name's Cupid."

"Then your mother is Venus, and the two of you —" Anger surged up in Psyche and she quickly bent over to pick up the dagger. "You planned this! You scared me half to death with all this snake business, and then you — you —" She stammered in her confusion. "I just don't believe it!"

The woman shrugged, the gesture causing the sheet to slip even farther. But Psyche refused to be distracted by the glimpse of Cupid's smooth brown skin glowing warm and dark in the dim light of the bedchamber. Looking away in determination, Psyche noticed for the first time the bow and arrows stacked in the corner of the room by the door. They looked real enough — but if this was Cupid, and Venus and Cupid had tricked her, then that was even worse than if she'd woken up next to a snake! How could she ever trust Cupid now? "I thought you were this fat little angel baby, with all these hearts and clouds and stuff! And you're — you're a girl!" she cried, pointing at the neat pile of arrows in the dainty white quiver.

"Excuse me, but I do work out on a regular basis," Cupid grumbled. "No extra fat here. See?" Psyche hurriedly averted her gaze from the splendid muscular torso displayed before her. Undaunted, Cupid went on, "Besides, can I help it if Mom decides to plaster that stupid baby picture all over the place? Jeez, she thinks I look cute like that. It's disgusting."

"Your mother!" Psyche hissed. "Your mother hates me! I'm sure she thinks this is hilarious, but —"

"Mom had nothing to do with it!" Cupid clutched the sheets tight and her eyes widened in fear. "All that stuff was just to make sure she wouldn't know! Honest!" She shook her head and muttered, "Boy, if she ever finds out, I'm in deep shit."

"But all those things you did." Psyche moaned. "Good grief, I thought you were my husband!" She plopped down on the bed, the dagger lying across her lap, and set the lamp back on the floor. Its flickering flame licked odd shadows into the corners of the room as she began to cry. "I'm so confused! I don't get any of this."

"Honey —" Cupid stroked her back and leaned closer, whispering in Psyche's ear. "It's still me here with you." The strokes became longer, firmer, as Cupid's fingers gently kneaded the soft flesh of Psyche's shoulders. "I'm still the one who made love to you each night in the darkness, the one who made you laugh with stupid jokes about Zeus, who takes care of you."

Psyche slowly began to relax beneath Cupid's hands. "They really are stupid jokes, you know."

"Well — there's other things I do better."

"Really?" It was hard for Psyche to concentrate, with Cupid's fingers circling her breast and teasing the nipple. "Like what?"

"Well, there's this," and Cupid proceeded to lick Psyche's neck while she slipped her other hand around Psyche's waist. Her tongue darted into

Psyche's ear, and suddenly Psyche decided it wasn't all that important to hold onto the dagger anymore. It clattered to the floor as Psyche leaned back, letting her back rest on Cupid's breasts.

"Believe me," Cupid murmured, "it took some doing to keep you in the dark — no pun intended." Her fingers began to tease the soft curls between Psyche's thighs. "Didn't you ever wonder why I wouldn't let you touch me?"

"Well, I thought you were a snake, so — oh, wow." Psyche lay down as Cupid moved down on the bed until her face was between Psyche's legs. "Won't — won't your arm hurt if you do this?"

"No big deal," Cupid muttered, her voice muffled. "I'm immortal." And then Psyche felt Cupid's tongue sliding across the nub of skin that kept getting harder and hotter beneath the divine ministrations of Cupid. Then Cupid's fingers probed into the warm, moist folds of skin just below her tongue. Psyche couldn't help gasping while Cupid gently inserted first two, then three fingers inside her and began slowly moving in and out and in again, each inward thrust going deeper, testing further.

"Could this be a snake, Psyche?" Cupid asked, raising her head for a moment to look at Psyche's face.

When Psyche tried to answer, Cupid bent down again and laved her tongue over Psyche's clitoris, increasing the pressure until Psyche cried out. As Psyche's body pulsed around her fingers, Cupid moved her fingers faster and faster, until they gleamed with moisture and slid in and out in rhythm to the surge of Psyche's hips.

"Ah!" Psyche sighed as her body, slick with sweat, kept writhing beneath Cupid until her orgasm spent itself. She opened her eyes to see Cupid still poised over her crotch, her face glazed and shining in the lamplight.

Seeing Cupid's smile, Psyche grinned and twisted out from under Cupid's embrace. "Hey!" Cupid, suddenly empty-handed, clutched at the air as Psyche nimbly grabbed her from behind. "What are you doing?"

"You'll see." Before Cupid could wiggle away from her, Psyche slipped her hands down around Cupid's hips as Cupid knelt on the bed, facing away from Psyche. "Just making sure you're not a snake," she whispered as her hands found slick hot skin between Cupid's legs.

Psyche felt Cupid's thighs tremble with each stroke of her palm against the warm round swell of Cupid's ass, and she teased her fingers between Cupid's labia. Cupid shuddered as Psyche bent forward and tongued the edges of her wet, swollen inner lips. Psyche slid one hand forward, rubbing her palm gently back and forth over the firm mound covered with dark damp curls. Cupid spread her legs farther apart, pushing back against Psyche's hands to feel their pressure, and Psyche caught up the motion, following Cupid's undulating lead. Psyche let her thumb trail downward, following the line traced between the round cheeks of Cupid's ass, until the tip of her thumb teased the sensitive circle that opened to her slightest touch.

Psyche couldn't see Cupid's face in the dark shadows of the bedchamber, but her sighs and small cries of excitement encouraged her. Strange — how simple, how natural it seemed, Psyche marveled. Was it just relief that she hadn't, in fact, sacrificed herself to a beast?

No, this was much more. As she looked down on Cupid arching her back, straining her entire body to receive her lover, Psyche felt her own desire rise up. Cupid threw her head back, her short dark hair curling down into those soft brown eyes, as she cried out, sated. "Psyche, Psyche," she murmured, collapsing into the sheets.

Psyche quietly moved up on the bed and cradled Cupid in her arms. How could she have been so blind? She closed her eyes and nestled close to — well, what the hell should she call Cupid now? Girlfriend? Main squeeze? Significant other?

She decided. "Husband," Psyche whispered, enjoying the sensation of her own breath brushing against Cupid's back. Why change things now? She planted a kiss on Cupid's shoulder and almost got tossed out of the bed.

"Sorry, babe, that oil burned me right there."

"Oh, honey, I'm so sorry!" Psyche peered through the dim light but couldn't see the burn. "I forgot all about it."

"Well, I guess we both got distracted." Cupid smiled and reached lazily for Psyche's hand.

They never got further than that, because the shutters suddenly burst open and a burst of cold wind blew into the room. The small flame from the lamp flickered, dancing strange shadows across the walls.

"Oh, Cupid, what's going on?'

"Hell if I know! Hang on!"

The wind began to die out. A spray of cold salt-water blew across the room, and a pale shimmering form took shape in the midst of the wind-tossed sea foam.

Cupid fell back against the pillows with a groan. "Hi, Mom." She sighed. "You could have called first, you know?"

PART THREE:
A Visit from Mother-in-Law

Venus spat out saltwater as she landed with a plop in the middle of the bedchamber. "Damn!" she hacked and coughed, struggling to regain her balance on the slippery stones. "I hate this seafoam clamshell shit. What the hell was that old fart Neptune thinking of, anyway?"

While Venus heaved and teetered, Psyche darted around her to one of the dark corners of the room. Before anyone could say Zeus she had slipped the white quiver over her shoulder and fitted an arrow to Cupid's bow.

"Hey, relax! It's just Mom!" Cupid looked up at her mother sheepishly, her dark face burning a deep red. "Guess you're not too happy with us, are you?"

In answer, Venus shook her auburn curls over her snowy white neck. Her lovely green eyes flared with celestial rage as she pulled a strap of her see-through tunic back over her shoulder. "Do you two have any idea how much shit you've gotten me in?" she yelled hoarsely. "Zeus is shitting bricks right now because you had to go and let everyone know you're not that fat little angel freak!"

Psyche aimed the arrow at her mother-in-law's back. "Stick 'em up, Venus," she said quietly, with as much authority as she could muster.

Venus turned, her pretty brow wrinkled in confusion, then started to laugh. "Yeah, right! As if that would do anything to me!" She stomped across the floor, seawater spitting out from under her delicate feet with each step. "I'm the one who invented those things, missy!" She grabbed the quiver from Psyche and yanked the bow from her hands, then stood back to regard Psyche. "I don't know why everyone thought you were competition for me," Venus muttered. "Look at those feet — size nine and a half, at least."

Cupid had taken advantage of the distraction Psyche presented to slip out of the bed and pull on a robe. It didn't last. Venus whirled around to glare at her daughter.

"And what the hell did you have to fall in love with this girl for?" she yelled. "I sent you on assignment to make her fall in love with that idiot shepherd kid, you remember —" She snapped her fingers, then remembered. "Yeah, the one who always picks his nose. You really screwed up, young lady!"

Cupid stood straight and folded her arms across her magnificent chest. "I fell in love with Psyche myself, Mom. I refuse to put on those wings anymore," and she wiggled her shoulders under her robe at the memory. "They itch like hell, anyway."

Venus put a dramatic hand to her forehead and moaned. "Oh, what am I to do? Once Cupid strikes the heart, there's no hope."

Cupid rolled her eyes. "Cut it out, Mom. Deal with it. I'm in love with Psyche, and she loves me."

Before Venus could respond, Psyche heard a commotion from another part of the castle. "Oh, no," she breathed. "It's probably my sisters and their husbands! They were going to pick me up after I killed the — the snake," she finished lamely, blushing furiously in the darkness and hoping Venus wouldn't notice.

"What? What snake?" Venus lifted her tunic and moved quickly around the room. "I don't see any snake."

"That's it!" Cupid grinned and took the bow and arrows from her mother. "Psyche, I never thought I'd say this, but your family is going to save us all," she whispered as she sped by to the door of the chamber. Then, louder, "Mom, I think I see the snake right behind you, in that corner there! We have to get out of here!"

"AAAGH! SNAKE!" Venus shrieked and barreled past the two lovers toward the door. Cupid stayed in the room long enough to give Psyche a quick wet kiss and darted after her mother.

"Terrific. Now what?" Psyche avoided the puddles of seawater Venus had left in her wake and tiptoed to the bedchamber's door. She could hear voices raised, echoing throughout the interior of the castle, but she couldn't make out the words.

"All right, that's it." Furious with the divine mother-and-daughter team that had deserted her,

Psyche marched out of the bedchamber and into the hall. As always, the torches and tapers lit themselves as she passed, lighting her way through the dark depths of Cupid's castle. Doors slammed open before her, and then shut quietly behind her angry progress. Psyche kept following the voices, and after a few moments she made out the flat nasal voice of Foolissima's husband, with the high-pitched rasp of Bitchiana's husband chorused in the background. Yes, she decided triumphantly, they must be gathered here — and she emerged from the corridors just outside the central courtyard.

Then there was an odd sound — not a voice at all, human or divine. What was that, anyway? Psyche stopped in her tracks just as her hand was about to open the gate to the courtyard, her fingers clenched on the wooden barrier. She strained to make out what the noise was. A sort of whooshing sound? Or a thrumming, as of a taut string plucked too hard?

The giggles that followed echoed off the high stone walls before tittering into silence. "I can't believe this," Psyche muttered, pushing her way through the gate into the sweet-smelling garden.

She still couldn't believe it when she saw her two brothers-in-law standing next to Venus, their arms encircling each other, simpering smiles plastered on their nondescript faces.

"All right, brat!" Venus yelled. Arms akimbo, she sighed and turned around. "Where the hell are you?" she yelled.

Cupid leaped down from a tree, bow still in hand, quiver slung over shoulder. Psyche couldn't be sure, but it certainly looked as though the number of

arrows had diminished. Weren't there at least five in
the quiver earlier? One, two — yes, there were only
three! But where —

The two men turned away, arms around each
others' shoulders, and started to walk past Psyche.
She could swear she saw one of them pat the other's
bottom, but then again, it was awfully dark. Then
she saw the slender carved shafts of the arrows
poking out through their clothes, and she knew.

"Cupid, you didn't!"

In answer, Cupid sighed and grinned, polishing
her nails on her tunic.

"Oh, yes, she did!" Venus stormed up to Psyche,
her glorious face reddened in anger. "That little brat
shot two arrows into those men, and of course the
first people they saw were each other! Oh, I could
just spit!" and she did so, right into Psyche's
rosebush. "Imagine, they have the goddess of love
standing right in front of them and they go after
each other's butt!"

"But my sisters — Cupid, what happened to
Bitchiana and Foolissima?" Psyche hurried away from
the enraged goddess to Cupid's side.

"Oh, they're probably going through your closet
right now. Especially since I told them about the
golden fleece you were having knitted into an
afghan." Cupid winked and put her arm around
Psyche.

"SHIT!" Psyche nervously glanced back at her
mother-in-law and saw that Venus was getting redder
and redder. In fact, she was so mad she was frothing
at the mouth — no, wait, that was sea foam! With a

burst of cold air the temper tantrum of the goddess turned into a spray of saltwater. A final shriek of fury, and she was gone.

Psyche stood trembling in the middle of the courtyard while Cupid tried to console her. "Come on, honey, it's not so bad. Your sisters will be thrilled to go over all the stuff in the castle, and their husbands are going to be occupied for a while."

"But — but your mother!" Psyche wailed, wiping her nose. "What in the world are we going to do about Venus? She really got pissed off!"

Cupid frowned. "Well, that is a bit of a problem." She puzzled for a moment, then her expression brightened. "Wait — I know! There's this little island we can go to. It isn't far from here." She grabbed Psyche in a hug. "We'll hide out until Mom cools off."

"Then you really do love me, Cupid?" Psyche smiled up at her lover through her tears. "Even if I used to think you were a snake?"

"Oh, that!" Cupid giggled. "I've been called a lot worse. Come on — we have to pack," and arm-in-arm they hurried back into the castle.

PART FOUR:
On a Desert Island

From a postcard sent by Psyche to her sisters Bitchiana and Foolissima:

Hope you're enjoying the castle — thanks for house-sitting. Did your husbands ever come out of the bedchamber?

The island is terrific. We go swimming all day, and Cupid's gotten a great tan. Sappho said we could stay here on Lesbos as long as we liked. Who would have thought such a famous poet could be so nice? And we've met so many friendly girls! The "X" on the postcard is our room.

By the way, we heard from Venus yesterday. The fake wedding went well, and she thinks everyone was fooled by the chubby guy they got to play Cupid's part. It's really hard to read her letters, though — they get so wet from all that sea foam and sand and stuff.

Gotta go — the girls are putting together a softball game. By the way, did you have any luck finding the fleece?

Love, Cupid and Psyche

Wild Waters
Janet McClellan

I'm sitting here holding a little pity party for myself. I've got a great view for it too. My cabin in this forty-acre little remote collection of bungalows over-looks the whole wide vista of Bear Paw Mountains. I've got a bottle of wine, a few smokes, some minor indulges of food, a cozy place by the fire and a new box of pop-up tissues. The cabins are placed a discrete distances from one another. That's handy, I wouldn't want anyone dropping in on me. I can't see my neighbors or even detect if I have any. No dogs barking, no motors running, no kids screaming, not even the high gaseous cloud vapors of jets mar the perfect sky. I'm perfectly alone and perfectly miserable.

I'm supposed to be working on the final chapters of the fifth rewrite for a book. It's a month or more overdue at my publishers. I'm in hot water with them too. I've begun collecting pissed-off people. Finishing this book, deciding if the heroine will live or die is what I promised I be doing. That was the excuse I'd given Carla when I left our house, left the state and drove as far and fast as I could. It was a cowardly act but I did not want a confrontation. I simply wanted to go. For revenge I may change the end of the book and kill all the characters outright. When you're on a roll, you might as well stick with it.

I'm no longer interested in pleasing Carla. Besides, I hadn't been able to please her for months. Nothing seemed to help. I tried taking on extra house chores. I hate housework but the division of labor had already shifted most of its load to me anyway. The accounting agency demands on her time had increased over the last two years while I struggled with my writing and felt more and more dispensable.

Thinking it might help, I tried to bring in a little extra money by selling a few short stories to a midtown paper. I even went so far as to pick up a creative writing class and teach aspiring authors, in hopes of guaranteeing a bit more steady income for my share of the bills. At several points I used my minor royalties to try to wine and dine her out of her absence from my bed. No effort seemed to work very well, last very long or reestablish the connections we once had. I had food, shelter, clothing and my work. I had the basics of life and nothing at all. I have the same things here. The addition of wine was a necessity. It seems to make things more tolerable while casting a soothing blue haze over my animosity.

We'd simply drifted apart and I had not noticed it until I could barely feel her waving to me from some different emotional shore. We'd both become caught up in our separate trials and tribulations. We did not drift apart. There had been a full tide and high winds. I was consumed by chapters to write, a series to push, galley proofs to scrutinize and a round or two of book signing in distant cities. She was busy trying to get her own career off the ground and into high gear. The problem was that while we charged forward, we failed to notice where we were going and what we were unintentionally leaving behind. I'm angry with the loss and at a loss as to what she might be thinking or feeling. We tumbled into the relationship, so I guess it's fitting that we ended the same way. Whatever we had faded like the early-morning fog out here as it hits the glare of the morning sun.

The last time I saw her, I was loading up my car to head here, to hide, sit and brood in the high rolling hills of Montana. She almost looked relived when I told her I'd be away for a month or two. I promised to call when I could but that she should try to entertain herself and not work too hard in my absence. I don't intend to let my mind wander or wonder about what or who that entertainment might be. Although I am just a bit curious. If I called and told her I was moving out and away for good, would her first and last question be, "Where do you want your stuff shipped?" Or, "Who did you say was calling?"

Tomorrow, if I survive the hangover my lassitude seems to be forcing on me, I think maybe I'll take a walk. If I can rise before noon, I'll walk toward the distant range of sloping mountains. Just me, a picnic basket, wine, a few more smokes, and chapter twenty where the heroine is supposed to get the girl. It needs work, a lot of it. It's going to be a little hard to write about passionate stimulations of love's first breathless encounter. You might say my heart's not really in it.

Angela Sterns raised her head from her journal and glanced over the last paragraph she had written. A frown creased her forehead. "Well, that's not the cheeriest little entry I've ever made," she said and slammed the journal closed. She raised her arms above her head and stretched her aching back. She stretched and tried to reassert her vertebrae into giving back her full original six-foot height. "Got to get up and move. If I sit any longer I'm going to solidify. If I do," she said looking at the dwindling fire, "fifty years from now, some poor camper will come along and find my bones amid the rubble of the cabin."

Angela walked over to the fireplace, tossed a couple of good-sized logs on the fire and closed the grate for safety. She looked around the room and couldn't decide what to do with herself. She knew what she did not want to do. She did not want to write in the journal anymore; it made her maudlin. She did not want to work on the book. She was in no mood to help the novel's ship captain, bold and lovely pirate Lucy Boundless, live happily ever after in the arms of her golden captive, the delectable Rachel Lowhan.

In exasperation, Angela grabbed a sling canteen, her binoculars, a cap and coat off the rack and walked out into the late-afternoon sun. She glanced toward a westerly gathering line of trees hiding a winding stream and decided to see what promise they might hold.

"A little late for bird-watching," she mumbled to herself as she stepped off the porch. The high warm sun felt good on her face, and she inhaled deeply as she pulled the cap down over her dark brown hair. A slight chill in the mountain breeze whispered up from the valley and caused her to pull the coat closed and button it up. She patted a jacket pocket and felt the pen and notepad snuggled deep in the material. "Never know when inspiration might strike," she said as she launched herself across the high meadow.

The altitude of the area gave mixed possibilities. It was a warm balmy day, but if she stood in the shadows the temperature dropped dramatically. It was the magic of the mountain air and rare light which had drawn her to Montana. It had pulled her back every summer for the last ten years. The same cabin, the same streams, the same stars in the sky and the same peaceful rising sensations made the area home away from home for her since her twenties. This time it was the only place she felt at home. This time it was the only home left to her. She'd been looking for an excuse to move to Montana for years. It simply wasn't the one she had expected.

An hour later she stood on the banks of the Little Bear Claw watching the waters trip over large boulders and slide above the clear deep sand-bottomed pools in the river. She let it pull her in. She walked into the groves of cottonwood, hackamore, pine and cedar trees that meandered down toward the stream's edge. Rounded smooth stones and flat pebbles laid down by the rise and fall of spring runoff tempted her to wade and provided steps around the rushing waters. Stepping through the brush, she found a small hillock rising green above the bank and scrambled onto it. The sun's full force warmed her and she lay down inhaling fully of the earth, sky and water surrounding her. In spite of her discontents the tiny river seemed to sweep away her immediate concerns. She became a part of the moment, the minute babbling song of the water, the hint of a breeze around her, and dozed contentedly on the green bosom of the earth.

When she awoke, it was to a sound like the lash of wings hissing softly in the sky beyond her. Angela opened first one eye, then the other as she tried to glimpse the path of the air-sailing bird. There were no birds as far as her eyes could see. Curious, she let her gaze drift toward the trees on the opposite shore but could not locate the source of the weird whip-hissing sounds. She rolled over and scooted toward the lip of the hillock above the small river. As she stole forward, she wondered if she would spy a hawk or eagle risking feather and wing to scoop fish from the water below.

Easing herself forward and over the edge of the hillock, she was careful to move silently. She did not want to expose herself and frighten any creature on the other side. As she approached, she caught sight of a dance of light swinging through the air like the loose strand on a spider's web. Angela watched as the web-like strand whipped, shimmered and danced in the air for a fraction of a second and then descended again to the water.

"Neither fish, nor fowl?" Angela whispered to the blades of grass near her mouth where she lay. She slowly reached behind her and grabbed the binoculars she'd brought with her.

At the end of what had appeared to be a cavorting spider's web stood a lone angler casting and teasing a lure to trout upstream. From where she lay, Angela watched the angler move in slow, steady quiet steps across the stream-bridging rocks. In the scrutiny of the binoculars, Angela saw the figure clamber onto a large boulder. The angler straightened up from the short climb, deftly shrugged out of the sleeveless multi-pocketed vest and navy wading jacket all the while managing to continue deftly casting upstream. The fly-casting angler's tanned arms worked in practiced concentrated rhythmic motions. The stance on the boulder hinted at confidence, competence, timing and control in the naturalist's pursuit. The clothes, shucked and sacrificed to the unsheltered glare of the sun, told Angela more of the angler's nature.

"Neither man, nor beast either," Angela murmured and smiled her broad smile beneath the lens of the binoculars. She steadied herself on her elbows and observed the enigmatic sensuous dance before her. She watched the slow physical inflection, the simple hip and shoulder gestures, and the sway of the woman's body as she practiced her lonesome sport. Two hundred and fifty feet away but with the aid of the binoculars Angela felt as though she could almost touch her with her eyes. A change in the angler's direction and the zoom feature on the binoculars let Angela catch a glimpse of the woman's face, the line of the chin, and the sweep of a thick crop of salt-and-pepper hair. A brimmed hat, shaded sunglasses and shadows cast by trees hid everything from Angela except the lines of earned merriment at the corners of the woman's eyes and her pert rounded small breasts.

Angela moved, re-set the focus of the binoculars and trained them on the woman's body. The sight of her smooth browned shoulders, straight back, firm rounded buttocks and long taut legs made her suck in her breath. It caught in her throat like a prayer or pleading before sweet release. Here before her was the next chapter in the novel, here was the spell-binding moment she wanted to translate from her mind to the paper. Maybe here, Angela thought, maybe here was the wizardry of motion and emotion she needed to rescue the book. She wanted the book to work. Writing was the only thing she loved that was still working. She fervently hoped she could transpose her covert spying on the woman's inadvertently sensual nature and meld it to the pages of the manuscript.

Angela let her mind take her on a fast-track fantasy wrapped around the woman and the characters in the novel. She welded them together and chanced upon a feel for the beginning love scene. She prayed she had chanced upon the right words to culminate the hunt and pairing of the lovers.

Captain Lucy Boundless barely managed to stop Lady Rachael Lowhan's hand from making its hard intended contact with her face. Lady Lowhan's effort had surprised her. Fortunately for both of them, the years of skill and speed wrought from wielding a sword served the captain well. She didn't want to think about what her anger might have led her to do or forcibly take from the good lady. Captain Lucy watched as the strap on the lady's gown slipped from her shoulder as she struggled in the firm grip of the captain.

"Stop," Captain Boundless commanded throatily. "You know, don't you. You can't help but know." She caressed the naked shoulder and moved the tips of her fingers down toward softer warm flesh. Boundless could feel the quivering beneath her fingertips and watched as the lady's breasts swelled in the restrictive bodice.

"Please. Don't, please . . ." The lady gasped as her body melted into the warm caress.

"Ask me again," Captain Boundless said as she

maneuvered the lady closer, letting their pelvises meet and press like a long-awaited kiss. Hips pressed toward hips and hungrily yielded to slow firm gyrations of desire. They fiercely sought each other's fire, held fast to each other's response and waited for each new tantalizing wave of pleasure.

The captain leaned forward and let her tongue run softly down the curve of the lady's neck and slip into the hollow of that delicious throat. Boundless released the captive hand of the lady, reached behind her, let her palm slip down to the small of the lady's back and onto the joy of her hips. Boundless raised her head and kissed the soft full lips presented to her. Her tongue glided to the edge of the lady's lips, past the small delicate teeth, and darted against the quivering pink pleasure hiding behind.

A moan escaped the lady, soft like a whisper, hard like a demand. Captain Boundless knew now that the lady wanted her. Wanted her hard, deep and willing. The captain, true to the code of the sea, knew that whatever the lady wanted, it was a captain's duty to give.

"Please," the lady softly entreated.

"Let you go?"

"No. Just please and please now," the lady urged the captain.

Angela looked at the quick notes on the paper and was satisfied that she had the dramatic hot movement she wanted. It was a step in the right direction. She liked to write the hot chapters. Or at least she had, when her lover had loved her in return. In those days she sometimes could hardly contain herself or wait for Carla to come home. But that was then and this was now. She had to be satisfied with the idea that the fly-fishing woman would be a good motivator for the final chapters of the book.

Angela watched the woman. The sunshine danced and reflected off the soft waves of the water, and time slipped sweetly by. She reached in her pocket and retrieved the notepad again and began writing about the living fantasy before her. She wanted to make notes on the most minute movement, carriage of form and turn of the head. The angler became a living portrait for the larger-than-life Captain Boundless. After a few moments, Angela shifted to get the advancing sun's glare out of the binocular lenses. She lowered the binoculars, moved a few pebbles away from her supporting elbows and made a few quick notes about the sheer chemistry she felt emanating from the woman. Satisfied with her articulation and the potential direction for the last chapters in her book, she returned the lenses to her eyes.

To Angela's surprise, she could not immediately relocate the woman or the boulder she had been standing on. Then she thought she located the boulder. It was the most prominent gray mass in the river, but there was no one there. Angela whipped the binoculars from her eyes and searched the far stream for the figure. The woman had disappeared.

Angela sat up. She used the binoculars to search up and down the banks of the river. Not a branch stirred, not a limb whispered; the surface of the water was calm. Nothing moved and yet the woman was gone. A small hammering panic set itself up in riotous commotion in Angela's chest. Had the woman fallen in? Was she now somewhere in a midnight-blue pool, trapped and drowning? Had she fallen off the boulder, struck her head and floated silently past her hillock without being able to call out for help?

"Shit. Oh, shit!" Angela worried aloud. She sat back on her heels frozen to the spot by indecision and dismay.

"I wouldn't recommend it on this bluff. Too many people might see you," a firm voice said behind Angela's back.

"Ahhalp!" Angela startled and toppled backward at the sound of the voice.

A firm hand grabbed her by her jacket and kept her from falling over. "Calm down," the woman smoothly insisted. "For a peeping thomasina you don't seem to much like having the tables turned on you. Do you?"

Angela looked up into a pair of green eyes set in a lightly lined tanned face. It was the face she'd seen through the binoculars. The woman had put her vest back on but the hint of the small round firm breasts peeked around the large armholes. The navy wading jacket hung through the shoulder straps of her catch case and she held the fly rod loose in her strong hand, balancing it with the ease of a French dueling master. Captain Boundless would have been proud, Angela's mind quipped excitedly to itself. As the other side of Angela's brain tried to think of an excuse that would fly for her invading the woman's privacy, she couldn't stop herself from grinning at the woman.

"Do you have an apology or excuse for your behavior? Or have you stopped taking some medication that you obviously ought to go back to? I promise to give fair consideration to a well-thought-out fabrication." The woman smiled tormentingly at Angela.

"I . . . ah. Well, you see, actually . . ." Angela stumbled and fumbled. *For heaven's sake, I can't tell her I was using her for a fantasy. I can't tell her I'm a writer. What would I do if she wanted to see what I'd been writing?*

"Yeah," the woman coaxed.

"I was taking nature notes. You know, birds, animals, little furred creatures and such. I wasn't spying on you. Really," Angela said in what she hoped was her most persuasive tone. She stood up thinking she might look more convincing at her full height. She felt her face flush as she looked back into the woman's eyes. "What makes you think I was spying on you?"

"Well, for one, the reflection of the sun off those binocular lenses. I could almost feel the heat on my back. It surprised me at first, and it frightened the fish away."

"Well, I am sorry about that. Now, if you'll excuse me, I have to get back to my cabin. It's getting late." As she walked past the woman she smelled a sweet tantalizing scent rising from the woman's body. She faltered in her tracks.

"I wouldn't want to keep you from any important

engagements you might have." The woman smiled tantalizingly at her.

Angela concentrated on putting one foot in front of the other and managed not to turn around all the way back to her cabin. And all the way back to the cabin, a silly chorus from a love song and her own immoderate romantic story themes buzzed in her head.

Angela poured herself another glass of wine, wrapped the large white terry robe about her and finally turned on the light next to the computer. It had gotten dark outside long before she managed to get undressed and push herself into a cool shower. She felt revived, refreshed, and had only the merest hint of the whimsical spider webs of lust evoked by the angler. She knew if she started writing now that she might get a rough draft for the twentieth chapter sometime before dawn. If she could do it, it would be a good night's work.

Taking a long sip of the wine, she walked over to the door where her coat hung and fished in the pocket for her notebook. She searched the waist pockets, breast pockets and inside pockets but it wasn't there. Holding down her panic, she went into the bathroom and dug through the pockets of her jeans. They were empty. She turned and fairly ran back to the door and her jacket, hoping she'd been too hurried with her first search. But she had not been mistaken; it was gone. Captain Boundless had slipped through her hands again. Angela stood by the door, fighting down the desire to go running into the night, across the meadow and down to the hillock that rose above the river. It had to be there, she prayed. She didn't want to have to coax the words from memory. She hoped her anxiety would be quieted by a little more wine and would let her wait to retrieve it in the morning.

The sudden knocking on the door where she stood startled her. "What?" she almost shouted in surprise.

"I have a notebook. The inside cover says it belongs to Angela. Would that be you?" a woman's voice called through the door.

Without hesitation, Angela turned on the porch light and flung the door open. Outside on the stoop, in the sudden blaze of light, stood the blinking green-eyed woman she'd spied on earlier in the day. She looked freshly scrubbed, and her salt-and-pepper hair seemed to sparkle with hidden lights of its own under the bare bulb. Angela noted that she had changed her clothes. The woman was wearing a pair of clean, pressed, faded blue jeans, a chambray shirt and a wide grin. It was the grin that reminded Angela that she was wearing her singularly short terry robe.

"Thank you," Angela said, forcing the words out from between clenched teeth. She reached out and took the proffered notebook. Angela tried very hard not to swallow noticeably as she attempted to wave a nonchalant hand toward the interior of the cabin. "Would you like to come in for a thank you of wine?"

"I'd like that. I'd like that very much," the woman said as she stepped over the threshold of the cabin.

"I'll get you a glass. Have a seat by the fire. I'll be right back." Angela smiled to herself as she walked toward the tiny kitchen. As she poured the wine, she realized she was humming and stopped in sudden embarrassment.

"I need to tell you that I took the liberty of reading your notebook," the woman said as Angela handed her the glass of wine.

"Oh?" Angela sat on the couch next to the woman.

"I normally wouldn't do that sort of thing. But you were gone so quickly, and then I wasn't really sure it belonged to you. It was Harvey, down at the manager's lodge, who told me that an Angela Sterns had rented his cabin. So I took a chance that it was you."

"How lucky for me that you're so resourceful. So, are you staying in the resort too?" Angela said, trying to hold herself in check. She wanted to touch her cheek, her hair, to trace her finger along the line of the full lower lip and feel her breath catch on her fingers.

"No. I found this community about twenty years ago while on vacation. I fell in love with it and moved out from Kansas City, Missouri. I own a small place over on the other side of the stream from where you were spying on me."

"I didn't mean to spy. Not really, it's just that I . . . Well, you looked so intent and I guess I found your intensity interesting."

"See anything else interesting?" the woman asked as she let her voice drop to a suggestive whisper.

Angela felt the heat rising in her face and her mouth went suddenly dry. "What do you do? For a living, that is?" she managed.

"Have you ever heard of BlueStem Pottery and Exterior Landscaping?" The woman ran her fingers through her salt-and-pepper hair.

"There is something I recall, vaguely."

"Well, that's what I do."

"You work there?"

"I work there and I own it. I employ ten other women, and between us we have a store in town and a successful mail-order business too. We do pottery, terra-cotta for interior and exterior garden landscaping and a line of outdoor furniture. The yuppies love it."

"That's how you have time for fly fishing," Angela said, giving in to her desire to lean forward.

"Exactly," the woman said as she followed Angela's lead and leaned ever so much closer. The woman's fingertips traced the blue veins on the back of Angela's hand. Then she tilted her head and looked into Angela's eyes.

We both want this, Angela thought. *We both want this, this moving forward, this presumptuous rising energy and heat between us. I wonder what her tongue feels like, I wonder what it wants to do, what it can do? Should I tell her what I could do to her, for her and how far I would take her tonight?*

"Is there anything else you'd like to know? Anything else you feel curious about," the woman said, her voice a husky whisper.

Angela inclined her body forward and let her lips graze the woman's cheek and slide to her succulent ear. "A name . . . I'd like to know your name," she pleaded as she inhaled the hot fragrance rising through the woman's open shirt collar.

"Morhan, sweetness. Lucy Morhan," she said as she pulled Angela's face to her and kissed her deeply.

Close enough, Angela thought electrically as she let herself flow willingly and eagerly into a fresh new realm of possibilities under the wide Montana sky.

Contrary Currents

Saxon Bennett

As suddenly as the wind had come up it died. They sat huddled in the blue and silver tent listening for the rise of the whirling sand and the uncanny howl of the wind as it screamed through the steep, narrow canyons of Lake Powell. But it didn't come. Wondering if this was a temporary lull, the eye of the storm giving them a moment of reprieve, the four women studied one another's faces. They'd been fooled before.

Earlier that day their kayaks, despite great physical energies to the contrary, had been smashed up against the walls of Powell's many-fingered canyons by the wind. The women had been forced to make camp. And then they had watched the wind pick up a sixteen-foot canoe off the beach and twirl it around like baton only to drop it on the rocky shore. They were naturally skeptical and highly respectful of the awesome power of the wind, especially Lucy, the team leader.

Lucy had been the first to venture from the tent, her long black braid the last they saw of her as she went on a reconnaissance mission.

"Well?" Crissy asked impatiently.

"Looks okay," Lucy replied, gazing up at the stars and seeing her favorite Pleiades, reassured by the discreet order of the otherwise chaotic universe, the kind of universe that threw curve balls with the childlike innocence of a five-year-old sadist who pulled the legs off crickets just to see what would happen.

"The wind must have tired of us and moved on to bigger and better playgrounds," Alex said, stretching her back and bending over to touch her toes.

"Yeah, probably went on to join the tornado seminar practicing moves somewhere over Kansas," Emily said, smiling at Alex.

"And spilling the drinks of well-tailored business-men sipping their martinis in first class as the wind knocks the plane about for kicks and giggles," Crissy joined in.

"You three have been in the tent for way too long," Lucy said, studying the sky. The clouds that

had threatened rain earlier had disappeared, leaving a
clear sky permeated with stars. Lucy wished
Cassandra had come so they could lie on their backs
and play connect-the-dots with the stars, but
Cassandra didn't like these death-defying eco-
challenge vacations. She stayed home with the cats
and her books, perfectly content to lie on the couch
with a six-hundred-page Irving novel and read herself
deep into the night, and like the cats she'd nap
during the day. That was her idea of a vacation. Not
that differing notions of vacations were a bad thing.
Cassandra had never begrudged her these trips.

"And to celebrate our release, I think a toast is in
order," Crissy said, going to retrieve the bottle of
tequila from the depths of the tent that was strewn
with playing cards, lesbian detective novels,
geographical maps of Lake Powell and Tootsie Roll
wrappers.

"I still don't trust our luck," Lucy said, naturally
suspicious of the whimsical nature of the weather.

"Naw, it's gone for good," Emily said.

"You can't trust Mother Nature," Lucy said,
remembering her younger, more optimistic days and
the trouble she'd gotten into by being ill-prepared.

"Why? Because she's woman and women are not
to be trusted, or is it just lesbians?" Alex teased.

"Regardless, let's take full advantage of the
present moment of fair weather and toast our good
fortune," Crissy said, passing out stainless steel shot
glasses filled to the wavering brim.

"Are you still suffering from your 'aversion to
lesbians' or whatever you call it?" Lucy asked.

"ATL syndrome. Yes, as a matter of fact my neurosis is progressing nicely. In fact, I think I've turned straight," Alex replied.

"Yeah, right," Crissy said, handing her a shot.

"I could be," Alex said indignantly, wondering for half a second if her life would be any easier.

"She hasn't dated a woman since the *incident*," Emily piped in.

"She's right, I haven't," Alex said.

"You're not *straight*," Crissy said, looking perturbed at the mere suggestion of such a thing.

"What! You wouldn't like me if I was a hasbian?"

"It's not as lighthearted an issue as it once was. It's turning into a fucking plague," Crissy said. She had an ex-lover who had suddenly decided she was heterosexual.

"All right, I'm not going straight but even *you* have to admit I don't make a very good lesbian," Alex said.

"The nomenclature does include a clause that mentions sleeping with women, which you haven't done in a while," Emily said.

"Isn't her vocabulary sexy?" Alex teased.

Emily blushed.

"No, I find it . . ." Crissy said.

"Disconcerting," Lucy suggested.

"You guys are on getting on my nerves. Why don't you just say what you mean," Crissy said.

"But then we would have to mean what we say," Alex replied. "You're missing the whole point of verbal repartee."

"Stop it! Can't you speak simply? I don't want to bring a dictionary on my vacation," Crissy said.

"Are we going to have that toast?" Emily asked. "Because if we are I'm going to need a refill."

Crissy peered into the nearly empty shot glass. She frowned and refilled it. "You're supposed to wait."

"Yes, but for how long?" Emily said.

"I'd like to propose the toast, if that's all right," Alex said.

"As long as it has nothing to do with being straight," Crissy said.

"It doesn't. In fact it's extremely lesbian-oriented."

"All right then," Crissy said, raising her glass with the others.

"To old lovers, may we learn to forget them and stop processing the process and turn our memories to more pleasant things like the string of orgasms they gave us," Alex said seriously.

Emily burst out laughing.

"What sort of a toast is that?" Crissy asked.

"From the heart," Alex said, covering hers with her fist and looking pensive.

"It was a good one," Emily said.

"It objectifies our lovers into mere physiological moments," Lucy said indignantly.

"Here we go again, from big words to seventies women's lib shit," Crissy said, drinking her tequila out of turn.

"You said we had to wait," Emily chided.

"How long?" Crissie retorted.

"I don't believe the word is *shit*. I believe it's referred to as rhetoric," Alex said.

"I give," Crissy said.

"I think trying to stop processing old love affairs

is good," Emily said, catching Alex's glance. Emily tried to keep from blushing. She'd had a crush on Alex for as long as she could remember. Of course there was always that one great impediment: being Sasha's lover and now her ex-lover, and that had kept her from anything more than sisterly flirtation with Alex.

It was Sasha who had so diligently tortured Alex that she shied away from relationships, casual dating and even anonymous sex. And it was Sasha who had introduced them. Emily secretly suspected it was Sasha's warped and twisted little way to keep tabs on Alex through her. Sasha feigned that a mutual interest in athletics made them perfect friends.

Each year Lucy organized a trip for them: biking or backpacking, or this year's adventure, kayaking on Lake Powell. Alex proved to be a valuable part of the team, and each year she faithfully helped gather equipment and organize supplies. The group didn't get together much during the year until spring, when they would begin planning the annual event.

Emily found herself itching for spring and the chance to see Alex. Emily made sure she got paired off with Alex, who was the perfect teammate — long and lean, good-natured, and a sharp outdoorswoman. Lucy and Crissy thought they bonded so well because of their mutual experience with Sasha, but Emily and Alex never talked about Sasha. It seemed an unwritten law between them.

There were so many times when she and Sasha were falling apart that Emily wished she could talk to Alex about it. Wished she could have called Alex and asked her about Sasha's oftentimes bizarre

behavior so she could make sure she wasn'
crazy one. Sasha made people feel crazy, l
knew now, Sasha was the one who needed .ıₑıp. But
Alex refused to talk about Sasha, referring to their
relationship as the "incident."

What Emily gleaned from Sasha was that the
relationship had been lengthy and, as Sasha so wittily
put it, "We prayed every Sunday to the Goddess of
Lesbian Longevity." It had been intense and their
breaking up difficult. If Sasha thought it was hard to
let go, it must have been devastating to Alex, whom
Emily saw as extremely sensitive in matters of the
heart. Otherwise, with Alex's good looks she should
have had a string of girlfriends, or at least casual
lovers, but instead she had a failed love affair and no
desire to start a new one.

Of course, that made her all the more attractive.
Because she wasn't looking for love, she had that
serene attitude of the well-contented. It made Emily
wish she had never seen Sasha's face so that she
wouldn't appear tainted to Alex. But Alex's ability to
remain aloof from the trials and tribulations of love
made her special. It wasn't often you met a woman
who didn't have a slew of old lovers, casual liaisons
and all the psycho-baggage that went with it. Part of
Emily didn't want to see that ruined . . . by anyone.

They gathered up driftwood from the shore and lit
a small fire. The wind was gone and they could hear
the gentle lapping of the water as it hit the beach in
even strokes. It seemed, as they sat around the
crackling fire, that the storm had been a bad dream,
and the tension of the day drained out of them.

Crissy passed the bottle around again in

celebration. "When are you going to start dating again?" Crissy asked Alex with a smirk.

"Are you trying to set me up?"

"We could try P-town for a couple weeks. Maybe a long-distance relationship is what you need. No pressure."

"Just lots of plane tickets and long-distance phone calls. I don't think so," Alex said.

Crissy studied Alex for a moment, thinking back to their wild college days when they'd organize class schedules, and work and apartment locations in accordance with their cruising time.

"What happened to you? You used to love to go out and chase women. You used to chase just to chase. I remember nights when you'd have more than one date, sometimes at the same bar."

"Thank God for multi-leveled bars," Alex said.

"But I thought you'd only gone out with Sasha," Emily said.

Crissy burst out laughing. "Shit, this woman's seen more pussy than a toilet seat."

Emily turned bright red.

"That was crude," Lucy said.

"Did Sasha tell you that?" Alex asked.

"Well . . . yes. She made it sound like she was the one great love of your life, and I thought that was why you didn't go out with women anymore. Because of what she had done to you," Emily said, feeling stupid for having built up this elaborate, virginal picture of Alex.

"Let me fill you in, kid. The only lesbian who doesn't have a past is twelve years old," Crissy said.

"So your not going out with women doesn't have

anything to do with Sasha . . . you're oversaturated and probably tired," Emily said, feeling her face getting red again.

"I am tired. I'm tired of all the drama. My life is a lot simpler now," Alex said, poking the fire with a stick, sending sparks of orange up into the sky.

"You can't be serious about throwing in the towel," Lucy said.

"I can," Alex said. "Who would I date?"

"I'm sure there are lots of nice women out there," Lucy said.

"Like you would know, Ms. Been-with-my-first-lover-since-the-beginning-of-time. Monogamy and longevity is all you know. It's not pretty out there anymore."

"Being monogamous for fifteen years has its own challenges, believe me," Lucy retorted.

"Such as?" Alex inquired.

"No sex," Crissy answered.

"We have sex!" Lucy answered indignantly.

"Yeah, twice a year whether you need it or not. Some people go to the dentist more often than a lot of you long-standing couples," Crissy said.

"That's not true. I can't believe how the community can be so unsupportive of couples who have managed to stay together. We should celebrate their stamina. Instead, you treat us like circus oddities," Lucy said.

"I think we hit a nerve," Alex said.

"You guys aren't being fair. Lucy's right. Longevity is a good thing," Emily said.

"Hopeless romantic," Crissy muttered.

"After Sasha that's an achievement," Alex said.

"Thank you," Emily said.

Alex smiled at her.

"I still think I'm right about the sex thing, though. Hang with someone long enough and the last thing you want to do is sleep with them," Crissy said.

"I disagree," Lucy said.

"All right, when was the last time you had sex?" Crissy asked.

"The night before we left, actually, we made love twice that day," Lucy said.

"Oh, well, that is rather impressive," Crissy conceded. "You know I'm just giving you a hard time. I'm jealous that you and Cassandra have managed what most of us only dream about."

"And they still like each other," Alex chimed in.

"I think it's beautiful. You two need to take lessons from Lucy and stop being so cynical," Emily lectured.

"Feel her forehead. She must have a fever," Alex teased.

"Or she's in a state of shock. No one walks away from Sasha and manages to remain enamored with the concept of true love," Crissy said.

"Maybe that's the secret. She was the one who walked," Alex said.

"A lesbian historical first," Lucy said snidely. She had never liked Sasha. That woman should have a biohazard sticker permanently attached to her forehead. Maybe that would stop nice women from inexplicably falling in love with her, Lucy thought.

"Quick! Pin the Purple Vulva on her. She's a hero," Alex said.

They laughed hysterically. Even tight-lipped Lucy cracked a smile.

Emily and Alex finished the bottle of tequila while Lucy sensibly went to bed, dragging Crissy with her because she'd already had more than enough to drink. They sat quietly watching the fire die down.

"Alex?"

"Hmm . . ." Alex said, looking up from the fire.

"Do you ever get lonely?"

"Sometimes. You have to keep busy, and after a while you forget about being alone, and then friends fill in a lot of those empty spaces."

Emily nodded.

"Do you miss her?" Alex asked.

"Not the abuse, but the warm snuggly body in my bed."

"I got the dogs, remember."

"I know, maybe I should get one."

Alex took her hand, "I know this is hard for you right now, but it will get better and one day you'll almost forget it happened."

Emily met her eyes. "Why can't you forget?"

"I have."

"Then why don't you fall in love again?"

"Because I don't trust love. It scares me."

"Do I scare you?" Emily asked, bringing Alex's hand closer to her mouth.

"No, I like you," Alex said, looking deep into

Emily's eyes as if trying to read what was written there.

"I'm glad," Emily said, gently putting Alex's finger in her mouth. She knew it was risky. She waited for Alex to stop her but she didn't. Instead, color rose to Alex's face and she swallowed hard. She closed her eyes and let Emily suck her fingers. Emily was afraid to say anything, afraid she'd break the spell. She kissed Alex's palms, her strong forearms, coming closer until she wrapped her body around Alex's. Alex opened her eyes and stared intently at Emily and then she kissed her.

Emily eased her back onto the sand, feeling her body on Alex's, Alex's push up against her. Alex pulled Emily's shorts off and then her own, and their wetness came together. Alex pulled Emily's buttocks in hard against her. Emily kissed her neck and breasts, making her way down until she kissed the wetness between swollen lips. Alex moaned softly, running her hands through Emily's hair. She almost came, Emily could feel her there and then Alex pulled her up toward her, kissing her, reaching for her.

"Let's do it together. I want to feel you," Alex whispered, running her hand down Emily's stomach and slowly entering her.

Emily waited for that precise moment, wavering, about to take flight, the moment between about to come and coming. She spread Alex's legs wider and moved eager fingers inside, filling her with her fingers, her mouth with her tongue, pressing hard

against her, their hips grinding in perfect
synchronicity, as if they'd made love a thousand times
before. Each of them seemed to know intuitively what
the other wanted. Alex bit her shoulder to keep from
crying out and Emily felt her own body soaring,
covered in the sharp, tingling sensation of complete
ecstasy.

Crissy slipped quietly out of the tent, looking back
inside fondly at Emily and Alex as they lay spooned
together, their two sleeping bags fused into one. She
rubbed her eyes, trying to adjust to the already
bright morning light. She'd slept later than they
should have, Crissy thought, briefly calculating the
angle of the sun. Lucy was already up and had the
coffee brewed. She was writing in her journal,
documenting their expedition and her feelings as they
went along. Crissy admired her diligence, her ability
to stick with something . . . or someone. You could
always count on Lucy to be there, to do things
methodically, to tough out a problem. She was a
trooper, a real trooper, Crissy thought. Not like the
rest of them. Crissy changed partners like her
underwear. Emily fell for bad women and then stayed
too long. Alex had no partners and refused all offers.
And there they were, a four-woman team of athletic
extremists who had nothing in common really except
these excursions designed to test their physical
prowess and inner spirit.

She poured herself a cup of coffee and smiled at Lucy, who looked up briefly, nodded and went on to finish her last few sentences before she came to join her.

"Did you see Alex and Emily in there? They look adorable and I bet that's the closest Alex has been to another woman in quite a while."

"Hmm . . ."

"It's a pity that's all she'll let herself do."

"Don't be too sure about that," Lucy said.

"What do you mean?"

"Come take a look at something," Lucy said, getting up.

They walked to the middle of the campsite near the firepit.

Lucy pointed. "See that?"

"What?"

"Look closely."

Crissy looked again. "I don't get it."

"What do you see?"

"Let me guess. A herd of wild elk went through and some of them took a nap. Tell me what I'm supposed to be seeing."

"Body prints," Lucy said, outlining pertinent places.

The light bulb went off. "Oh, I get it," Crissy said, pointing her thumb in the direction of the tent. "Well, I'll be damned."

Lucy nodded knowingly.

"You're quite the little observer."

"I didn't study animal tracks for nothing."

"What would you classify these as . . . snail trails."

"Don't be crude," Lucy said, putting her hands on her hips and pursing her lips.

"You really think they got together?"

"I wouldn't exactly call these snow- or rather sand-angel prints."

Crissy smiled. "Neither would I."

The Bonfire
Lisa Shapiro

We always ended the season with a bonfire. Flames in the cement-rimmed pit, feeding on driftwood, leapt as high as the beach cottage. At the deli-market, we stocked our coolers with beer and piled grocery bags full of chips and marshmallows. Our group was evenly divided between the beer-swillers and the marshmallow-toasters. Someone was always good enough to remember hot dogs, which the drunkards waggled at each other but no one ate. At least, I couldn't remember eating dogs since college, when it was still cool to eat kid food.

Now, professionals that we were, we grilled steak and swordfish and sipped chilled Chardonnay on the cottage deck. Afterward, relaxed and excited, we trundled the coolers and goodies down to the sand and spread blankets around the firepit. I was always happy and sad at the same time. By late August, the end of summer was more than a date on the calendar. It was a feel in the evening — like cool sand, damp fog, daylight that lingered without July's warm afterglow.

Our last stop after the deli-mart was the liquor store, where we bought gin and then scrounged for empty cardboard cartons. When we built a bonfire, we built it high.

Cass and I were the ringleaders, having started the bonfire tradition in high school. In college we couldn't afford a cottage, but on summer break we'd dragged our girlfriends to the beach for all-night parties. We were too old now for that nonsense — old enough to be comfortable, settled enough to have permanent partners. At least, everyone but me. Even Cass had been faithful to Marilyn going on three years. Cass had been my compatriot since the tenth grade, when we'd first been drawn together through a shared, intense worship of girls. Even Cass was monogamous now.

I dug my toes into the sand and stared at the ocean. Back at the cottage, my friends were bumping hips in the kitchen, tossing salad and pouring wine. On the deck, Cass was standing guard over the charcoal briquettes. Her girlfriend, Marilyn, could have stoked the grill. She owned a restaurant in

Hillcrest. Three years ago when Cass had arrived in
her coveralls to fix the plumbing, it had been love at
first service call. I thought it was nice of Marilyn to
let Cass handle the fire.

Jan and Sandy, the other cottage couple, had
come to my aid with boxes of tissue last winter,
nursing me through the absolute wretchedness when
Lake left. Lake, damn her. I rarely thought of her
without the epithet. For two years, Lake was the
lover I'd brought to the cottage. Then, before I'd had
time to absorb her whim, she was gone, gone and
living in Colorado.

"I always knew I was meant to live in the
mountains," she'd said.

She hadn't asked if I also felt destined for the
Rockies. Would I have left San Diego and moved to
Denver? No. I loved the ocean. But following Lake
hadn't been an option.

Her parting words had been, "I'm sorry, Heather.
I don't love you anymore."

Lake was good at making friends, though, and I'd
inherited Jan and Sandy from her. She'd known them
first but I was the one who got dumped, so I won
their comfort.

"She really loved you," Jan soothed.

But love had faded, soured, curdled and just plain
changed. What I felt now was close to hate, which
probably meant I wasn't over her yet, but what the
hell. Cass and I had rented the beach cottage for two
weeks, the same as every summer. I came without
Lake, and Jan and Sandy came, too, because they
were my friends now.

Sandy had invited a friend for the weekend, our last few days together. The guest was a pale, willowy woman who wore sunblock under a full-length caftan and read thick books with academic titles. She was a professor, and back-to-school days were nearly upon us. She'd arrived on Friday and, beyond introductions, we hadn't shared a word until Saturday morning.

She'd come into the kitchen while I was grinding coffee beans. Sometimes I thought Marilyn took the gourmet thing too far.

"Sorry," I said, not really meaning it. "I guess I woke you." As the latecomer, she'd been relegated to the pullout couch.

"I was awake," she said. "I was just starting to think I'd grind those damn beans myself and screw the sleepyheads."

Cass and Marilyn were screwing — I could hear them, which was why I'd gotten up. I looked at — Ellen, was that her name? It was a nice, ordinary name. Why had I fallen for a woman named Lake? Damn her. I looked at Ellen and it dawned on me that she was pretty. This was the first time I'd seen her *sans* caftan. She'd been sleeping in shorts and a tank top and it was clear why she had to be careful about the sun. She had the attributes of the ultra-fair — pale skin, her face still slightly pink-tinged from her pillow. Her hair was white-gold, her eyes bleached-out blue. She had long limbs; at five-ten, not many women are as tall as me, but she was staring straight into my eyes.

I don't know why, but when she reached out and
touched my face, it felt natural. I didn't flinch. The
gesture simply didn't surprise me. All four of her
fingertips brushed my cheek, then moved to my
messy curls.

She said, "I wish I could tan like you. For that
matter, I'd give anything for naturally curly hair."

I tossed my head and her fingers slipped away. "I
always used to wish for long, straight hair."

She smiled. "Do you still?"

"No." I was suddenly glad that I had curls. I had
something she coveted. I wasn't sure why that gave
me satisfaction, but it did.

I dumped the ground coffee into a filter and got
the pot brewing. I interrupted the drip long enough
to pour two mugs, then carried them to the deck.
Ellen had her caftan on and her nose in a book.

"Thanks," she said, when I put the mug beside
her.

"Cream or sugar?" I wasn't usually so solicitous.

"No, thanks." She went back to her reading.

Fuck her, I thought, and carried my coffee over
the breakwater and down to the sand.

On Saturday evening I was on the sand again,
standing by the firepit, having slunk out on the
dinner preparations. The joviality in the cottage was
grating on my nerves. It was the end of summer and
if that wasn't an excuse for being surly, what was?

"I love late summer," a soft voice behind me said.

I turned and there was Ellen. She wore shorts
and a sweatshirt with the sleeves cut off. The

evening's fog didn't threaten her complexion. It was still a shock to meet her eyes. I wasn't used to tall women. Lake, damn her, had been petite.

"The end of summer always depresses me," I said and went back to studying the waves.

"Want to take a walk?"

"Sure." I didn't care about her company, one way or the other, but it was better than going back inside for Chardonnay. I wasn't hungry and I didn't even feel like getting drunk.

It hit me then why I was sad. All summer long, I'd harbored a fantasy that Lake would come home. She'd come back to the beach house — how could she pass it up? But it was Saturday night, the last weekend at the cottage, and I knew she was a no-show. She wouldn't be waving from the deck when I turned around, calling me up for dinner. She was gone. Lake was gone.

I reached for Ellen's hand. "Come on. Let's walk down by the water."

At the water's edge, I cuffed my jeans and let the cool waves creep up my feet. Ellen's bare legs shone palely. The sun had already banked itself behind low clouds. A few shafts of sunset broke through, crowning the horizon, but wispy fog was swirling in. The glow would soon go out of the sky.

Ellen moved to stand beside me. "What kind of work do you do?"

"I'm an assistant editor at *Harbor Magazine*."

"Posh rag."

I couldn't tell if she was teasing. The magazine was all about chic restaurants and trendy clubs.

Tourists loved it. Natives disdained it. But it paid well so I hung on to the work.

Lake had loved the magazine. It was how we met — at a party given by the senior editor. I remembered with a sour taste on my tongue that Lake had landed in San Diego fresh from an affair in Taos.

"Damn her."

"Who?"

I hadn't realized I'd said it aloud. "No one."

Ellen began walking toward the jetty. Reluctantly, I followed. From a step and a half behind, I focused on her figure. In spite of our being the same height, she was lankier. I probably had fifteen pounds on her — muscle, I assured myself. I kept fit. Ellen's physique was naturally more slender. Lake had been slender, too, although inches shorter, with red hair and freckled skin. Before Lake, I'd never thought of freckles as sexy. Probably, I never would again.

I was being morose. Worse, I was bad company. Ellen would report back to Sandy and I'd catch hell.

There's no excuse for being rude to a woman. It was Sandy's philosophy. *No matter how messed up your love life is.*

I called, "Hey, wait up."

Ellen skimmed a glance over her shoulder. "Are you still back there?"

I caught up. "Couldn't you feel me pouting three paces behind?"

"Now that you mention it, you're very glum."

"I got dumped recently. I'd rather be PMS with a hangover than feel like this."

"Sandy said your girlfriend left last New Year's."

I nodded. "I was dressing for a party when she told me. Instead of ringing in the year together, she had her bags packed and I drove her to the airport. It all happened before midnight."

"That was eight months ago," she observed. "You're still pining."

I was starting to feel murderous toward Sandy. What right did she have to tell this ivory academic, this judgmental bitch, about my relationship. So what if it had ended before the Champagne corks had popped. It was nobody's business but mine, I fumed.

I stopped walking, hoping Miss Fairlegs would disappear into the fog. Or waves. Anything to get her out of my sight. I was facing the ocean and she came around and stood in front of me, blocking my view. Water splashed around our ankles.

I stared at my feet. "We should head back. They'll grill the steaks and eat without us."

She said, "I never should have come this weekend. I knew I'd hate it."

That caught my attention. I'd been so absorbed in my own misery, I hadn't stopped to consider anyone else's. After mine, could there be any unhappiness left to go around?

I finally looked at her. "What are you so bummed about?"

"I hate the beach. I should never have let Sandy talk me into it."

"Where're you from?"

"Phoenix."

"Desert heat. You have to wear sunblock there,

too." For some reason, I was still obsessing about her skin.

"In Arizona, it's acceptable to stay indoors. People here act like you're a sinner if you shun the sun."

I laughed. "So why'd you come to the cottage?"

"I have a hard time . . . meeting people."

My mouth was dry. I wished I was back on the deck so I could open a beer. I didn't know what to say.

She said, "Shyness is like having a stammer. Sometimes you have to join in the conversation and hope for the best." She hesitated, then took the plunge. "How come you're flogging a dead relationship?"

I told her the truth. "I hoped she'd come back."

"Are you still waiting?"

I took a breath and let it out. "No. But it took me the whole summer to figure that out."

Ellen was looking at me intently. "Sandy wanted me to meet you. Until this minute, I couldn't understand why."

"Sandy wanted — what are you talking about?"

"She wanted me to meet you."

I'd heard her the first time. "What is this — some kind of setup?"

"Don't act so offended. You're harder to approach than I am."

"I've been preoccupied." Why was I defending myself? I shot back, "You've had your face in a book for two days. Is that how you get to know someone?"

"I told you I'm no good at it."

"Did you think I'd flop down beside you in a

matching caftan and say, `Oh, my. What are you reading?' "

I was getting nasty but she smiled. "That was plan A. Plan B was to ask you for a walk. And here we are."

I didn't know whether to be pissed or flattered. But I'd already spent months being angry. The flattery was kind of nice, and I realized I felt like responding.

I took her hand. "Plan B. Keep walking."

The jetty was a hundred yards ahead. After a dozen strides, I slowed so that I wasn't pulling. We matched paces, still holding hands. She was easy to walk with.

I glanced at her sidelong, still absorbing her beauty and my attraction to it. "Why did you leave Phoenix?"

She sighed. "I got dumped, too. We taught on the same campus and it took me forever to find a job in another town."

"What happened?"

She didn't answer right away. Just when I thought she might not, she murmured, "I'm shy about a lot of things. She wasn't . . . satisfied." She slipped her hand from mine.

I could only imagine what it had cost her to make such a confession. "You've got guts," I said. "I'm glad you asked me for a walk."

"I believe it's easier to change old habits in a new environment. At least, that's what I keep telling myself I'm trying to do."

I pondered her remark. Maybe I should have skipped the beach and taken my vacation in Phoenix.

I asked, "Why do you think Sandy wanted us to meet?"

"We're both loners and we hate the beach."

"I don't hate the beach."

"You will, if it's where you're stuck."

We'd reached the jetty and I stopped to inspect a few pieces of driftwood. I didn't hate the beach. I'd prove it.

I tugged a piece of wood free of the sand. "I'll show you what the beach is about. Let's make a fire."

"This bonfire thing. Would you mind explaining it?"

"It's a tradition." I began dragging the wood toward an empty firepit. "Actually, it's a juvenile holdover from when Cass and I were in high school. We hung with a group that always ended the summer with a bonfire."

That's right. I'd been part of a group. I wasn't a loner, either. But the group, for me, had been a way of staying safe, of avoiding notice. I'd surrounded myself with people and bonded to Cass. When Lake had come along, she took charge of making friends. Like Jan and Sandy.

I dropped the wood by the firepit, brushed my hands on my jeans and gazed at Ellen. The breeze tugged her hair in wisps around her face. She caught a few strands and pulled them back.

I said, "I guess you never had a group to hang out with."

"I can't stand a lot of noise."

"You must hate it at the cottage." Cass and Marilyn did everything loudly. Talk. Fight. Fuck.

She said, "It's kind of awful."

"So, I guess you're not looking forward to the bonfire."

"I thought I'd leave early."

"No way." I gathered up my wooden booty and heaved it into the pit.

Other rings, up the beach, were dotted with cozy flames. Smoke and the smell of seaweed permeated the air. Along the jetty, waves broke on the rocks, drowning the sounds of music and laughter. Our ring was closest to the jetty and too low to the tidal mark for comfort. But the tide was out, the sun had set and it was the only firepit left. I needed kindling and I headed toward a nearby garbage can.

"Wait here," I instructed. "Guard the wood."

She called after me. "Heather?" I turned. "What are you doing?"

"I'm building you a fire. I'll be right back."

Sure enough, the can was full of crumpled food bags and, as luck would have it, a ditched newspaper. Without a second thought, I toppled the can to reach the bounty.

Ellen had trailed after me. "I can't believe you're doing this."

"Quick. Get back to the pit and guard the wood."

She made a point of turning her head to one side and then the other. Even though it was dark, she shaded her eyes. "From whom?"

"Rival bonfire-builders, that's who." There was no one even close to our pit, but it was part of the tradition. Someone always had to guard the wood. I said, "For the best bonfires, you need cardboard boxes. Those go flaming up to heaven."

"You're really into this."

"You bet I am."

I didn't give another thought to rejoining Cass and company. Let them dine on double helpings of steak and fish. Let them get plastered on wine, beer and gin. They could pitch marshmallows into the biggest bonfire in history. I wasn't interested. There was only one point of interest, one thing to stay focused on. I was guarding a lonely firepit, a piece of driftwood that was probably too damp to light, and trying to prove myself to one painfully shy woman who'd asked me for a walk. Somehow, out of that equation, I came up with the logic that I was destined to build her a fire.

Patiently, as I had done year after year during summers since my youth, I scrunched McDonald's bags into tight cones and rolled newspaper into twisted logs. Fortunately, at the deli-mart, I'd stocked up on matches. I pulled a book from my hip pocket.

I placed the paper at strategic points under the wood and said a prayer. "Please light."

I went through half a book of matches and had to go back to the garbage can to ferret out more lunch bags, but eventually the wood stopped smoking and caught the flame. I settled back, wiping the grime from my hands onto my jeans.

Ellen was laughing. "I don't think cavemen had to work so hard."

I grunted, reached up and yanked her down. The sand was cool and the fire had begun to blaze. Yellow and red flames licked the rim of the pit.

"It won't last," I said. "Once it really gets going, it'll burn fast."

"It smells good," she said. I turned to watch as she inhaled. She laughed again. "It's wonderful."

"Thanks." I felt wonderful.

I'd never been so happy to build a fire. Never mind that it had taken half an hour. Never mind that we'd missed dinner and Sandy and Cass would tease me mercilessly when I finally reappeared at the cottage. Never mind that I'd built a mediocre beach fire, a far cry from the glorious inferno I'd envisioned, had been imagining all season. Never mind any of that. I'd built a pissant fire for Ellen and I felt good.

I felt very good, and it took a minute to realize that the delightful sensation stealing my breath and goading my pulse was from her lips on my cheek. She leaned closer and kissed my neck.

I pulled back slightly and met her questioning gaze with one of my own. "Are you getting over being shy?"

The fire alternately lit then shadowed her face. Her features looked warm — from the heat or a blush, I couldn't tell.

Her smile broke slowly, teeth gleaming against the orange flames, the blue night. "I didn't know how else to repay such tremendous effort. No one's ever built me a bonfire before."

"It's not really —"

"Heather, shush. This isn't easy." She kissed me softly. Our tongues touched briefly.

It occurred to me that she might not really be shy. Perhaps, sensing my gloomy reticence, she'd merely played the part of the reluctant academic. Maybe I'd been conned. Seduced.

"Are you seducing me?" I blurted the question against her lips.

Her voice was low. "You built the fire. I thought you were doing the seducing."

Wind roared in my ears, although the breeze coming off the water was mild. The spitting fire sounded very loud. I lay back, pulling her on top.

Our lovemaking happened fast. My hands were dirty, my clothes full of sand. I was afraid to touch her with anything but my mouth. I hiked up her sweatshirt and gobbled her breasts, then pulled her shorts down. She stayed above me the whole time. As I lifted my head to suck her in, I saw the fire burning behind her, the flames leaping high into the night.

She came quickly but seemed in no hurry to get up. Her hips rotated gently, her cunt still wet on my tongue. I ate her slowly. She caught her breath suddenly, arched and began to move hard. I grabbed her hips and stayed with her, sucking and licking for all I was worth. She came again, as sweetly as the first time.

Her hands were planted in the sand on either side of my head. Her stomach convulsed as she gasped, then tightened as she raised herself off. She pulled her shorts up and sat beside me, still panting lightly.

I ran my tongue over my lips, savoring her flavor. She leaned to me and I caught her for a kiss before

I saw the doubt in her eyes. I dropped my hand to her leg. Her skin was cool.

"Maybe I could teach you to like the beach."

"Why don't you come home with me?" She said it lightly.

"You don't owe me anything," I responded. "I loved this. I don't need anything else."

She got to her feet. "You need a new environment, too. Let's get the hell out of here." She pulled me up and helped me brush the sand off. "Do you need to stop at the cottage?"

I shook my head. If I wasn't back in the morning, Cass would pack my stuff. Sandy would deliver it to my door and demand the details. What would I tell her? That Ellen, her weekend guest, had confided to me that she wasn't having a good time. In a fit of bravado, I'd built her a fire, although I had a feeling that, even if I hadn't ignited the driftwood, she'd have ended up sitting on my face all the same. Still, in spite of the sand and the garbage, I was glad we'd had the fire.

We held hands and hiked to the alley where our cars were parked.

I said, "Shit. My keys are inside."

I didn't want to go in. I didn't want to have to deal with my friends. I didn't want to face their questions or congratulatory teasing. Yeah, I was getting over Lake. Yeah, I was getting laid with Ellen. I didn't want to talk about it. Ellen was right. Crowds were noisy. I wanted to leave the cottage and my gloomy thoughts as though they were smoke billowing from a firepit, blowing into the ocean fog.

Ellen searched in her pockets and came up with a key ring. "Thank goodness I didn't lose them."

"Do you always carry your car keys when you go for a beach walk?"

She pointed to her packed bag on the back seat. "With or without you, I wasn't going to stay another night." We climbed in and she started the motor. "Are you sure you don't mind leaving early?"

I shrugged. "You've seen one bonfire, you've seen 'em all. Can I take a shower when we get to your place?" The sand in my jeans was beginning to itch.

As the car pulled out, I looked back. Was it my imagination, or could I see sparks shooting into the sky above the cottage. Yes, of course. This year's blaze was bigger than ever. I turned my back on it. By tomorrow morning the firepit, like my memories, would be cold, the pain, like burned driftwood, reduced to ash. I was with Ellen now, and the beach season was over.

About the Authors

LAURA ADAMS — Once a Girl Guide, always a Girl Guide. Earnest and prepared, and loving the company of the other girls, Laura, at the age of twelve, declared in her journal that she would like to remain twelve all her life. At nineteen, loving the company of other women, she recorded in her journal that she'd always like to be nineteen. Looking back from thirty-something she tells Journal, an overly fluffy tabby who adopted Laura during the Broken Icebox/Salmon Glut of 1993, that no one could pay her enough to be nineteen again. She wouldn't want to relive most of the experiences that led her to knowing what she knows now. Laura Adams is the closely guarded *nom de plume* of a famous lesbian romance writer. Her works for Naiad include *Night Vision*, *Christabel*, and the forthcoming *The Dawning*.

SAXON BENNETT lives in Phoenix, Arizona, for purposes of sun worship and Technicolor dreaming with her darling partner and their beloved cat. Phoenix is a place full of human oddities and transcendental tree huggers. And like the middle of an Oreo cookie, she feels perfectly at home. She is the author of *The Wish List, Old Ties,* and *A Question of Love.*

DIANA BRAUND is a transplant to rural northern Maine where the rugged coastline and spectacular ocean views allow her to live her days inside a picture postcard. In past lives she has worked as a college professor, reporter, business-woman and bon vivant. She is at work on her second Naiad novel, *Wicked Good Fun.*

KAYE DAVIS is a criminalist in a Texas Department of Public Safety regional crime laboratory with twenty years experience. Her areas of expertise include the analysis of drugs, the examination of paint samples and the comparison of shoeprint and tire track evidence. She has testified in court over three hundred and fifty times and has participated in numerous crime scene investigations. Kaye is a native Texan and lives in the Dallas area with her partner of seventeen years and two dogs, Trooper and Dispatcher. She is the author of the Maris Middleton mysteries, *Devil's Leg Crossing, Possessions,* and *Until the End,* all published by Naiad Press.

LYN DENISON decided she wanted to be a writer when she was still at school. She thought writers led such exciting lives and didn't have to go to work. She finds it very ironic that when reality struck she had chosen to write romantic fiction. She was born in Brisbane, the capital city of Queensland, Australia's Sunshine State and was a librarian for twenty-one years before becoming a full-time writer. She loves reading, cross stitching, traveling, modern country music, line dancing and her partner of ten years — not necessarily in that order. She lives with her partner in a colonial worker's cottage, which they have renovated, in a historic suburb near Brisbane's city center. The latest addition to their family is a very fast Subaru Impreza WRX hatch, known affectionately as the menopausemobile.

CATHERINE ENNIS is a Southerner by birth, and still lives in the deep south with her long-time lover and an assortment of pets. She has enjoyed many pastimes including gardening, gourmet cooking, fishing, and working on her Model A Ford coupe. Catherine's books are set in the locales with which she is most familiar: the New Orleans area, the Memphis–Nashville area and the Louisiana Cajun country. Her early work experience included wholesale florist and research office manager, medical illustrator and teacher, followed by some years on the arts and crafts show circuit. Finally she started her own business utilizing her art background, making her work even more enjoyable because obviously, no one could have a better boss. Writing has become her favorite hobby.

PENNY HAYES was born in Johnson City, New York, February 10, 1940. As a child she lived on a farm near Binghamton, New York. She later attended college in Utica and Buffalo, NY, and in Huntington, WV, graduating with degrees in art, nursery school education, and elementary and special education. She recently retired from public school teaching and now devotes her time to writing and anything to do with the outdoors and good conversation. Her novels include *The Long Trail, Yellowthroat, Montana Feathers, Grassy Flats, Kathleen O'Donald, Now and Then* and most recently *City Lights/Country Candles*. Her eighth novel, *Omaha's Bell*, is due out in March 1999. She has also written short stories for *The Erotic Naiad, The Romantic Naiad, The Mysterious Naiad, The First Time Ever, Dancing in the Dark* and *Lady Be Good*.

PEGGY J. HERRING is the author of *Once More with Feeling, Love's Harvest, Hot Check* and *A Moment's Indiscretion*. She has also contributed to the Naiad anthologies *The First Time Ever, Dancing in the Dark* and *Lady Be Good*. Peggy lives in South Texas with her partner, Frankie J. Jones, and likes spending time at Textures Books & Gifts, the feminist bookstore they own together. Peggy's next novel, *Those Who Wait*, will be released by Naiad Press in 1999, and she's currently working on *To Have and to Hold* for publication in 2000.

LINDA HILL, originally from the Midwest, now makes her home in the Boston area. Her biggest complaint in life is that there are never enough hours in the day to squeeze in everything she wants to do. When not writing, Linda spends a great portion of her time doing computer work — sometimes just for fun. When not in front of a monitor, she enjoys antiquing, woodworking, golfing, the Celtics, and an occasional trip to the casino. She is the author of *Never Say Never, Class Reunion* and *Just Yesterday,* all published by Naiad Press. Wearing another hat, Linda is the Naiad Webmistress at www.naiadpress.com.

BARBARA JOHNSON doesn't own a Le Baron con-vertible, but she'd sure like to know someone who does. Without those magical car rides to distract her, she's managed to write three novels for Naiad Press: *Stonehurst, The Beach Affair,* and *Bad Moon Rising.*

FRANKIE J. JONES grew up between the soybean rows and cotton stalks of Southeast Missouri, better known to its inhabitants as the Bootheel. While in the Army she met her life partner, Peggy J. Herring. They currently live in South Texas as far away from cotton stalks as Frankie can get. When not working at her eight-to-five job or writing, Frankie spends her time working in the bookstore she and Peggy own. When she finds a free moment she likes to spend it reading, metal detecting, or researching the numerous shipwrecks off the Texas coast. Frankie is the author of *Rhythm Tide.* Her second novel, *Whispers in the Wind* is due to be released in 1998.

KARIN KALLMAKER was born in 1960 and raised by her loving, middle-class parents in California's Central Valley. The physician's Statement of Live Birth plainly states "Sex: Female" and "Cry: Lusty." Both are still true. From a normal childhood and equally unremarkable public school adolescence, she went on to obtain an ordinary Bachelor's degree from the California State University at Sacramento. At the age of 16, eyes wide open, she fell into the arms of her first and only sweetheart. Ten years later, after seeing the film *Desert Hearts,* her sweetheart descended on the Berkeley Public Library determined to find some of "those" books. "Rule, Jane" led to "Lesbianism — Fiction" and then on to book after self-affirming book by and about lesbians. These books were the encouragement Karin needed to forget the so-called "mainstream" and spin her first romance for lesbians. That manuscript became her first Naiad Press book, *In Every Port*. She now lives in Oakland with that very same sweetheart; she is a one-woman woman. The happily-ever-after couple celebrated their Twentieth Anniversary in 1997, and are mothers of two quite remarkable children, Kelson and Eleanor. In addition to *In Every Port*, she has authored the best-selling *Touchwood, Paperback Romance, Car Pool, Painted Moon, Wild Things, Embrace in Motion*, and *Making Up for Lost Time*. In 1999, look for *Watermark*.

MARIANNE K. MARTIN is the author of *Legacy of Love* and *Love in the Balance*, both published by Naiad Press. Her short story *By the Light of the Moon* was included in Naiad's 1997 anthology, *Lady Be Good*. For a number of years she taught and coached in the public school system, before turning her hobbies into a career as a photo-journalist. She has coached at both the amateur and collegiate levels and enjoys participating in a number of sports. She currently resides in Michigan as a writer and professional photographer.

JANET McCLELLAN began her career in law enforce-ment at the age of nineteen. During the next twenty-six years she worked as a narcotics investigator, patrol officer, detective, college professor, and prison administrator. All of which her mother refers to as her checkered past. When not writing mysteries, she spends her time traveling and investigating the mysteries of Dallas, Texas; Kansas City, Missouri; and Eagles Nest, New Mexico. Her three mysteries, *K.C. Bomber, Penn Valley*

Phoenix, and *River Quay,* featuring Detective Tru North, and a romance, *Windrow Garden,* have all been published by Naiad Press.

ANN O'LEARY was born in Melbourne, Australia. Following a career in film, advertising and audio production, Ann is now a full-time writer, living in Melbourne with her partner. She is the author of *Letting Go* and *Julia's Song.*

TRACEY RICHARDSON was inspired to write "She Shoots, She Scores" after watching those awesome women on skates at the 1997 Women's World Hockey Championships. Her partner, Sandra, kept a tight rein on her that weekend. Tracey's other short stories have appeared in *Lady Be Good* and *Dancing in the Dark.* Her first novel for Naiad was the romance *Northern Blue,* published in 1996. Her mystery *Last Rites* was published in 1997, followed by *Over the Line* in 1998. Tracey and Sandra live in Ontario, Canada.

LISA SHAPIRO is the author of *The Color of Winter, Sea to Shining Sea,* and *Endless Love,* all published by Naiad Press. She lives with her cherished lover, Lynne in Tampa, Florida.

THERESE SZYMANSKI finds most of her past too strange to share with anyone until at least the second date. An award-winning playwright who works in advertising and plays in theater (with both *Alternating Currents* and *Pissed Off Wimmin*) to the best of her knowledge, she has never made it with a DJ, although she has oft been propositioned by a certain Dangerous Voice from Motor City radio. She is the author of the Brett Higgins mysteries *When the Dancing Stops* and *When the Dead Speak* and the forthcoming *When Some Body Disappears* (due out in January 1999).

JULIA WATTS is the author of three novels, *Wildwood Flowers*, *Phases of the Moon* and *Piece of My Heart*. Though her story "Manicure" is fictional, she does admit to owning many bottles of nail polish in a wide range of hues.

PAT WELCH lives and works in the San Francisco Bay Area, where she writes the Helen Black mystery series for Naiad Press. Her sixth novel in the series, *Fallen from Grace*, was released in July 1998. She is currently at work on the seventh entry in the series, titled *Snake Eyes*. A Southern Lady transplanted to the West Coast, she can be found in her natural habitat of bookstores and coffee shops in Berkeley when she's not writing her Great American Novel.

LAURA DeHART YOUNG currently has four romance novels published by Naiad Press: *There Will Be No Goodbyes*, *Family Secrets*, *Love on the Line*, and her newest book, *Private Passions*. Her fifth romance novel, *Intimate Stranger*, will be published by Naiad Press in 1999.

"Enough Said," the short story appearing in this anthology, was inspired by Laura's friends Sandy and Deanna. When not writing for Naiad, Laura works as a communications manager for a worldwide information company. She lives in Atlanta, Georgia, with her Pug, Dudley.

LOOKING FOR NAIAD?

Buy our books at
www.naiadpress.com

or call our toll-free number
1-800-533-1973

or by fax (24 hours a day)
1-850-539-9731

A few of the publications of
THE NAIAD PRESS, INC.
P.O. Box 10543   Tallahassee, Florida 32302
Phone (850) 539-5965
Toll-Free Order Number: 1-800-533-1973
Web Site: WWW.NAIADPRESS.COM
Mail orders welcome. Please include 15% postage.
Write or call for our free catalog which also features an
incredible selection of lesbian videos.

FIFTH WHEEL by Kate Calloway. 224 pp. 5th Cassidy James
mystery.   ISBN 1-56280-218-6 $11.95

JUST YESTERDAY by Linda Hill. 176 pp. Reliving all the
passion of yesterday.   ISBN 1-56280-219-4   11.95

THE TOUCH OF YOUR HAND edited by Barbara Grier and
Christine Cassidy. 304 pp. Erotic love stories by Naiad Press
authors.   ISBN 1-56280-220-8   14.95

WINDROW GARDEN by Janet McClellan. 192 pp. They discover
a passion they never dreamed possible.   ISBN 1-56280-216-X   11.95

PAST DUE by Claire McNab. 224 pp. 10th Carol Ashton
mystery.   ISBN 1-56280-217-8   11.95

CHRISTABEL by Laura Adams. 224 pp. Two captive hearts and
the passion that will set them free.   ISBN 1-56280-214-3   11.95

PRIVATE PASSIONS by Laura DeHart Young. 192 pp. An
unforgettable new portrait of lesbian love . . .   ISBN 1-56280-215-1   11.95

BAD MOON RISING by Barbara Johnson. 208 pp. 2nd Colleen
Fitzgerald mystery.   ISBN 1-56280-211-9   11.95

RIVER QUAY by Janet McClellan. 208 pp. 3rd Tru North
mystery.   ISBN 1-56280-212-7   11.95

ENDLESS LOVE by Lisa Shapiro. 272 pp. To believe, once
again, that love can be forever.   ISBN 1-56280-213-5   11.95

FALLEN FROM GRACE by Pat Welch. 256 pp. 6th Helen Black
mystery.   ISBN 1-56280-209-7   11.95

THE NAKED EYE by Catherine Ennis. 208 pp. Her lover in the
camera's eye . . .   ISBN 1-56280-210-0   11.95

OVER THE LINE by Tracey Richardson. 176 pp. 2nd Stevie
Houston mystery.   ISBN 1-56280-202-X   11.95

JULIA'S SONG by Ann O'Leary. 208 pp. Strangely
disturbing . . . strangely exciting.   ISBN 1-56280-197-X   11.95

MAKING UP FOR LOST TIME by Karin Kallmaker. 240 pp.
Nobody does it better . . .   ISBN 1-56280-196-1   11.95

GOLD FEVER by Lyn Denison. 224 pp. By author of *Dream Lover*.   ISBN 1-56280-201-1   11.95

WHEN THE DEAD SPEAK by Therese Szymanski. 224 pp. 2nd
Brett Higgins mystery.   ISBN 1-56280-198-8   11.95

FOURTH DOWN by Kate Calloway. 240 pp. 4th Cassidy James
mystery.   ISBN 1-56280-205-4   11.95

A MOMENT'S INDISCRETION by Peggy J. Herring. 176 pp.
There's a fine line between love and lust . . .   ISBN 1-56280-194-5   11.95

CITY LIGHTS/COUNTRY CANDLES by Penny Hayes. 208 pp.
About the women she has known . . .   ISBN 1-56280-195-3   11.95

POSSESSIONS by Kaye Davis. 240 pp. 2nd Maris Middleton
mystery.   ISBN 1-56280-192-9   11.95

A QUESTION OF LOVE by Saxon Bennett. 208 pp. Every
woman is granted one great love.   ISBN 1-56280-205-4   11.95

RHYTHM TIDE by Frankie J. Jones. 160 pp.   . . . to desire
passionately and be passionately desired.   ISBN 1-56280-189-9   11.95

PENN VALLEY PHOENIX by Janet McClellan. 208 pp. 2nd
Tru North Mystery.   ISBN 1-56280-200-3   11.95

BY RESERVATION ONLY by Jackie Calhoun. 240 pp. A
chance for true happiness.   ISBN 1-56280-191-0   11.95

OLD BLACK MAGIC by Jaye Maiman. 272 pp. 9th Robin
Miller mystery.   ISBN 1-56280-175-9   11.95

LEGACY OF LOVE by Marianne K. Martin. 240 pp. Women
will do anything for her . . .   ISBN 1-56280-184-8   11.95

LETTING GO by Ann O'Leary. 160 pp. Laura, at 39, in love
with 23-year-old Kate.   ISBN 1-56280-183-X   11.95

LADY BE GOOD edited by Barbara Grier and Christine Cassidy.
288 pp. Erotic stories by Naiad Press authors.   ISBN 1-56280-180-5   14.95

CHAIN LETTER by Claire McNab. 288 pp. 9th Carol Ashton
mystery.   ISBN 1-56280-181-3   11.95

NIGHT VISION by Laura Adams. 256 pp. Erotic fantasy romance
by "famous" author.   ISBN 1-56280-182-1   11.95

SEA TO SHINING SEA by Lisa Shapiro. 256 pp. Unable to resist
the raging passion . . .   ISBN 1-56280-177-5   11.95

THIRD DEGREE by Kate Calloway. 224 pp. 3rd Cassidy James
mystery.   ISBN 1-56280-185-6   11.95

WHEN THE DANCING STOPS by Therese Szymanski. 272 pp.
1st Brett Higgins mystery.   ISBN 1-56280-186-4   11.95

PHASES OF THE MOON by Julia Watts. 192 pp. . . . . . hungry
for everything life has to offer.   ISBN 1-56280-176-7   11.95

BABY IT'S COLD by Jaye Maiman. 256 pp. 5th Robin Miller mystery.   ISBN 1-56280-156-2   10.95

CLASS REUNION by Linda Hill. 176 pp. The girl from her past . . .   ISBN 1-56280-178-3   11.95

DREAM LOVER by Lyn Denison. 224 pp. A soft, sensuous, romantic fantasy.   ISBN 1-56280-173-1   11.95

FORTY LOVE by Diana Simmonds. 288 pp. Joyous, heart-warming romance.   ISBN 1-56280-171-6   11.95

IN THE MOOD by Robbi Sommers. 160 pp. The queen of erotic tension!   ISBN 1-56280-172-4   11.95

SWIMMING CAT COVE by Lauren Douglas. 192 pp. 2nd Allison O'Neil Mystery.   ISBN 1-56280-168-6   11.95

THE LOVING LESBIAN by Claire McNab and Sharon Gedan. 240 pp. Explore the experiences that make lesbian love unique.
                                                                    ISBN 1-56280-169-4   14.95

COURTED by Celia Cohen. 160 pp. Sparkling romantic encounter.   ISBN 1-56280-166-X   11.95

SEASONS OF THE HEART by Jackie Calhoun. 240 pp. Romance through the years.   ISBN 1-56280-167-8   11.95

K. C. BOMBER by Janet McClellan. 208 pp. 1st Tru North mystery.   ISBN 1-56280-157-0   11.95

LAST RITES by Tracey Richardson. 192 pp. 1st Stevie Houston mystery.   ISBN 1-56280-164-3   11.95

EMBRACE IN MOTION by Karin Kallmaker. 256 pp. A whirlwind love affair.   ISBN 1-56280-165-1   11.95

HOT CHECK by Peggy J. Herring. 192 pp. Will workaholic Alice fall for guitarist Ricky?   ISBN 1-56280-163-5   11.95

OLD TIES by Saxon Bennett. 176 pp. Can Cleo surrender to a passionate new love?   ISBN 1-56280-159-7   11.95

LOVE ON THE LINE by Laura DeHart Young. 176 pp. Will Stef win Kay's heart?   ISBN 1-56280-162-7   11.95

DEVIL'S LEG CROSSING by Kaye Davis. 192 pp. 1st Maris Middleton mystery.   ISBN 1-56280-158-9   11.95

COSTA BRAVA by Marta Balletbo Coll. 144 pp. Read the book, see the movie!   ISBN 1-56280-153-8   11.95

MEETING MAGDALENE & OTHER STORIES by Marilyn Freeman. 144 pp. Read the book, see the movie!
                                                                    ISBN 1-56280-170-8   11.95

SECOND FIDDLE by Kate 208 pp. 2nd P.I. Cassidy James mystery.   ISBN 1-56280-169-6   11.95

LAUREL by Isabel Miller. 128 pp. By the author of the beloved *Patience and Sarah*.   ISBN 1-56280-146-5   10.95

LOVE OR MONEY by Jackie Calhoun. 240 pp. The romance of
real life.   ISBN 1-56280-147-3   10.95

SMOKE AND MIRRORS by Pat Welch. 224 pp. 5th Helen Black
Mystery.   ISBN 1-56280-143-0   10.95

DANCING IN THE DARK edited by Barbara Grier & Christine
Cassidy. 272 pp. Erotic love stories by Naiad Press authors.
                                                  ISBN 1-56280-144-9   14.95

TIME AND TIME AGAIN by Catherine Ennis. 176 pp. Passionate
love affair.   ISBN 1-56280-145-7   10.95

PAXTON COURT by Diane Salvatore. 256 pp. Erotic and wickedly
funny contemporary tale about the business of learning to live
together.   ISBN 1-56280-114-7   10.95

INNER CIRCLE by Claire McNab. 208 pp. 8th Carol Ashton
Mystery.   ISBN 1-56280-135-X   11.95

LESBIAN SEX: AN ORAL HISTORY by Susan Johnson.
240 pp. Need we say more?   ISBN 1-56280-142-2   14.95

WILD THINGS by Karin Kallmaker. 240 pp. By the undisputed
mistress of lesbian romance.   ISBN 1-56280-139-2   11.95

THE GIRL NEXT DOOR by Mindy Kaplan. 208 pp. Just what
you d expect.   ISBN 1-56280-140-6   11.95

NOW AND THEN by Penny Hayes. 240 pp. Romance on the
westward journey.   ISBN 1-56280-121-X   11.95

HEART ON FIRE by Diana Simmonds. 176 pp. The romantic and
erotic rival of *Curious Wine*.   ISBN 1-56280-152-X   11.95

DEATH AT LAVENDER BAY by Lauren Wright Douglas. 208 pp.
1st Allison O'Neil Mystery.   ISBN 1-56280-085-X   11.95

YES I SAID YES I WILL by Judith McDaniel. 272 pp. Hot
romance by famous author.   ISBN 1-56280-138-4   11.95

FORBIDDEN FIRES by Margaret C. Anderson. Edited by Mathilda
Hills. 176 pp. Famous author's "unpublished" Lesbian romance.
                                                  ISBN 1-56280-123-6   21.95

SIDE TRACKS by Teresa Stores. 160 pp. Gender-bending
Lesbians on the road.   ISBN 1-56280-122-8   10.95

HOODED MURDER by Annette Van Dyke. 176 pp. 1st Jessie
Batelle Mystery.   ISBN 1-56280-134-1   10.95

WILDWOOD FLOWERS by Julia Watts. 208 pp. Hilarious and
heart-warming tale of true love.   ISBN 1-56280-127-9   10.95

NEVER SAY NEVER by Linda Hill. 224 pp. Rule #1: Never get
involved with . . .   ISBN 1-56280-126-0   11.95

THE SEARCH by Melanie McAllester. 240 pp. Exciting top cop
Tenny Mendoza case.   ISBN 1-56280-150-3   10.95

THE WISH LIST by Saxon Bennett. 192 pp. Romance through the years.   ISBN 1-56280-125-2   10.95

FIRST IMPRESSIONS by Kate 208 pp. 1st P.I. Cassidy James mystery.   ISBN 1-56280-133-3   10.95

OUT OF THE NIGHT by Kris Bruyer. 192 pp. Spine-tingling thriller.   ISBN 1-56280-120-1   10.95

NORTHERN BLUE by Tracey Richardson. 224 pp. Police recruits Miki & Miranda — passion in the line of fire.   ISBN 1-56280-118-X   10.95

LOVE'S HARVEST by Peggy J. Herring. 176 pp. by the author of *Once More With Feeling*.   ISBN 1-56280-117-1   10.95

THE COLOR OF WINTER by Lisa Shapiro. 208 pp. Romantic love beyond your wildest dreams.   ISBN 1-56280-116-3   10.95

FAMILY SECRETS by Laura DeHart Young. 208 pp. Enthralling romance and suspense.   ISBN 1-56280-119-8   10.95

INLAND PASSAGE by Jane Rule. 288 pp. Tales exploring conventional & unconventional relationships.   ISBN 0-930044-56-8   10.95

DOUBLE BLUFF by Claire McNab. 208 pp. 7th Carol Ashton Mystery.   ISBN 1-56280-096-5   10.95

BAR GIRLS by Lauran Hoffman. 176 pp. See the movie, read the book!   ISBN 1-56280-115-5   10.95

THE FIRST TIME EVER edited by Barbara Grier & Christine Cassidy. 272 pp. Love stories by Naiad Press authors. ISBN 1-56280-086-8   14.95

MISS PETTIBONE AND MISS McGRAW by Brenda Weathers. 208 pp. A charming ghostly love story.   ISBN 1-56280-151-1   10.95

CHANGES by Jackie Calhoun. 208 pp. Involved romance and relationships.   ISBN 1-56280-083-3   10.95

FAIR PLAY by Rose Beecham. 256 pp. An Amanda Valentine Mystery.   ISBN 1-56280-081-7   10.95

PAYBACK by Celia Cohen. 176 pp. A gripping thriller of romance, revenge and betrayal.   ISBN 1-56280-084-1   10.95

THE BEACH AFFAIR by Barbara Johnson. 224 pp. Sizzling summer romance/mystery/intrigue.   ISBN 1-56280-090-6   10.95

GETTING THERE by Robbi Sommers. 192 pp. Nobody does it like Robbi!   ISBN 1-56280-099-X   10.95

FINAL CUT by Lisa Haddock. 208 pp. 2nd Carmen Ramirez Mystery.   ISBN 1-56280-088-4   10.95

FLASHPOINT by Katherine V. Forrest. 256 pp. A Lesbian blockbuster!   ISBN 1-56280-079-5   10.95

CLAIRE OF THE MOON by Nicole Conn. Audio Book — Read by Marianne Hyatt.   ISBN 1-56280-113-9   16.95

FOR LOVE AND FOR LIFE: INTIMATE PORTRAITS OF
LESBIAN COUPLES by Susan Johnson. 224 pp.
ISBN 1-56280-091-4   14.95

DEVOTION by Mindy Kaplan. 192 pp. See the movie — read
the book!
ISBN 1-56280-093-0   10.95

SOMEONE TO WATCH by Jaye Maiman. 272 pp. 4th Robin
Miller Mystery.
ISBN 1-56280-095-7   10.95

GREENER THAN GRASS by Jennifer Fulton. 208 pp. A young
woman — a stranger in her bed.
ISBN 1-56280-092-2   10.95

TRAVELS WITH DIANA HUNTER by Regine Sands. Erotic
lesbian romp. Audio Book (2 cassettes)   ISBN 1-56280-107-4   16.95

CABIN FEVER by Carol Schmidt. 256 pp. Sizzling suspense
and passion.
ISBN 1-56280-089-1   10.95

THERE WILL BE NO GOODBYES by Laura DeHart Young. 192
pp. Romantic love, strength, and friendship.   ISBN 1-56280-103-1   10.95

FAULTLINE by Sheila Ortiz Taylor. 144 pp. Joyous comic
lesbian novel.
ISBN 1-56280-108-2   9.95

OPEN HOUSE by Pat Welch. 176 pp. 4th Helen Black Mystery.
ISBN 1-56280-102-3   10.95

ONCE MORE WITH FEELING by Peggy J. Herring. 240 pp.
Lighthearted, loving romantic adventure.   ISBN 1-56280-089-2   11.95

FOREVER by Evelyn Kennedy. 224 pp. Passionate romance — love
overcoming all obstacles.
ISBN 1-56280-094-9   10.95

WHISPERS by Kris Bruyer. 176 pp. Romantic ghost story.
ISBN 1-56280-082-5   10.95

NIGHT SONGS by Penny Mickelbury. 224 pp. 2nd Gianna
Maglione Mystery.
ISBN 1-56280-097-3   10.95

GETTING TO THE POINT by Teresa Stores. 256 pp. Classic
southern Lesbian novel.
ISBN 1-56280-100-7   10.95

PAINTED MOON by Karin Kallmaker. 224 pp. Delicious
Kallmaker romance.
ISBN 1-56280-075-2   11.95

THE MYSTERIOUS NAIAD edited by Katherine V. Forrest &
Barbara Grier. 320 pp. Love stories by Naiad Press authors.
ISBN 1-56280-074-4   14.95

DAUGHTERS OF A CORAL DAWN by Katherine V. Forrest.
240 pp. Tenth Annivesay Edition.   ISBN 1-56280-104-X   11.95

BODY GUARD by Claire McNab. 208 pp. 6th Carol Ashton
Mystery.
ISBN 1-56280-073-6   11.95

CACTUS LOVE by Lee Lynch. 192 pp. Stories by the beloved
storyteller.
ISBN 1-56280-071-X   9.95

SECOND GUESS by Rose Beecham. 216 pp. An Amanda
Valentine Mystery.
ISBN 1-56280-069-8   9.95

A RAGE OF MAIDENS by Lauren Wright Douglas. 240 pp.
6th Caitlin Reece Mystery. ISBN 1-56280-068-X 10.95

TRIPLE EXPOSURE by Jackie Calhoun. 224 pp. Romantic
drama involving many characters. ISBN 1-56280-067-1 10.95

PERSONAL ADS by Robbi Sommers. 176 pp. Sizzling short
stories. ISBN 1-56280-059-0 11.95

CROSSWORDS by Penny Sumner. 256 pp. 2nd Victoria Cross
Mystery. ISBN 1-56280-064-7 9.95

SWEET CHERRY WINE by Carol Schmidt. 224 pp. A novel of
suspense. ISBN 1-56280-063-9 9.95

CERTAIN SMILES by Dorothy Tell. 160 pp. Erotic short stories.
ISBN 1-56280-066-3 9.95

EDITED OUT by Lisa Haddock. 224 pp. 1st Carmen Ramirez
Mystery. ISBN 1-56280-077-9 9.95

WEDNESDAY NIGHTS by Camarin Grae. 288 pp. Sexy
adventure. ISBN 1-56280-060-4 11.95

SMOKEY O by Celia Cohen. 176 pp. Relationships on the
playing field. ISBN 1-56280-057-4 9.95

KATHLEEN O'DONALD by Penny Hayes. 256 pp. Rose and
Kathleen find each other and employment in 1909 NYC.
ISBN 1-56280-070-1 9.95

STAYING HOME by Elisabeth Nonas. 256 pp. Molly and Alix
want a baby . . . or do they? ISBN 1-56280-076-0 10.95

TRUE LOVE by Jennifer Fulton. 240 pp. Six lesbians searching
for love in all the "right" places. ISBN 1-56280-035-3 11.95

KEEPING SECRETS by Penny Mickelbury. 208 pp. 1st Gianna
Maglione Mystery. ISBN 1-56280-052-3 9.95

THE ROMANTIC NAIAD edited by Katherine V. Forrest &
Barbara Grier. 336 pp. Love stories by Naiad Press authors.
ISBN 1-56280-054-X 14.95

UNDER MY SKIN by Jaye Maiman. 336 pp. 3rd Robin Miller
Mystery. ISBN 1-56280-049-3. 11.95

CAR POOL by Karin Kallmaker. 272pp. Lesbians on wheels
and then some! ISBN 1-56280-048-5 11.95

NOT TELLING MOTHER: STORIES FROM A LIFE by Diane
Salvatore. 176 pp. Her 3rd novel. ISBN 1-56280-044-2 9.95

GOBLIN MARKET by Lauren Wright Douglas. 240pp. 5th Caitlin
Reece Mystery. ISBN 1-56280-047-7 10.95

FRIENDS AND LOVERS by Jackie Calhoun. 224 pp. Mid-
western Lesbian lives and loves. ISBN 1-56280-041-8 11.95

BEHIND CLOSED DOORS by Robbi Sommers. 192 pp. Hot,
erotic short stories. ISBN 1-56280-039-6 11.95

CLAIRE OF THE MOON by Nicole Conn. 192 pp. See the
movie — read the book!   ISBN 1-56280-038-8   11.95

SILENT HEART by Claire McNab. 192 pp. Exotic Lesbian
romance.   ISBN 1-56280-036-1   11.95

THE SPY IN QUESTION by Amanda Kyle Williams. 256 pp.
A Madison McGuire Mystery.   ISBN 1-56280-037-X   9.95

SAVING GRACE by Jennifer Fulton. 240 pp. Adventure and
romantic entanglement.   ISBN 1-56280-051-5   11.95

CURIOUS WINE by Katherine V. Forrest. 176 pp. Tenth Anniversary Edition. The most popular contemporary Lesbian love story.
     ISBN 1-56280-053-1   11.95
     Audio Book (2 cassettes)   ISBN 1-56280-105-8   16.95

CHAUTAUQUA by Catherine Ennis. 192 pp. Exciting, romantic
adventure.   ISBN 1-56280-032-9   9.95

A PROPER BURIAL by Pat Welch. 192 pp. 3rd Helen Black
Mystery.   ISBN 1-56280-033-7   9.95

SILVERLAKE HEAT: A Novel of Suspense by Carol Schmidt.
240 pp. Rhonda is as hot as Laney's dreams.   ISBN 1-56280-031-0   9.95

LOVE, ZENA BETH by Diane Salvatore. 224 pp. The most talked
about lesbian novel of the nineties!   ISBN 1-56280-030-2   10.95

A DOORYARD FULL OF FLOWERS by Isabel Miller. 160 pp.
Stories incl. 2 sequels to *Patience and Sarah.*   ISBN 1-56280-029-9   9.95

MURDER BY TRADITION by Katherine V. Forrest. 288 pp. 4th
Kate Delafield Mystery.   ISBN 1-56280-002-7   11.95

THE EROTIC NAIAD edited by Katherine V. Forrest & Barbara
Grier. 224 pp. Love stories by Naiad Press authors.
     ISBN 1-56280-026-4   14.95

DEAD CERTAIN by Claire McNab. 224 pp. 5th Carol Ashton
Mystery.   ISBN 1-56280-027-2   9.95

CRAZY FOR LOVING by Jaye Maiman. 320 pp. 2nd Robin Miller
Mystery.   ISBN 1-56280-025-6   11.95

UNCERTAIN COMPANIONS by Robbi Sommers. 204 pp.
Steamy, erotic novel.   ISBN 1-56280-017-5   11.95

A TIGER'S HEART by Lauren W. Douglas. 240 pp. 4th Caitlin
Reece Mystery.   ISBN 1-56280-018-3   9.95

PAPERBACK ROMANCE by Karin Kallmaker. 256 pp. A
delicious romance.   ISBN 1-56280-019-1   10.95

THE LAVENDER HOUSE MURDER by Nikki Baker. 224 pp.
2nd Virginia Kelly Mystery.   ISBN 1-56280-012-4   9.95

PASSION BAY by Jennifer Fulton. 224 pp. Passionate romance,
virgin beaches, tropical skies.   ISBN 1-56280-028-0   10.95

STICKS AND STONES by Jackie Calhoun. 208 pp. Contemporary lesbian lives and loves.
ISBN 1-56280-020-5   9.95
Audio Book (2 cassettes)
ISBN 1-56280-106-6   16.95

UNDER THE SOUTHERN CROSS by Claire McNab. 192 pp. Romantic nights Down Under.
ISBN 1-56280-011-6   11.95

GRASSY FLATS by Penny Hayes. 256 pp. Lesbian romance in the '30s.
ISBN 1-56280-010-8   9.95

THE END OF APRIL by Penny Sumner. 240 pp. 1st Victoria Cross Mystery.
ISBN 1-56280-007-8   8.95

KISS AND TELL by Robbi Sommers. 192 pp. Scorching stories by the author of *Pleasures*.
ISBN 1-56280-005-1   11.95

STILL WATERS by Pat Welch. 208 pp. 2nd Helen Black Mystery.
ISBN 0-941483-97-5   9.95

TO LOVE AGAIN by Evelyn Kennedy. 208 pp. Wildly romantic love story.
ISBN 0-941483-85-1   11.95

IN THE GAME by Nikki Baker. 192 pp. 1st Virginia Kelly Mystery.
ISBN 1-56280-004-3   9.95

STRANDED by Camarin Grae. 320 pp. Entertaining, riveting adventure.
ISBN 0-941483-99-1   9.95

THE DAUGHTERS OF ARTEMIS by Lauren Wright Douglas. 240 pp. 3rd Caitlin Reece Mystery.
ISBN 0-941483-95-9   9.95

CLEARWATER by Catherine Ennis. 176 pp. Romantic secrets of a small Louisiana town.
ISBN 0-941483-65-7   8.95

THE HALLELUJAH MURDERS by Dorothy Tell. 176 pp. 2nd Poppy Dillworth Mystery.
ISBN 0-941483-88-6   8.95

SECOND CHANCE by Jackie Calhoun. 256 pp. Contemporary Lesbian lives and loves.
ISBN 0-941483-93-2   9.95

BENEDICTION by Diane Salvatore. 272 pp. Striking, contemporary romantic novel.
ISBN 0-941483-90-8   11.95

TOUCHWOOD by Karin Kallmaker. 240 pp. Loving, May/December romance.
ISBN 0-941483-76-2   11.95

COP OUT by Claire McNab. 208 pp. 4th Carol Ashton Mystery.
ISBN 0-941483-84-3   10.95

THE BEVERLY MALIBU by Katherine V. Forrest. 288 pp. 3rd Kate Delafield Mystery.
ISBN 0-941483-48-7   11.95

THE PROVIDENCE FILE by Amanda Kyle Williams. 256 pp. A Madison McGuire Mystery.
ISBN 0-941483-92-4   8.95

I LEFT MY HEART by Jaye Maiman. 320 pp. 1st Robin Miller Mystery.
ISBN 0-941483-72-X   11.95

THE PRICE OF SALT by Patricia Highsmith (writing as Claire Morgan). 288 pp. Classic lesbian novel, first issued in 1952 . . .

acknowledged by its author under her own, very famous, name.
ISBN 1-56280-003-5   11.95

SIDE BY SIDE by Isabel Miller. 256 pp. From beloved author of
Patience and Sarah.   ISBN 0-941483-77-0   10.95

STAYING POWER: LONG TERM LESBIAN COUPLES by
Susan E. Johnson. 352 pp. Joys of coupledom. ISBN 0-941-483-75-4   14.95

SLICK by Camarin Grae. 304 pp. Exotic, erotic adventure.
ISBN 0-941483-74-6   9.95

NINTH LIFE by Lauren Wright Douglas. 256 pp. 2nd Caitlin
Reece Mystery.   ISBN 0-941483-50-9   9.95

PLAYERS by Robbi Sommers. 192 pp. Sizzling, erotic novel.
ISBN 0-941483-73-8   9.95

MURDER AT RED ROOK RANCH by Dorothy Tell. 224 pp.
1st Poppy Dillworth Mystery.   ISBN 0-941483-80-0   8.95

A ROOM FULL OF WOMEN by Elisabeth Nonas. 256 pp.
Contemporary Lesbian lives.   ISBN 0-941483-69-X   9.95

THEME FOR DIVERSE INSTRUMENTS by Jane Rule. 208 pp.
Powerful romantic lesbian stories.   ISBN 0-941483-63-0   8.95

CLUB 12 by Amanda Kyle Williams. 288 pp. Espionage thriller
featuring a lesbian agent!   ISBN 0-941483-64-9   9.95

DEATH DOWN UNDER by Claire McNab. 240 pp. 3rd Carol
Ashton Mystery.   ISBN 0-941483-39-8   10.95

MONTANA FEATHERS by Penny Hayes. 256 pp. Vivian and
Elizabeth find love in frontier Montana.   ISBN 0-941483-61-4   9.95

LIFESTYLES by Jackie Calhoun. 224 pp. Contemporary Lesbian
lives and loves.   ISBN 0-941483-57-6   10.95

MURDER BY THE BOOK by Pat Welch. 256 pp. 1st Helen
Black Mystery.   ISBN 0-941483-59-2   9.95

THERE'S SOMETHING I'VE BEEN MEANING TO TELL YOU
Ed. by Loralee MacPike. 288 pp. Gay men and lesbians coming out
to their children.   ISBN 0-941483-44-4   9.95

LIFTING BELLY by Gertrude Stein. Ed. by Rebecca Mark. 104 pp.
Erotic poetry.   ISBN 0-941483-51-7   10.95

AFTER THE FIRE by Jane Rule. 256 pp. Warm, human novel by
this incomparable author.   ISBN 0-941483-45-2   8.95

PLEASURES by Robbi Sommers. 204 pp. Unprecedented
eroticism.   ISBN 0-941483-49-5   11.95

EDGEWISE by Camarin Grae. 372 pp. Spellbinding
adventure.   ISBN 0-941483-19-3   9.95

FATAL REUNION by Claire McNab. 224 pp. 2nd Carol Ashton
Mystery.   ISBN 0-941483-40-1   11.95

IN EVERY PORT by Karin Kallmaker. 228 pp. Jessica's sexy, adventuresome travels. ISBN 0-941483-37-7 11.95

OF LOVE AND GLORY by Evelyn Kennedy. 192 pp. Exciting WWII romance. ISBN 0-941483-32-0 10.95

CLICKING STONES by Nancy Tyler Glenn. 288 pp. Love transcending time. ISBN 0-941483-31-2 9.95

SOUTH OF THE LINE by Catherine Ennis. 216 pp. Civil War adventure. ISBN 0-941483-29-0 8.95

WOMAN PLUS WOMAN by Dolores Klaich. 300 pp. Supurb Lesbian overview. ISBN 0-941483-28-2 9.95

THE FINER GRAIN by Denise Ohio. 216 pp. Brilliant young college lesbian novel. ISBN 0-941483-11-8 8.95

LESSONS IN MURDER by Claire McNab. 216 pp. 1st Carol Ashton Mystery. ISBN 0-941483-14-2 10.95

YELLOWTHROAT by Penny Hayes. 240 pp. Margarita, bandit, kidnaps Julia. ISBN 0-941483-10-X 8.95

SAPPHISTRY: THE BOOK OF LESBIAN SEXUALITY by Pat Califia. 3d edition, revised. 208 pp. ISBN 0-941483-24-X 12.95

CHERISHED LOVE by Evelyn Kennedy. 192 pp. Erotic Lesbian love story. ISBN 0-941483-08-8 11.95

THE SECRET IN THE BIRD by Camarin Grae. 312 pp. Striking, psychological suspense novel. ISBN 0-941483-05-3 8.95

TO THE LIGHTNING by Catherine Ennis. 208 pp. Romantic Lesbian `Robinson Crusoe adventure. ISBN 0-941483-06-1 8.95

DREAMS AND SWORDS by Katherine V. Forrest. 192 pp. Romantic, erotic, imaginative stories. ISBN 0-941483-03-7 11.95

MEMORY BOARD by Jane Rule. 336 pp. Memorable novel about an aging Lesbian couple. ISBN 0-941483-02-9 12.95

THE ALWAYS ANONYMOUS BEAST by Lauren Wright Douglas. 224 pp. 1st Caitlin Reece Mystery. ISBN 0-941483-04-5 8.95

MURDER AT THE NIGHTWOOD BAR by Katherine V. Forrest. 240 pp. 2nd Kate Delafield Mystery. ISBN 0-930044-92-4 11.95

WINGED DANCER by Camarin Grae. 228 pp. Erotic Lesbian adventure story. ISBN 0-930044-88-6 8.95

PAZ by Camarin Grae. 336 pp. Romantic Lesbian adventurer with the power to change the world. ISBN 0-930044-89-4 8.95

SOUL SNATCHER by Camarin Grae. 224 pp. A puzzle, an adventure, a mystery — Lesbian romance. ISBN 0-930044-90-8 8.95

THE LOVE OF GOOD WOMEN by Isabel Miller. 224 pp. Long-awaited new novel by the author of the beloved *Patience and Sarah*. ISBN 0-930044-81-9 8.95

THE LONG TRAIL by Penny Hayes. 248 pp. Vivid adventures of two women in love in the old west. ISBN 0-930044-76-2   8.95

AN EMERGENCE OF GREEN by Katherine V. Forrest. 288 pp. Powerful novel of sexual discovery. ISBN 0-930044-69-X   11.95

DESERT OF THE HEART by Jane Rule. 224 pp. A classic; basis for the movie *Desert Hearts*. ISBN 0-930044-73-8   10.95

SEX VARIANT WOMEN IN LITERATURE by Jeannette Howard Foster. 448 pp. Literary history. ISBN 0-930044-65-7   8.95

A HOT-EYED MODERATE by Jane Rule. 252 pp. Hard-hitting essays on gay life; writing; art. ISBN 0-930044-57-6   7.95

AMATEUR CITY by Katherine V. Forrest. 224 pp. 1st Kate Delafield Mystery. ISBN 0-930044-55-X   10.95

THE SOPHIE HOROWITZ STORY by Sarah Schulman. 176 pp. Engaging novel of madcap intrigue. ISBN 0-930044-54-1   7.95

THE YOUNG IN ONE ANOTHER'S ARMS by Jane Rule. 224 pp. Classic Jane Rule. ISBN 0-930044-53-3   9.95

AGAINST THE SEASON by Jane Rule. 224 pp. Luminous, complex novel of interrelationships. ISBN 0-930044-48-7   8.95

LOVERS IN THE PRESENT AFTERNOON by Kathleen Fleming. 288 pp. A novel about recovery and growth. ISBN 0-930044-46-0   8.95

THIS IS NOT FOR YOU by Jane Rule. 284 pp. A letter to a beloved is also an intricate novel. ISBN 0-930044-25-8   8.95

OUTLANDER by Jane Rule. 207 pp. Short stories and essays by one of our finest writers. ISBN 0-930044-17-7   8.95

These are just a few of the many Naiad Press titles — we are the oldest and largest lesbian/feminist publishing company in the world. We also offer an enormous selection of lesbian video products. Please request a complete catalog. We offer personal service; we encourage and welcome direct mail orders from individuals who have limited access to bookstores carrying our publications.